Stage Blood

A Kayne Sorenson Mystery

Thomas Paul Severino

Stage Blood

A Kayne Sorenson Mystery

Thomas Paul Severino

Copyright 2018

By Thomas Paul Severino

Pollywog Pond Communications, Wilton Manors, FL

www.tomseverino.com

tomseverino100@gmail.com

Cover painting: *King Lear: Cordelia's Farewell* by Edwin Austin Abbey, 1898.

ISBN-978-7322278-6-6

Stage Blood

Also by Thomas Paul Severino

The Kayne Sorenson Mysteries: The Quartet of Blood

Seed Blood

Tribal Blood

Stage Blood

Ancient Blood

The Kayne Sorenson Mysteries: The Quartet of Evil

The Evil Genius

The Shadow of Evil

The Pearl of Great Evil

The Evil League

The Kayne Sorenson Mysteries: The New Adventures

The Crystal Orb

The Flower of Gold

The Amazing Adventures of Rebecca Quinto

The Frozen Diva

The Lost Museum

The Last Maya

Thomas Severino

Stage Blood

For

Anton Wallner

Robert F. Siccone

and

The Very Rev. John F. Costello

Thomas Severino

Art is not a mirror held up to reality but a hammer with which to shape it. — Bertolt Brecht

Murder has no tongue, but miraculously, it still finds a way to speak. —William Shakespeare, *Hamlet*, Act II, Scene 2

Thomas Severino

Prologue

The tutor roughly deposited the battling boy on the tack room floor. The boy tumbled into a sprawl. His father stood with arms crossed, incensed at the behavior of the seventeen-year-old.

"Where did you find him?"

"It was as I said. He was at the airport."

The boy stood up and brushed the dirt from his clothes. His father walked to him and stood within an arm's reach. He refused to meet the man's searing gaze.

The tutor rubbed his shoulder, where the boy had clipped him. The kid was a superb athlete, and it took all he had to bring the boy here, including a restraining rope.

The man said nothing, studying his errant son. He knew the boy's brothers were hiding out in the lofts of the adjacent barn, observing the scene below from knotholes through the shared wall. It was a secret they shared and one they thought their father was unaware of.

"That will be all, Mr. Logan. I will take it from here. Thank you."

He surreptitiously gestured to the wall up and behind him and softly instructed, "See if you can do something about that, please."

Alone in the room, the silence between the man and boy bespoke of an isolation that began years back. The man could not call the boy by the name he had given him at birth. Too much had happened between them for the boy to address the man as 'father.'

The man turned his back on his son, who only then raised his eyes to take in his father. With a surly boldness, he addressed the man.

"So, is it to be the strap again?" He looked at the equipment on the walls. "Like so many times before?"

There was no response.

"Or the paddle. That's always been your favorite."

The man was silent. Then he said quietly, "He's dead. By his own hand."

The boy said nothing. He hung his head but felt no sorrow, only a cold numbness.

"You did this thing. I told you not to continue. I told you to stop."

The man spoke softly but spun around and pointed at the boy, taking a step toward him. His rage was palpable.

"But you would have none of it. You tormented him even after we all knew."

"He was mine. You will never understand what he meant to me. Never."

The boy's eyes were filled with rage.

"Yes!" the father yelled. "He was your toy, your plaything. You tormented him just the way you destroyed your other amusements, your brothers, schoolmates, everyone. You delighted in making him suffer from that first time. You are a monstrous cat toying with your victim. Even in the throes of death."

He stopped as words began to get away from him.

"You are missing some vital pieces of a human-- inside of you."

The boy smirked, "If I am incomplete... whose fault is that? You made me."

It was an accusation.

The boy changed the expression in his voice to fake a juvenile tone, "Anyway, I am a minor. I am not responsible for...."

His father raised his hand to strike his son but froze.

The boy lowered his eyes into menacing slits and taunted, "Go ahead, Big Rancher Boss. Do you think it matters? You know it stopped hurting a long time ago."

Unable to resist the taunting, the man caved in.

"YOU *ARE* RESPONSIBLE. YOU COULD HAVE STOPPED."

Broken, the father covered his face with his hands and waited to regain his composure before speaking again. This was a man who despised weakness in himself and others. That the boy had caused him to weep would be remembered for a long time. There was no forgiving this.

"I am so ashamed of you. This is beyond words. He had a wife and a small son, and you took him from them. You persisted and would not break it off. He could not face the consequences."

"And what else?"

The young man's tone lent a Satanic dimension to the whole scene, evil and perverse, taunting his raging father. He toyed with his father.

With his back to the boy, the man brought two strong arms up and slammed his hands down on a sturdy work table.

The overwhelmed man roared, defeated by rising emotion. When next he spoke, it was soft and pitiful.

"He was my friend."

The boy whispered with a frighteningly victorious quality to his voice. "I know."

Two men entered the tack room and stood next to the door, silently and with folded arms.

With perceived difficulty but with the discipline of a soldier, the man struggled to switch into a role he knew well, that of a business administrator.

"I am sending you away to school. You need to be away from the authorities for your own good and away from the rest of us if we are to regain some sanity in this family. I will send orders for your next steps upon your completion of secondary school."

He now commanded with even more authority in his voice, "If you bolt, you are on your own, and I will make no attempt to find you or protect you. I will deny you completely.

He finished, "You have brought this crisis upon my family, and it cannot be fixed as long as either of us is alive."

The emotion of what was happening returned. Anguish in his soul prevailed as he addressed the boy for the last time.

"You are no longer a part of me. We share no parts in common. I deny you."

He signaled to the men.

"Take him. I will not see him again."

The men led the boy from the room.

Chapter One: Honor

Nick Sechi's Journal

"You have offended the integrity of my family, Sir, and I demand satisfaction."

"I simply asked that you remove your hand from the backside of my boyfriend, bud."

The thickly accented voice came back through the mesh visor of the fencing helmet as the man stood defiantly. He corrected, "This magnificent man is no one's boy, boy, and I suggest you learn to respect and treat him as such. Your ignorance is appalling, as befits most of those of Italian descent."

I felt my blood rise, knowing I was turning my signature frustration color, crimson red. I noticed that the jerk had the voice of an adolescent male just finding its manly depth.

Kayne, his fencing helmet under one arm, placed what he hoped was a pacifying hand on my chest as I took a step toward the arrogant stranger.

"Nick, easy. Please allow me to introduce His Excellency, Count Krisztian Lajovic, a descendant of the Royal House of Carinthia, a full-blooded Slovenian and, as such, not a friend to the Italians, historic foes of the nation."

Kayne suppressed a somewhat comical smile at the Count as I extended my hand.

"Italian idiots. Never quite able to conquer my people. Insulting by their very existence."

The Count removed his fencing glove and whacked me across the face with it.

"Will you fight, Sir, or, like so many of your countrymen, play the coward?"

I wanted to take this jerk apart with my bare hands, but Kayne pushed me back with urgent protests and a curious smile.

"Nick, you are greatly unmatched here. Stand down. His Excellency is a master with the sword."

My fencing skills were newly learned as we traveled through Europe, seeking relaxation and diversion from a very violent case in Colorado. I was totally jazzed at every opportunity to become a better swordsman. It was clear that this dude was adept. Nevertheless, with a heap of D'Artagnan-like swagger, I picked up my helmet and *épée* from a nearby bench and performed the customary salute.

"*En garde*, asswipe."

Before my opponent could respond, a club referee stepped forward to offer her assistance. Agreeing to forego the lame, conductive bib, electric mask, and specialized weapon, we moved to a practice area. Remarkably, I lost track of Kayne for a few moments but focused on the Count, who was taking practice swipes and lunges before turning to the duel at hand.

"Shall we say the best of five touches for this bout, gentlemen?" We nodded in agreement.

Kayne returned just as the referee gave the required commands.

"*En garde. Êtes-vous prêts? Allez!*"

The Count attacked with a straight thrust, which I easily parried, deflecting the blade away from my body. I came back with what I thought was an excellent riposte. I was surprised at the Count's unsophisticated first move. If he was indeed that good, he was playing with me.

My opponent caught the tip of my *épée* in a circle parry, batting it away from its intended target. He countered with a beat attack, knocking back my blade and scoring a single touch near my collarbone.

He stepped back, shaking his head and spreading wide his hands.

"But this is too easy, you hot red devil. You are not in fencing school today, boy. Try to be a man."

14

I thought, *Getting cocky, jerkwad?* Focusing, I assumed my stance.

We began the second round with my opponent stamping his foot to the ground directly from the *en garde* position. His appel was intended to distract me. He jumped forward and lunged, but I backed up and turned to the side, grazing his blade with mine and causing him to miss.

He countered with a feign and moved into beating back my counter-attack. I ducked his next thrust, but he managed to flick his weapon like a whip, bending his blade to catch me on my right butt cheek. I heard laughter from the spectators.

"*Touché*, gentlemen." The ref extended her arm and hand to my side, indicating I had been hit.

I pulled off my helmet, my face steeped in my usual annoying blushing, and turned my back to my opponent, trying to control my temper. Observers continued to murmur, and even Kayne was doing his damnedest to suppress a chuckle. He made a hand signal, which translated as, *Calm down, Nick boy.*

Beneath his mask, the Count was laughing girlishly at my embarrassment. He said nothing but motioned to the referee for a continuance.

The following two points went to me in what I thought was an excellent series of attacks, riposts, parries, and feigns– one to his thigh and another to his shoulder as he stumbled awkwardly. I danced at him in a rather balletic move, remembered from my training with Cirque du Soleil in my undergraduate years. I was bigger than the Count and used my athletic training to gain the advantage and score points.

The crowd of observers along the *piste*, the playing area, had gotten larger. I scanned for Kayne. Gone again.

What's up with that? Very strange.

"You are lucky but hardly skilled, boy."

We saluted and began the match point at the ref's command.

I began with an aggressive lunge. The Count used leverage to counter the strength of my attack in a brilliant opposition parry and a swift, deadly riposte, almost throwing my blade. As he cut across me, I dropped a hand to the floor and ducked my body under his *épée*.

From a low position, I straightened my sword arm, attempting a hit. The Count spun away and covered his vulnerable side with a semi-circular parry. He feigned expertly and returned to *en garde*. The crowd murmured in admiration.

The smug bastard!

I moved in for a renewal, attacking with a simple lunge to his torso. He again parried, feigned, and pushed my open shoulder with his free hand, unbalancing my stance. The referee protested.

I redoubled with way too much aggression, slashing with what is called a "wrathful strike." He engaged, parried down, and to the outside, attempting to control my weapon. The Count then let me in close and flicked my *épée* away using a body spin as leverage. It clattered to the floor as the ref called, "Halt!"

Professional, my ass...

As I removed my mask and stooped to retrieve my weapon, I looked back to see the Count, still helmeted, moving over to resume his contact with the astonished Kayne.

The bastard!

Leaving my sword, I rushed him. With his back to me, he side-stepped, tripped me as I passed, and caused me to tumble to the floor.

I looked pretty ridiculous sitting on my ass amid the howling, pointing athletes and spectators. I was a bit dazed as Kayne and my opponent came up to me. The Count caught my hand and pulled his head close to my red face.

Through the wire of his mask came the jaw-dropping words, "Calm down, Nicky. You are making a spectacle. You merely zigged when you should have zagged, Darling."

Chapter Two: The Reveal
From the Case Notes of Kayne Sorenson, Ph.D.

Nick has asked me to supplement his journal notes, so I am complying. My case records have documented my observations, which have heretofore been protected due to the sensitive nature of much of their contents. The most notorious investigations extend back almost twenty years. Recently, my intimate partnership with Officer Nicola Sechi of the Wilton Manors, Florida Police Department has caused me to add to his memoirs of two rather chilling adventures in South Florida and in Aspen, Colorado.

Nick has chosen to name the former "Seed Blood," and the latter he titled "Tribal Blood." He is attempting to log our exploits for prosperity. Why? I do not know. Why anyone would want to follow our exploits is a mystery in itself.

I must confess that although I pride myself on the meticulousness of my detective work, my notetaking is often a cause for the befuddlement of readers. I promise to keep my Australian slang out of these reports. Nick tends to record the more heartfelt aspects of our work and our relationship. My mind works differently. I suppose I should ask for forbearance. Cheers.

***

I pulled Nick into the changing room of the fencing club following his duel with the mysterious and very sexy Count Krisztian Lajovic. My lovely man was physically worn out and highly frustrated. The fencing match had caused him to lose his rather famous temper, especially over the revelation that concluded the encounter.

I unclasped his fencing jacket and pulled him against me, kissing him passionately, disregarding the expression on the faces of changing athletes in the locker room. We continued to be the club's center of attention.

"Did you know?" He gasped between our very passionate mouthing, pushing my pesky black forelock out of the way.

17

I put my hand behind his head of short-cropped, red-blond hair, placing my mouth next to his ear with watchful eyes upon our observers.

"Not a word, my love. Not here, not now."

I stepped back and placed my index finger against his moist lips. He was still visibly shaken but showed signs of recovery. The tangy smell of his sweat was intoxicating. I remember thinking I wanted him to stay slightly edgy, at least for a bit.

The Count, now unmasked, strode by and paused to say, "Sipon Café, Radnigerstrasse, near Hut Ab. Say 40 minutes, *Ja*?" He winked at Nick.

I nodded. Nick just stared at the beautiful featured, dark-haired boy in the fencing kit. His hair was styled in loose black curls on top, a hard side part, and a low fade-- ultra-chic. The Count moved to one of the private changing booths, detaching his fencing jacket as he pulled the curtain, his helmet, and *épée* disappearing with him.

We undressed and headed to the wet rooms. Our shower stalls were side-by-side. Nick walked in and closed his curtain. I waited a moment and then opened it and stepped in. I pulled the curtain behind me. The expression on his face said, "WTF?"

He turned his back against me, rubbing the soap between his hands into a lather. My hands moved down his wet shoulders to his muscled back. I pressed my hungry mouth to his ear. "You can defend my honor any time, Big Boy."

***

The Austrian municipality of Hermagor-Pressegger See is in the lower Gail valley at the northern foot of the Carnic Alps. To the south, the district is connected through the Nassfeld pass to the Italian municipality of Pontebba in the *Provinicia di Venezia*. In the north, the Gailtal Alps ringed the horizon. Beyond the beautiful mountains, Lake Weissensee glistened in the summer sunlight. Here in this famous ski resort area, we sought the comfort of its warm springs and verdant hiking trails.

Set in the Duchy of Carinthia, Hermagor shares direct connections to the Slovenian capital of Ljubljana and to *La Serenissima*, Venice, in the *Veneto*. The picturesque area also offered proximity to the Balkan peninsula and the northern ports of the Adriatic Sea. More than once, the borders of the Duchy had switched from Austria to Slovenia and back again. The Italians were their long-time rivals going back to Roman times.

Throughout the centuries, Hermagor continued to set the stage for international intrigue. Historically, it was a strategic area for the Austro-Hungarian Empire as a mustering station for the Imperial Army close to the Italian front. Critical to two World Wars and countless border skirmishes, the countryside bristled with intrigue. Spies, oligarchs, drug lords, corporate heads, diplomats, and deposed royalty all seemed to find their way to this Alpine region, now a part of southern Austria.

Nick was six months through his year off from the Wilton Manors Police Force. I was taking a leave from my teaching duties in criminology at Florida Global University. Nick had been a student in my class, and I confess the attraction was epic, and our adventures were fraught with terror and death. I believe I will leave the details of our personal life to his more amorous writing.

***

"Look to the south, Nick. You can see Mt. Gartnerkofel in the Carnic Alps near our hotel. There is the Möderndorf Castle – an amazing museum of regional folk culture. We must come to ski here in winter and see more of this beautiful region."

"Cool tour, Kayne, but we need to talk. I have a few significant questions." He was pouting.

"As do I, my love. Let's let the Count explain. And … speak of the devil."

Count Krisztian Lajovic moved gracefully up the street and approached our table at the Sipon Café. I stood and exchanged triple kisses, saying, "My dear, you will never pass as a man if you cannot remember what I taught you about man-swagger. You are much too lithe and sensuous. We will work on the butch factor, yes?"

The "Count" waved a hand at me and turned to Nick to exchange the European greeting, a triple kiss.

"Nicky, Darling, I apologize sincerely. Will you forgive your Rebecca, her little charade? I have an excellent reason, I assure you, Darling."

Nick, trancelike, said, "Um, what... Girl? This had better be good."

Turning to me, our beautiful friend with sparkling eyes advised, "Darling, spend the rest of the afternoon shagging this gorgeous boy into a stupor. It will clear his head, among other things."

Turning to Nick, she added, "Oh wait, according to the gossip in the men's changing room, Officer Sechi's shag therapy has already begun. Really, Darlings, shower sex? So unabashedly animal and straight Austrian men are so easily appalled."

I was gratified that Nick smiled at the lewd implications of our dear friend.

The waiter approached, and I waved away the menus. I pointed to each of us in turn as I said, *"Kaisermelange, Maria Theresia und Türkischer, bitte."*

"Darling, a raw egg in your coffee, seriously?"

"Exquisite. And my man needs the boldness, strength, and endurance of the 'Turkish One.' That is if we are going to follow your advice and sex up all afternoon. A prospect I am very much looking forward to. I want him savage." I winked at Nick. "I do have some romantic ideas for our evening, coincidentally."

Nick interrupted impatiently, "OK. OK. Why the disguise, and what the fuck are you doing here? The Alps? Fencing? Man drag? Let's go, Rebecca. Explanation, please."

"First, my Nicky Darling, you are very good for a novice swordsman. But keep your cool, baby. The sport of fencing requires a very calm approach. My instructors in Salamanca impressed that disciplinary strategy on me when I was a mere slip of a girl at the university."

She looked a bit nostalgic for a second but came back with more.

"So, next-- I am supposedly doing research for an exhibit on the lost treasures of Imperial Russia for the Museum. You remember, Kayne, back in 2007, during, shall we say, your Hungarian exploits? When we met, I was researching art recovery for a historical reappropriation project for the Russian Republic."

My thoughts went to Major Ádám Haagen, my "Golden Hussar," and our extended interlude. Still, I quickly brushed aside both the remembrance and the emotion – quite useless.

"Back then, I was experimenting with a male *alter ego,* and honestly, Darling, thanks to your mentoring, getting away with it. Remember?"

I chuckled, "There is something so decadent about woman-to-man masquerading in the European *demi-monde* – so Marlene Dietrich."

Nick asked, "Why now? Surely, your research work for your museum does not require a false identity. You are up to something, girl."

Rebecca looked around at the very empty café. "Truthfully, I have been recruited for a rather special assignment through my connections with the FBI. This is very much on the down-low, Darlings,-- unofficial. Mark would have a shit fit if he knew."

Mark Gadarn was Rebecca Quinto's latest love, a reporter for CBN Cable News currently on assignment in Turkey.

"You are aware that certain Asian and European ultra-conservative regimes are imprisoning and executing homosexuals by the hundreds. In September 2017, the Toronto-based nonprofit Rainbow Railroad made public that the Canadian government was working with them. They are quietly allowing gay men and lesbians from Chechnya to seek safety in Canada. As of June 2017, safe passage had been secured for 22 people deemed government-assisted refugees. But there are a few who need some extraordinary rescue operations because of who they are...."

Our waiter returned, and the conversation stopped.

"Try this, Nicky. The orange liqueur is delicious." Rebecca handed Nick her *Maria Theresia.*

"Mmm. Mine is making my hair hurt. Wow! Caffeine on steroids, boys and girls."

I redirected our attention away from our coffee as the waiter retreated. "Continue, my dear. Allow me to add that I already fear you are in grave danger."

Rebecca shrugged off my concern. "I am a key operative in a case related to the imprisonment of three gays in the concentration camps in the Caucasus, two men and a woman, leaders in the fields of medical technology at the submicroscopic level. Their captors may be selling them to the highest bidder. My contacts want to get them to the West and to freedom.

"This drag gig opens doors that are closed to females. My interests are taken seriously, and the anonymity of my work is paramount. No one wants to come forward on behalf of these prisoners. There are landmines everywhere."

Rebecca stirred her coffee and continued. "As His Excellency Krisztian Lajovic, I have had some fun gender-bending here in the divine decadence of Old Europe. Being a spy is so Mata Hari, Darling, but boring as shit sometimes. I would say almost as dull as being the Director and Head Curator of the Fritcher Museum of Art in Ft. Lauderdale. Still, our recent adventures show that to be far from true."

She mused wistfully, "Doing male drag in exclusive men's sports clubs is my favorite. I love to criticize the stereotypical roles of women and men. You both know how less than normal I can be. I want to ridicule and destroy the whole bullshit cosmology of restrictive sex roles and sexual identification. Part of my radical politics. Plus, you get to see a lot of gorgeous man butts."

Kayne interjected with a smile, "We have to work on the male objectifying thing if you are going to be an authentic advocate for equality."

Again, she brushed off his comment. "So, I'm evolving. But enough about this bad girl. Look at these folks."

Rebecca passed me her mobile, and the pictures of the aforementioned scientists came into view. Nick leaned in to share as I scrolled.

I added my commentary. "These scientists are internationally renowned nanotechnologists. Their research involves the direct control of matter on the atomic scale. They have even taken the field to the sub-nano level. We are talking smaller than the quantum-realm scale."

Nick excitedly commented, "Wow. I've been reading up on this nano stuff. This research will end up making existing medical applications cheaper and easier to access. Cars are already being manufactured with nanomaterials, so they need fewer metals and less fuel and operate on clean power. Talkin' clothing that lasts longer, even bandages infused with nanoparticles that enable faster healing. It is awesome."

I added, "It is an exciting field. Nanobiotics is the spin-off application that creates subatomic robots that can splice genes and remove and replace defective DNA. Think of the medical implications. Nick, these are extremely important people."

"It all means next to nothing to me, darling boys. For my two cents, these are persecuted people, and we need to get them to safety."

I handed her back her phone and looked around the empty bistro before I said, "Rebecca, this is dangerous. Again, let me say that your life is on the line here. Espionage is one deadly game."

"I have protection, Kayne. That dude you were eyeballing at the match, the one who kept dodging into the shadows while Nick and I were dueling– he's my bodyguard, though he keeps at a distance. Extremely good at it, by the way, former MI-6."

Nick said, "Let me understand this, James Bond is on the case with you?"

"Yep. To be exact, he is just down the Strasse watching us."

I turned but saw nothing. The street was empty. This guy was good.

"Why not Kayne and me? We got your back. We have been an excellent team in the past. We're as good as it gets."

Rebecca looked like the proverbial cat who swallowed the canary. Moving her gaze from Nick to me, she reached out and took each of our hands.

"Together, we are truly amazing, Darlings. Superspy is my ace in the hole. My loves, my confederate in this operation is…."

We waited for the other shoe to drop. Looking at me, Rebecca said, "Darling, he's your brother."

Chapter Three: Spy Games
Nick Sechi's Journal

Rebecca's revelation of the identity of her associate had absolutely no visible effect on Kayne. He enigmatically raised his *Kaisermelange* and took a sip. He brushed back a floppy bang of his jet-back hair with his left hand. The only change in his face was an almost imperceptible darkening of his ice-blue eyes.

I was stunned. My thoughts turned to our recent adventures in Colorado.

"Which one? Kick? Mitch?"

Rebecca turned from Kayne and looked me directly in the eyes.

"The black sheep himself, Eric James Sorenson."

"Holy shit!"

Kayne still showed no reaction except to remove Rebecca's hand from his.

As if on cue, a tall man in torn-at-the-knees jeans and a white t-shirt seemed to appear out of nowhere. He approached our table, placing a hand on his brother's shoulder.

He was indeed Kayne's identical triplet with the same build, coloring, and eye shape as Kayne and Thomas, aka Kick. His face was disfigured on the right side by a scar that started at the outside corner of his almond-shaped left eye and coursed across his sharp cheekbone to the edge of his mouth. I presumed that the trauma that caused the disfigurement resulted in a silver cast in the pupil of his left eye. The right was colored in the Sorenson Siberian Husky ice-blue.

Eric had a tattoo on the side of his neck of what appeared to be a scorpion, partially hidden by the crew neck of his t-shirt. A band of Latin words encircled his muscled bicep below the tight left sleeve. *Melius est regnare in inferno quam servire in caelo*. It is better to reign in Hell than to serve in Heaven-- Milton.

His hair was buzzed short like mine, jet black with a hard part high on the right temple. He moved with the grace of a trained athlete. Eric was a tall, lean-muscled man, like Kayne, but sharper around the edges. The overall effect was, *Fuck with me at your peril.*

"How are you, brother?" His voice was a deep baritone, edged with a world-weariness and a bluntly honest attitude. This was a man who did not give a damn what anyone thought of him.

No one said anything or did anything for about a minute.

Rebecca started, "Eric, this is....."

Kayne stood slowly, removed his brother's hand from his shoulder, tossed his napkin on the table, and said to no one in particular, "Will you excuse me, please?" He turned and started to the *Strasse.*

Eric did an about-face and followed him.

Rebecca and I watched as Eric caught his brother by the upper arm a few feet from us, attempting to turn him back around and start a conversation. Kayne protested and pushed him away. The black sheep persisted but not without scanning the area for observers.

The brothers exchanged heated remarks illustrated by sharp, hostile hand gestures and the primal body language of two rival males of the species. At one point, Kayne pointed to Rebecca and aggressively tapped his brother's chest, making a very passionate point. Eric managed to move them both into the shadows of the trees on the side of the Sipon Café.

The posturing, displays, and trials of strength in the words and gestures of the reuniting brothers were filled with anger and frustration. Eric made an aggressive move, his face inches from his brother's. My "spider-sense" was tingling big time. No one was going to physically assault Kayne. My body tensed. I stood and made for the pair.

"Yo, asshole!"

Three blue eyes and one silver eye caught sight of me.

Rebecca reached out and held me back.

"No, Nick. Easy Darling. Kayne is not in danger."

26

"I do not like this guy, Rebecca."

The Brothers Sorenson continued their excited interchange. As I sat back down, she kept a hand on my arm.

With exasperation, Rebecca said, "Well, I think this is going very well, don't you, Darling?"

The "Count" put her head in her hands. "Sweet Jesus, I so totally fucked this up."

***

When they returned to the table, neither brother's face was readable-- two masks of emotional repression. In Kayne's visage, I recognized a force of sheer will, attempting to control the cold drip of his anger. Eric's look was apathetic and flat, as if the emotional motivation behind his gaze was blunted.

The four of us remained silent for about a minute. I attempted to gain Kayne's gaze, but he avoided eye contact. Eric, on the other hand, was directly assessing his brother's lover and partner in detective consultation with a peeling, piercing look. My attempt to charge into the disagreement seemed a challenge to his superiority.

Eric extended a hand to me at the end of a muscled arm and fixed my gaze.

"You are aware of me, my boy, but have heard little about me from the members of my family, I'll wager. Shame prevents disclosure of my exploits and of my very existence. Of this, I have been aware for some time now.

"I am Eric. I am the fallen angel of the Sorenson brood. And you are Nicola Michael Sechi of the Wilton Manors Police Force in Florida, USA. The sexy cover boy. I will call you Nick."

His tone was sardonic and slightly mocking. His gaze was intense and somewhat chilling. Eric's "tell" was not the forelock shoot of his brother or the hyper-energetic, center-of-attention style of the last of the triplets, Kick. The former agent had a habit of repeatedly clenching his very strong-looking hands.

As we shook, I returned the strength of his grip. A glint in his blue eye seemed to indicate that he was impressed with the manliness of his brother's associate. His examining look lingered. *Ouch! Cruised by the devil incarnate.*

My thoughts continued, *These Sorensons are a whole lot of drama. So much light and darkness.*

I attempted a friendly retort, "Well, this completes the meeting-the-family part of the relationship, I guess. Kayne and I spent the spring at the Aerie."

Eric chuckled and lit a cigarette. He raised it to his lips back-handed, European villain style, like the Nazi Major Heinrich Strasser, played by Conrad Veidt in "Casablanca."

"Ahh, yes, the happy couple, Kick and Mitch." He leaned back in his chair and assumed an Alpha position, arms behind his head, t-shirt stretched from his flat abdomen to his broad pecs-- a mocking, dark prince.

Kanye raised his eyes to mine. His glance communicated silently. *Stop assessing his triceps, Nick.*

Kayne knows me well and can read my lustful thoughts with ease.

The ultra-spy drew on his Murad, spiraling the smoke over our heads, and looked to the sky. He said the next two words very slowly.

"And, Ace ..."

He pronounced his father's nickname with an unmistakable hiss.

At the mention of the Sorenson *Paterfamilias*, I nodded and said, "Yeah, quite a guy."

Eric brought his arms back to the table and uttered a deathly chuckle. He lowered his voice and said,

"So much for family remembrances. They are of no consequence. Let's move this along, then. Plainly said, my beautiful Count here, and I need you both in on this affair if we are to succeed."

He leaned forward, saying, "I do not want to go into the details here, so I would like to propose a trip this evening whereby we can dissect the matters at hand." Again, his eyes darted for eavesdroppers. Eric gave one the sense that he was hyper-aware of his surroundings while never actually turning his head.

He continued, looking at each of us in turn. "The great Serbian actress, Mira Savic, appears tomorrow night at the Volkstheater in Vienna performing in Brecht's *Mutter Courage und Ihre Kinder*. It is her farewell performance. I have four tickets for tomorrow, including passage to Vienna on the night train. It leaves at midnight. We can conspire in a private cabin concerning the Count's little project."

Rebecca said, "So totally *Murder on the Orient Express*, right, Kayne Darling? Daring, intrigue, adventure – you love that." She attempted to break through Kayne's mental cloak of ice. He said nothing.

"My beloved brother, I know how much you love the dramatic. This performance is not to be missed." Eric placed his hand on his stoic brother's back but spoke to me.

"Nick, you in?"

I did not answer but looked to Kayne for a reaction.

He shifted in his chair, turning in such a way as to free himself from his brother's touch. Kayne locked eyes with his brother.

"Show me."

His tone was quietly insistent.

No response.

Now Kayne's voice was raised in anger that came from a weariness of years of dealing with intense family issues, love imprisoned by fear, and hatred.

"Show me, Eric. Fuckin' do it, ya bleedin' brogan!"

The errant brother drew back to glare murderously at his triplet and did nothing for about 60 seconds. Finally, he slapped the table aggressively, stood up, and turned his back to us. I thought he was going to leave.

For a moment, I was distracted again by the man's physique-- broad back in a tight t-shirt and rocking a hot butt in tight jeans, so identical to his beautiful brother but with an aura of monstrous power. I watched a similar reaction creep over the visage of the "Count." We were transfixed.

Eric stopped, reached into his jeans pocket, and withdrew a folder of pills, which he tossed on the table.

He turned back to Kayne with a furious look.

"Zyprexa. Twice a day. Mother's genetic legacy, eh?"

He turned back, placed both fists on the table, leaned down into the defiant stare of his brother, and spoke with a soft menace.

"Are you satisfied, my beloved brother?"

Chapter Four: The Morning Star

Nick Sechi's Journal

Kayne, Rebecca, and I stepped from the express train after a short trip to the Nassfeld district near the Italian border. Kayne had barely spoken since we left his brother, who moved down the street away from the Café Sipon in Hermagor and seemed to disappear. The Millennium Express III left us in the foothills of Mt. Gartnerkofel in the Carnic Alps. Our suite in the Kaiserin Elisabeth Hotel was a short walk from the train station.

We had a few hours of daylight left, plenty of time for dinner, and then a return to Hermagor and the night train to Vienna. The afternoon was warm and sunny. The mountain air, fresh with the scent of new-mown grass and wildflowers, was alive with brightly colored pollinators. Butterflies and honeybees danced in the golden sun.

Instead of taking the horse-drawn cart to the hotel, Kayne detoured us to the ski lift. He wrapped an assuring arm around my shoulders as we walked towards the aerial transport. Soon, we found the ground falling away beneath our feet as we ascended into the verdant alpine countryside.

Damn, I felt it coming on again. Nick the Wuss here, boys and girls.

"Easy, my love. I have you." Kayne added with a whisper, "Nothing's going to harm you while I am around," as he kept his strong arm around my shoulder. I was rigid with acrophobic anxiety. I tried to butch it up. I hated appearing weak and passive under any circumstances. Poor fit for my superhero aspirations.

Rebecca chatted away, "I should have brought a guitar and donned a dirndl. We all could have sung 'Do, Re, Mi,' Darlings."

She aped a Julie Andrews/Maria von Trapp, "Shall I teach you to sing?"

As we ascended to the snow-capped peaks rising above green meadows and sparkling lakes, Kayne reminded her, "You are aware of our performance abilities, my dear. None of us has stage fright. Remember how we brought down the house at Quarto Bar in Ft. Lauderdale? We were a rippa. Bob's your uncle."

He did his signature forelock sweep with his right hand.

I remembered that Kayne, when tired or tipsy, slipped into his almost untranslatable 'Strine – Australian slang. I attempted not to look down but stared at the sharp surfaces of the mountains, like facets of gigantic gemstones, dusted with snow and getting closer as we ascended.

Rebecca snuggled close to me and pulled a silver flask from her jacket. "Here, Nicky. This will take the edge off."

I swigged the delicious liquid and passed the flask to Kayne. He took a pull, handed the container back to Rebecca, and commented, "Ahh, *Bierbrand*. Excellent, my dear. Schnapps made from distilled beer. Now, this almost gets you off the hook."

She gave him the finger and turned back to the dazzling scenery.

Our chair seemed to bring the ground up to our feet as we slid into the landing area and took off for a casual hike, the sun lowering over the snowy range. The mountains to the south were breathtaking, towering over the mountain pass which led to Italy. We found a small outcropping of rocks in a verdant meadow and sat down to deconstruct the morning's events.

Children and family members chased each other or just sat and enjoyed the lengthening afternoon sun on the slanting lawns that, when carpeted with snow in a few months, would draw skiers and winter sports enthusiasts from all over the globe. Kayne pointed out a soaring raptor who flew in widening circles against the azure sky, surveying the grass for mice and rabbits.

"*Aquila chrysaetos*, Nick, the Golden Eagle, found everywhere in the heraldry of the old Austro-Hungarian Empire."

Rebecca, stretching out on the green carpet of grass and edelweiss, addressed the matter most on all our minds.

"I apologize, Kayne, Darling. I had no idea of the extent of the bad blood between you and your brother. This rescue attempt is highly secretive, so I hesitated to inform you. I realize now that I should have handled this differently."

"What's done is done, my dear. Let's see it through, eh?"

Again, he accepted the offered flask of schnapps and raised it in a forgiving toast before drinking.

"*Prosit.*"

I dropped behind him in the grass, resting my head on his lap, rising only to sip and pass along the libation. The liquor was calming down the rollicking residue of my fear of heights. *We were so walking back.*

The view was just as intoxicating, and the events of this afternoon seemed to fade in their intensity. Kayne ran his hand over my head in a casual caress, his blue eyes alternating from my face to the rivaling blue of the sky.

"What's Eric's problem, Boss, and why does no one in your family talk about it? Full disclosure, please."

Kayne sighed and turned towards the lowering sun.

"Are we really going to do this? You have met quite a few compelling characters in the Sorenson family, my love. The members seem to get madder than a wet dingo with each introduction."

"I think he is adorable, Darling. Sort of, anyway. Such a delicious bad boy."

"My dear friend, I have, up until this moment, held your intelligence in extremely high regard. Your masculine drag seems to have brought with it the baffling male ability to think with the little head and not with the big head."

He shot me a knowing look.

"However anatomically impossible that would be."

"Hold on there, Darling. Are you saying that a woman is not capable of the follies associated with her, um … libido?"

I held up a hand, "OK. OK, before we get into a revival of *The Vagina Monologues*, let's go. Eric Sorenson – the Dark Side of the Force. Wassup with all of that?"

Kayne spoke in a monotone that began to unlock years of uncomfortable memories.

"He got the biceps tattoo at the ripe old age of 15. The Latin phrase, *Non-Serviam,* circling his upper left arm, is attributed to Lucifer, The Morning Star. He was said to have spoken these words to express his refusal to serve God in the heavenly kingdom."

"Ace?"

"Correct, Boyo. Former AU Marine and Master of Inala, the largest cattle station in Central Australia."

"So, there is no love lost between your father and your brother, Darling?"

Kayne shook his head, "*Fathers and Sons*, more nihilism than even Turgenev could handle... I am afraid their relationship reached the mortal enemies' level early on. The tattoo was a grand 'fuck you' to Da. You see, something happened."

His hand seemed to tremble as he raised the flask for additional fortification.

I reached for his free hand.

"Eric was rebellious from the start. Our childhood was filled with rage and frustration between him and my father. From his youth, he seemed to be embroiled in fights, thievery, and acts of cunning malevolence, frustrating his brothers, Ace, and a line of countless tutors.

"Kick was often the target of his evil designs partially because Kick's condition required patience and focused guidance. Kick is an imp. Eric is Satan. In Da's absence, Mitch was the only one who could keep the Dark Prince from causing havoc. Eric, in those days, called our adopted brother the 'The Archangel,' referring to his status as Da's right-hand bloke and deputy."

"My God, it's like Milton revisited – *Paradise Lost*, Lucifer expelled from the Heavens and cast into Hell, Darling."

I said, "Kayne, you seemed to have referred to an incident. I assume it was the straw that broke the camel's back. What happened?"

"Quite that, Nick. First, you know of our DNA issues, yes? We are identical triplets, and we share the genetic makeup that has produced three variations of a neurotic disorder. I keep my ADHD under control through meditation and extreme mental discipline. Kick takes his lithium for his bipolar disorder. Mitch keeps him focused and true to his promise to take his medication."

"Ouch! Eric is a psychopath. Holy shit, but...."

"Close, Nick, and that, in fact, is most likely true." He checked in to see that Rebecca was following carefully.

"His mental disorder is quite complicated. Hostility and intensely aggressive rebellion peaked in his teens, along with pubescent sexual desires of a most peculiar nature. There are not many opportunities in the Outback for counseling and psychotherapy. Ace did what he could, but they were consistently at loggerheads.

"My father's temper is biblical in intensity, I am afraid, and he believed in corporal punishment for his four sons. Having said that, I assure you that Mitch never felt the bite of the strap. Eric was entirely at the other end of the spectrum. He was frequently made to report for corrective measures in the tack room. Da's strap use seemed only to further alienate my rebellious brother. As we grew older, his continued discipline sessions had the reverse effect. Eric became even more filled with emotional pain and hatred."

The swooping eagle caught a plump, scampering rodent and soared into the sky to the dismaying cries of observing children.

"Ace had a few former Marine buds working at the station. Eric had a torrid affair with one of them. He was remarkably cognizant of his behavior and the pending consequences, even at the age of fifteen. I have no doubt that my brother seduced the older man. Ace found out and confronted both his son and his friend, demanding a cessation of activities. Eric disobeyed the order to desist and continued the sexual liaison with a real relish for his defiance and its primal intensity.

"Morally, it was well beyond the abuse of a minor. Eric was sixteen when it all came out. Consent in Australia is seventeen. My brother possessed an adult's intelligence, cunning, and lust in these matters. There was never any doubt."

Kayne paused to gather his thoughts, searching our faces for a reaction. He continued saying, "The veteran had a wife and a ten-year-old son. He took his own life when the shame of the relationship with my brother started to become known. Eric was banished to a military school in Switzerland. He returned to the US for four semesters with us at Notre Dame. But there was more trouble at the end of our second year with an assistant soccer coach. A significant gift to endow a department chair at the University smoothed over that scandal. Ace was furious.

"My errant brother lost his scholarship and returned to Europe to finish University in Berlin. His exploits in the leather clubs of the German capital's Nollendorfplatz in the Schöneberg district are legendary. While in Germany, he enrolled in a mercenary training program, which equipped him for his work in espionage. The details of his life since have been cloaked in silence. Assassination, revenge, treachery, and theft are his stock in trade."

Turning to Rebecca, Kayne added, "His medication apparently does much to control his mental disorder, which, by some expert stealth, he has kept from his superiors for years."

He took her hand. "So, you see, my dear, you have literally allied yourself with the devil. Have a care. He is driven by the most demonic forces when he is not himself … or should I say when he *is* himself… which is quite often, I'm afraid."

The sun blazed as it slowly fell off its mountain perch and descended behind the western peaks. The mountain air began to cool. A few lights glimmered like settling fireflies in the village, nestled in the shadows below.

Rebecca protested, "Kayne, your brother holds all the cards in this affair. He has the ability to locate and secure the release of these scientists from their captivity. His skills and contacts in the spy game are being used for the good of this operation."

"I realize that, my dear. Eric is a very skilled mercenary. Despite his covert aura, I have been able over the years to contact him, learn of some of his exploits, and, in one case, engage him in addressing some rather nasty business for NATO, missing plans for an integrated air defense network. But the price of his engagement is very high. He leaves death and destruction in his wake."

I spoke up, "We need to talk more about this. The dude sounds like a time bomb if you ask me. Hey, any chance we can head back down? Twilight's coming on quickly, it seems, and apparently, we have a train to catch tonight."

"My Darlings, I have much to think about before our midnight rendezvous at the train station. I will take a cab to my hotel and meet you at the Hermagor station at 11:45 PM."

The three of us started down the mountain, following the trail lit by the lights of the overhead chairlift. As we reached the base, now taking on the first darkening coverings of the evening, we walked the few blocks to the hotel and secured a cab for Rebecca. As her taxi sped away, my phone voicemail feature chirped.

"Mother."

Thomas Severino

Chapter Five: Viola

Nick Sechi's Journal

"Nicola, I have been trying to contact you all day. Why have you delayed returning my calls?"

"Sorry, Mom. We were sorta mountain climbing and, well, you know, no cell phone towers."

"So, are you still in Colorado, baby? I thought you were leaving after all that trouble. How is your Kanye? Portia tells me you both had yet another brush with death?"

"It's Kayne, Mom. Kanye is the rapper. Think of the dude in the bible who killed his brother Able, only spelled differently."

I regretted that last statement as soon as the words left my mouth. Looking at Kayne, I saw him smile ruefully.

"Nick, I do not like the sound of that at all. Be careful. When are you coming back east?"

"As a matter of fact, we are in Europe, Austria, to be exact. We hit the EU about three weeks ago and...."

I heard my mother say to my sister, "Portia, your brother is in Austria with that Kanye person. He skipped the Bronx altogether. Do you believe it?"

"Nick, we are heading to Europe in a few days, as a matter of fact. It will be so great to see you."

"What? Where and why?"

"Your sister is producing a Shakespearian festival production as part of Ars Europa. I have been asked to be one of the guest directors. 'Lear,' Nick Baby. My favorite. We start previews in the Czech Republic next week. The tour includes Bratislava, Budapest, and somewhere in Slovenia. Seven weeks total. Just in time to get me back to NYU for the fall semester."

Holy shit! To quote my mother's Handbook of Sayings, "This is all I need."

"Nicola, we will be together at last and very soon. And I can meet your Kanye."

"Kayne, Mom. Kayne."

"Yes, yes, of course. Kayne. Your sisters squeal every time they pull up his picture on the web. They are so jealous of you and your choice of men. Tell me, dear, are you OK? Happy? The break-up, I mean."

Wow, I did not want to go there. I hadn't thought of my ex in a while. The past was over and done.

Kayne had stepped a bit ahead of me and was also taking a call.

"All good, Mom. Please ask Portia to forward your itinerary so we can meet. We are actually headed to Vienna to see *Mother Courage* tonight. I will tell you all about it."

"Ahh, *La Divina Savic*. I have been following that production. The reviews coming out of Vienna are astounding. Tony Kushner's translation of the Brechtian masterpiece is monumental. Meryl Streep did it in Central Park a few years back. Brilliant. You will love it, dear. The topic for our discussion when we meet will be, is *Mother Courage and Her Children* really an anti-war piece?"

Always the college professor, my mother loved challenging her students, family, and friends to think critically about theater's social messages. Since my father died when I was 13, her career has taken off. Viola Sechi, Ph.D., had achieved the distinction of being one of the world's eminent Shakespearean scholars. In recent years, with six grown children, my mother had reached the apex of her career. In addition to teaching, research, and publishing, she often served as production director in collaboration with my older sister, the theatrical producer Portia Sechi.

"Great, Mom. Listen, it will be great to see you guys. I am going to ring off and…. "

"Fine, dear. OK. Say hello to your new man for me."

"I will. Please give my love to my sisters and the rest of the family."

"See you soon. I love you, dear."

"I love you too, Mom."

***

Kayne was finishing his call as we stepped under the entrance marquee outside the Kaiserin Elisabeth Hotel.

"Good, Scott. Thanks very much. I look forward to your report. Please give Gints our love."

Standing on the steps of the hotel, he rang off and said, "Scott... for research on the imbroglio we are about to undertake. I will tell you all about it in a bit. And I want to hear about your call with Dr. Sechi, but first...."

He placed an index finger against my lips, his signal for "No words, now." With a chaste kiss, Kayne replaced his cautionary digit and bounded up the stairs with me in tow, getting a wink from the doorman.

He stepped up to Hotel Guest Services and said in German,

"Please ask Chef Kempf to prepare our in-room dinner for two. I'd like it brought up in...."

He turned to me and looked me up and down like appraising an escort and causing me to blush. He knocked back his forelock.

"Hmm ... right ... Say in two hours. We will start with Carelian Caviar and Beluga Noble Gold Line Vodka, both sub-zero cold. Then the Bavarian Lamb with Arctic raspberries, boiled rosemary potatoes, and the chef's signature sauerkraut dish. I would like him to pair the entrée with the best German wine. He can select. Send the vodka and caviar immediately and...."

He leered sinfully at me before adding, "We will make our own dessert."

Yep, I completely reddened down to my socks.

The Service Director leaned forward over her monitor to look me over and said, "*Ja, Doktor Sorenson. Sofort, mein Herr.*"

"*Vielen Dank.*"

I playfully socked him and said, "Feeling so dirty right now, Boss."

He pulled me close.

"You just wait 10 minutes, mate."

We bounded to the elevator.

Chapter Six: Repast

From the Case Notes of Kayne Sorenson, Ph.D.

Nick jumped over me and grabbed a towel. Wrapping it around his waist, he accepted the cart of vodka and caviar and turned back to hand the steward a gratuity. We shot back the delicious appetizer and toasted with a shot of Russia's most excellent spirits.

I saluted, "*Na zdorovie, tovarich*. And make a note, my love, that this will signal the end of the preliminaries."

He dropped the towel and sat naked with me on the edge of the bed, his body moist from our initial romancing. I ran an index finger along his sweat-soaked shoulders and muscled back. Tasting him rivaled the exotic intoxication and flavors of the vodka.

He chuckled, "You are a frisky boyo, Mate. Moving as fast as a ginkgo in heat."

His 'Strine was a sincere attempt for a Yank.

"Dingo, my love."

He continued, "Kayne, do you know the definition of Italian foreplay?"

"Tell me."

"Here it is."

Nick jumped up and stood with his legs apart. He snapped his fingers and pointed commandingly to his tumescent genitals.

"Get on."

I roared with laughter and pushed him back on the bed.

By the time dinner arrived, we had easily broken some long-standing shagging records, including a few innovative ways to do shots. Some of which I remembered from my earlier days on the continent with four members of the Czech National Gymnastic Team.

"Kayne, I have done navel shots before, but I never... there?... Oh, shit... that feels... Oh, wow. That's smoking hot! ... ummm. Yeah, Boss."

Our sexual chemistry was well-paired for many reasons. First, we both enjoyed sexual intimacy immensely. We agreed that sex should be and indeed was a great deal of fun.

Second, we liked the yin and yang relationship dynamic, pivoting the enjoyment of intense sexual behavior with the tender romance it had the potential to bring to flower. Appropriate kisses and touching outside the bedroom created an intimate physicality to our shared life. And, as Nick would express it, we could give a fuck if the haters didn't like it.

Finally, we were both healthy males with very high libidos and fantastic endurance. We liked fit men, so playful cruising and frisky engagement spiced up our time together. However, I often reminded Nick that a switch to intellectual functions assured more objectivity and accuracy in judgment. Cognitive vs. carnal – a rippa of a struggle, mate.

I read the passionate mind of the hot young man in his sleepy reverie with his head on my abs. I watched his face as beta brainwaves teased the onset of deep sleep.

"He was on 'the juice' for a time."

"Who?" He raised his head, turned, and looked at me.

"Eric. I can read the thoughts behind your previous leering, Nick. We have been together long enough for me to use my psychic abilities and know when you are sizing up a hot man. You were so thinking of him right now."

He sat up and looked at me with more than a bit of astonishment. "Fuckin' mind reader. Scaring me, Boss."

"A rather simple observation, you were tracing your left index finger from the outside corner of your eye to your mouth, mapping that plane of his face. Would not be surprised if, during our lovemaking, you were imagining what...."

He reached up to lightly cuff me and grinned. "OK. So, I call BS on that. You always have my attention when we sex up, Boss. You are an awesome man-beast.

Now very alert, he added, "But wow, Eric... steroids, huh? Some of my gym buds are on testosterone, Trenbolone, and HGH. Goin' monsta. So, the Euro-spy is sporting shrunken balls, huh? I would think that anabolics would be the last thing the men in your family need, Handsome. You all being so fit as fuck and all."

He ran a hand over my torso.

I sat up a bit and said, "You are such a young randy pup. It's all good. But like I said, Eric took steroids in our younger years. I saw him briefly when I was in Copenhagen doing graduate work. He had gone bloody bestial– clothes that hardly fit, rages, and everything. Because of his career aspirations, he cycled off soon after that. The boys with whom he was playing-- my brother does not date... such extreme sessions... they ended up looking like tortured submissives from gay bondage porn."

Nick said, "Having appraised," He finger-counted. "five of the Sorenson males, some in very unique situations, I have to say that my preferred selection is the one who is naked and with me now."

I mocked an accusation, "Hah! You say that now, but...."

He covered my mouth with his and pulled me under him as if to say, "Now be quiet and...."

Thomas Severino

Chapter Seven: Night Train

From the Case Notes of Kayne Sorenson, Ph.D.

"This coach will go straight through to Vienna. You will not have to change trains in Villach. The car will be transferred to the Vienna train. Mr. Garber is in number four, and His Grace is in number six. You have the number five, Herr Doktor and Herr Sechi. We arrive at Dietersplatz Stadtbahn Station, Vienna, at 9 AM. Just ring when you would like your compartment converted to the sleeper."

"Thank you, Petr."

Rebecca chose to keep to her male drag for the trip to Vienna with one modification. In our side of the connected cabins, the Count unleashed her bosom beneath her oxford shirt.

"Darling, it is absolute torture strapping my breasts down. I just need a few hours to relax a bit. Please pass the champagne, Nicky, Darling. Kayne, your brother is divine to have arranged all this. Scary as all get out, but…. Did he tell you that this was one of the cars used in the movie? The original, not the remake."

My brother, traveling as Paul Garber, excused himself before the train left Hermagor to take a few calls. I observed him walking the platform outside, finding a secluded corner, and speaking into his mobile with his eye on the windows of our car.

"Highly unlikely, my dear. I would imagine those coaches are in some railway museum in Paris or Hollywood. Please take what he says with a grain of salt."

Nick handed me a flute of the Moët & Chandon Imperial. Our room service dinner at the Kaiserin Elisabeth was delightful. We were sated in more ways than one.

"Do you intend to do the *Victor/Victoria* gig throughout your entire European stay, my dear?"

My brother's voice came behind me.

"We are in the clear, Rebecca. The operative that was tailing you in Hermagor has been eliminated. So he will not be following us to Vienna. We have eluded detection."

He stepped into the compartment and closed the door behind him. As we contemplated the meaning of "eliminated," he crossed into the tight space to lower the window shade.

Nick offered Eric a drink, which he waved away. I turned to my brother and said, "The tall blonde?"

"Precisely. Familiar, my dear brother?"

I settled into the club chair for our war council, and Nick dropped next to me on the floor with his champagne. He instinctively leaned against me with an arm on my thigh as I lightly touched his shoulder.

Eric did not sit on the couch next to Rebecca. He leaned against the compartment's exterior wall. He carefully moved the edge of the shade every so often to view the platform. Eric's body gave the illusion that he was relaxed, but in reality, he was coiled like an animal about to pounce. Ever since I could remember, this was his usual posture.

"Let me give you a hint. You were quite naked when last you encountered each other. Or should I say, when you were fleeing him?"

Rebecca gasped.

"He is dead, Eric."

"Let it be as you say then, Kayne. But allow me to convey that in the evil darkness of ancient European cities, the dead often prey on the living once more."

He adjusted the shade as the train began to move.

Nick looked at me for an explanation, but I avoided his gaze and insisted, "Enough with the cat and mouse. What is the plan? And please provide the security details if we are to become involved in human trafficking over the next few weeks."

"Always direct and bull shit free, my brother. Honorable to a fault. I remember. Oh, how well I remember. How do you manage to be so bloody moral all the time?"

Nick stood up and said with increasing passion, "Listen. This operation, as you call it, sounds very serious and dangerous. If the two of you are going to dredge up the past and spar with each other for the rest of the gig, it will put us all in harm's way. Can we agree to leave the past behind and focus on freeing those scientists as a team?"

Eric sneered, "Perhaps the boy is right, Kayne. Wherever did you find such a ballsy but intelligent beauty?" He mocked in an Australian accent, "Fulla piss and vinegar, eh lad?"

Before I could intervene, Nick started toward the insulting Eric. He placed an index finger on my brother's chest. He said through clenched teeth and a florid countenance, "Look, Agent Zero or whoever the fuck you are, I am nobody's boy, and anytime you would like to find out why we can take it outside."

Watching Eric clench and unclench his hands, I said quietly, "Nick."

He tapped his index finger on my brother's sternum as he made his point. "Simply put, you fuckin' psycho, I'm his man, and he is mine. None of this boy shit. Am I clear here?"

Eric's left eye with the silver-white pupil seemed to glimmer as he locked onto the gaze of the hostile young cop inches away, breathing fire. He had killed for lesser insults. His mouth formed a challenging sneer as Nick extended his other arm backward and waved his hand to indicate me.

"Just so you know, all of that is of exceptional interest to me. Kayne's safety, honor, and fantastic intelligence are of primary importance. You best respect that if we are going to work together and not get each other killed. And all of what I just said goes for Rebecca, also. We *all* go home, Wenceslaus. No casualties. Do you understand me?"

He punctuated his last point by drawing his face closer and applying more pressure to my brother's chest.

As Rebecca stood up to come between the furious bantam and the cunning scorpion, Eric took Nick's hand from his chest and raised it to his mouth.

He hissed like a deadly cobra saying, "My ssssincere apologiesss, Officer Ssssechi."

Locking eyes with Nick, Eric placed Nick's finger into his open mouth up to the last joint. His expression was at once ice-cold and scorching hot.

***

Rebecca and I quickly did a double insertion, keeping the two would-be fighters apart. I pulled Nick and his raised fists to the opposite side of the compartment before he could make the first strike. Rebecca brought the full effect of her gaze and womanly presence to meet the demon in the corner, pushing him backward.

She said with frosty seriousness, "Enough! What the fuck is it with men? Have you any intelligence at all? Jesus! Lives are at stake here while you three are in a deadly game to see who is the top dog. Or, more aptly, whose dick is bigger. This shit stops right now.

"We are three intelligent and capable people who care about justice being served as an essential matter of human rights...."

Eric made a sound, but she ignored him and continued, "This thing is more significant than any of us and our sibling rivalries or our need to dominate. It deserves fuckin' respect for the work and for each other, damn it.

"To be exact and incredibly precise, stop this, or I am leaving the three of you behind. I am not saying I'm out. I am letting you know I will get this done without you and your fuckin' testosterone."

Rebecca sat back on the couch, tossed back her flute, and held it out empty.

We shamed males said nothing for a bit. I reached over and filled Rebecca's glass, which she raised elegantly.

"Thank you, Kayne, Darling."

Chapter Eight: Ransom Games

Nick Sechi's Journal

After an altercation regarding rules of engagement, we settled in our compartment to create a plan for rescuing the scientists. Kayne upended the bottles of champagne in the ice bucket. The steward brought a late-night repast, Austrian-style tapas, and delicious German wine. Eric did not partake.

Most likely only feeds on blood. Note to self: locate a crucifix.

He said, "It is a ransom game but far from simple. The fact that these three scientists are members of the gay community is merely an excuse to keep them prisoner. Europe and the Caucasus are rife with homophobia. The internment camps are filling up."

Eric continued, "As I said, LGBTQ+ is not the issue. The bad guys want their technology, specifically the nanotechnology related to gene splicing. The price? Well, you take it from here, Rebecca."

"I came to this project because of an unofficial interest on the part of the FBI, the CIA, and the International Criminal Police Organization, INTERPOL. I say 'unofficial' because of their reluctance to undertake direct political, military, religious, or racial interventions. Incarceration of gays throughout most of the world is defended on religious grounds."

Kayne added, "Correct. INTERPOL focuses primarily on public safety and battles transnational crimes against humanity, including, it should be noted, genocide, human trafficking, and the illegal commerce traffic in works of art. I would estimate these are the very atrocities in which we are about to be involved."

"Exactly, Darling. So, through Eric's contacts, we have found out that a certain Eastern European and very mysterious businessman... can you say 'oligarch?'... let it be known that he is offering the lives of Ruslan Dudayev, Eteri Patarava, and Ioane Abkhazi for a very rare manuscript."

I asked, "The lives of three cutting-edge scientists for a book? Sounds pretty whack job."

"The work in question, Nicky Darling, is not just any book. "The Booke of Sir Thomas More" is the only surviving literary manuscript in Shakespeare's hand. Researchers have theorized that he served as one of a few editors on the text of this rarely performed play. It was stolen from the London Shakespeare Museum in January 2016 and was quite nowhere to be found. The black market included and no arrests ever made."

"This is where I come in," Eric interjected. "I was able to arrange a meeting between Count Lajovic here and an agent for someone who has the manuscript. Initial negotiations did not result in its coming into our possession, but showed promise. Recently, I took another meeting with the intermediary, and somehow, he became willing to provide me with the treasure."

I found this Eric somewhat different from the asshole I had challenged a few minutes ago. He seemed focused entirely on the plan and unconcerned with his jealous rivalries. But I avoided thinking of his methods of coercion that resulted in the black market agent's change of heart.

I asked, "So we are going to trade a stolen manuscript for the release of the scientists? And INTERPOL is on board with this? I find this hard to...."

"Not exactly, Nick. The plan is to switch a copy for the original."

"And this copy is coming from where?"

"Me. Darling, in my work, one encounters many forgeries and forgers. The copy is close to being finished, and it promises to be an excellent replication."

Kayne said, "Pretty risky for my two cents. The switch is a major obstacle, I would suggest. Won't a fake be anticipated?"

"Correct, brother dear. I believe, however, that it will be easily done. The text in question is only four pages long. Rebecca's forger truly is an expert with a family pedigree of providing papers for refugees from the Nazis. I have earned the trust of the ahhh... businessman holding the gay scientists and will handle that part myself."

"Where do we come in?" I asked.

"Ars Europa."

The conversation momentarily stopped.

"Nah, nah, nah, boys and girls, I know where this is going, and it's not going to happen." I folded my arms across my chest.

Eric continued, "The multinational theater project has few restrictions in the European community, although its leftist leanings and inclusivity are suspect in most of the arch-conservative countries. They can come and go and cross borders easily. Once we have the three, we insert them among the cast and crew of this summer's productions and get them to a more accepting country that will ship them off to Canada. Our Canadian partners are ready to receive the scientists."

Eric continued, "Nick, your mother and…."

I stood up and held up a hand. "Listen to me carefully, and I will say it in only one word. NO FUCKIN' WAY!"

"Nicky, Darling…."

"Technically, that is three words, but we get the point, my love."

"No, Rebecca, we're out."

I looked at Kayne for instant support. He was staring at the dark Austrian countryside, racing past the window of our compartment. He swept his forelock, an indiscernible expression on his handsome face.

Rebecca and Eric joined me in looking at the pensive professor.

"Kayne …"

After a bit, he stood up and looked at his watch. "The hour is very late, and Vienna is coming up in just a few. Clearer heads will prevail in the morning."

I started to protest.

He continued, "Sherlock Holmes would have said that this is a three-pipe problem and retired to his study to stare at the fire. The Great Detective would have contemplated the case's complexities wreathed in dense tobacco smoke. And so must I."

Eric stood and pulled out a cigarette. He exited our compartment and headed back to the rear observation platform without a word.

Rebecca stood up and kissed Kayne good night. She pulled me into a hug up and said, "Good night, Darling."

Chapter Nine: City of Dreams

The Case Files of Kayne Sorenson, Ph.D.

"Did I really call him 'Wenceslaus?'"

"Yes, Nick, and 'Agent Zero.' You were madder than a rained-on rooster, my Boyo. Very intense and very furious."

I was propped up on pillows on our compartment's narrow bed. Nick lay with his head on my chest, and I caressed my handsome man as he drifted close to sleep.

"Jesus, Kayne. I was apeshit over that asshole. Not thinking clearly."

"Yes, my love. That famous Sechi temper again. Try to sleep, Nick. This has been a very frustrating day, my love."

His regular breathing soon indicated that he had slipped into the arms of Morpheus. I stared for a time at the variant shades of night, sliding past our compartment's window. Near dawn, I moved into a restless sleep.

***

"Come down from there, young masters, and go back to the house. Master Mitch, you should know better than to spy on your father."

"Mr. Quince, is Da going to beat Eric again?

"Master Thomas, please do as you're told. This is a bad business, and it is between your father and your brother right now."

"Man, ya blockhead, for the hundredth time, I like to be called Kick."

"Let's go, Kick Boyo."

"Keep your bleedin' hands offa me, Kayne, ya goodie two shoes."

"Gentlemen, please."

"I got this, Kayne. Kick, listen to your big bro. Time for medicine and for you and me to hit the sack. Gimme your hand, lad."

"Mitch, Eric is gonna get punished again. Doing the nasty with the Marine guy, yes?"

"Not our business, Mess. Let's go before I do my own beating on your arse."

Eric's bed was empty... for hours. Our shared room seems like a tomb with him gone.

Hiding in Ace's office closet behind the louver doors... I'm only in my PJ bottoms... shivering.

"It's done, Sir."

Ace pours a glass of Japanese whiskey.

"Darana, handle the details of his support from here on out. I don't want to know under any circumstances. His name is never to be mentioned at Inala."

"I understand, Captain Sorenson."

Ace alone.

He drinks in the troubled night.

Stares straight ahead at the closet door.

He slowly stands and approaches, his hand reaching for the knob.

"Kayne!"

***

"Kayne!"

Nick shook me awake into the bright morning light of the train compartment.

Kissing me, he said, "Dreaming again and talking in your sleep."

I blinked and tried to bring the morning into focus.

"Damn, Kayne, you're sweating like a Republican at a gay bar. You OK?"

I chuckled and rubbed my eyes. "Just a stupid dream. You cleaned up and dressed already?"

"Right on that, mate," he teased. "Best be moving your Aussie arse. The train is pulling into Dietersplatz Stadtbahn Station. Vienna is at our feet."

He cut a dashing figure mimicking a Viennese waltz across the cabin floor, humming Straussian strains. A knock at the door brought Eric into the compartment smelling of Turkish tobacco.

"Get your clothes on, dear brother. Two European capitals viewing naked Sorenson butt in one lifetime is two too many."

"Are we doomed to discuss past improprieties of our lusty youth? Budapest was eight years ago. I can think of a few bare-arsed episodes in your randy years. Let's not forget Notre Dame."

"Somebody's naked in here, Darlings? Why was I not invited?"

Rebecca swept in through the connecting door, finally in female dress. She sported an attractive sky-blue, full skirt and white, short-sleeved blouse ensemble with a complimentary neckerchief and broad straw hat, which she held in one hand. Her bobbed hair finished the effect.

Nick smiled, "Audrey Hepburn, *Roman Holiday.* Girl, nice."

She did a twirl, pointed to each of us in turn, and said, "Clothes. Clothes. No clothes. Delicious, Darling Kayne, but the Viennese are rather modest, I hear."

Eric said, "I have business in the city today. I will meet you at the Ferdinand Raimund Monument in front of the theater." He tossed three tickets on the unmade lower berth.

Ignoring Rebecca and looking us both up and down, he added, "You do know the upper berth pulls down. Hardly room for a decent shag cramped up in just the one. What happened, lads, struggle for bottom?"

He turned to exit and swatted me on my arse. It was not a playful gesture. I leaned off the bed, grabbed a shoe, and threw it at the door just as he closed it behind him.

Rebecca said, "Ish! Why do I feel like I need a shower after he has been around?"

I retrieved my knickers and signaled with an index finger that she should turn around. She smiled, repeated my finger gesture, and stared intently at my reverse striptease.

I chided, "Now, who's thinking all hormonally, most divine woman? First, you're all, 'he's one hot profiteer,' and now it's 'Lordy, I can't stand to be near that scallywag.' Make up your mind, Miss Scarlett."

"You are so impossible, Kayne Darling. Nick, please get your man in suitable shape for the faded glory of a once imperial capital. I will let Petr know concerning the destination of our luggage. I want to have breakfast in the shadow of that."

She pointed to the window and the beautiful church beyond, turned, and exited into her cabin.

I followed her to the doorway.

"Rebecca, our steward, Petr, is sure to wonder who did away with the Count. I am afraid you will be the prime suspect, my Countess."

I vocalized the suspenseful chords of the score of *Murder on the Orient Express* and ducked as a hairbrush came sailing through the open door.

Chapter Ten: The Plague Church
Nick Sechi's Journal

The 18th-century baroque/rococo masterpiece, Rektoratskirche St. Dieter Borromäus, commonly called the Dieterskirche, rose above an oval reflecting pool at the south end of Resselpark directly across from the train station. As we walked, Kayne waved at a woman, a young cleric, and a picnic basket seated on a bench among the park's trees with a full view of the cathedral. He introduced Professor Sandra Mayd from the Technische Universität, Wien-- Vienna University of Technology, and Prälat *Tomás Sanger* of the Catholic Order of the Crusaders of the Red Star.

"*Guten Morgen, Herr Doktor.* We have the breakfast for you and your friends from the Café-Restaurant Resselpark." Dr. Mayd gestured to the bistro partially hidden among the park trees as the young prelate unfolded a blanket in the nearby shade.

"*Bitte.*"

We settled on the blanket. The morning was warm and bright. The sunshine took on a luminosity surrounding the jewel of marble and gold that dominated our southern view.

"How are your cats, Doctor?"

"Thank you for asking, Dr. Kayne. My little family grows by leaps and bounds despite our very scientific approach to controlling the urban feral cats."

Kayne explained that Dr. Mayd served additionally as the University's volunteer in charge of the feral cats that found their way to the park and the campus. The tiny woman said, "We run a catch, neuter/spay, and release program. Cats are territorial, and keeping a clowder of cats on site prevents an explosion in the feline population. It is a lesson in the principles of environmental biology. The students are a tremendous help."

I thought of my dog, Chouko, back in Florida and how I missed my "Beautiful Butterfly."

Rebecca helped the young priest pass around the delicious Austrian breakfast fare. The pastries and sausage rolls were astounding, as was the strong hot coffee. As we made a bit of small talk, Kayne's gaze searched the surrounding park for unusual occupants.

I imagined our young male friend as the reincarnation of Rolf, the messenger boy in the *Sound of Music*, so classically blonde and clean were his looks. Perhaps the prayers of the good sisters at Maria's abbey saved him from his fascist leanings, and here he was, having entered religious life. I chuckled inwardly at my fantasy.

He wore a traditional Roman cassock and cincture. As he pushed the sleeve of his soutane up to serve us, I noticed that the inside of his forearm bore a scarlet tattoo, a Maltese Cross above a six-pointed star. He appeared to be all of 19 or 20 with distinct Hapsburgian features.

Rebecca accepted a china cup of the morning brew. "Thank you, Father Darling."

Kayne raised an eyebrow at me and pushed off his forehead bang. His cocked expression was a response to Rebecca's very comic form of address.

She continued, "Please tell us about your magnificent church."

The young priest smiled and said, "Is this your first visit to 'The Imperial City,' my friends?"

I spoke up, "Kayne and Rebecca have been here before. This is my first visit."

"Austria's capital offers a unique blend of glamor, mystery, and an intriguingly stunning past. We are famous for our cultural events, imperial sights, coffee houses, cozy wine taverns, and extraordinary Viennese charm. Music, theater, art, and architecture in Vienna are like no other. And, there is no place better to start your tour than here at the Dieterskirche."

The young man pointed to the massive church. He said, "In 1713, one year after the last great black plague epidemic, Charles VI, the Holy

Roman Emperor, pledged to build a church for his patron saint, Charles Borromeo. The saint was revered as a healer for plague sufferers. Construction began in 1716 and was completed in 1737.

"The church initially possessed a direct line of sight to the Hofburg, the palace of the Hapsburgs, and the government center for the empire." He pointed to the northwest before adding, "Dieterskirche was also, until 1918, the imperial patron parish church, the Emperor's parish church."

I was fascinated as he continued.

"From here, you can see the architecture unites the most diverse of elements. The façade in the center, which leads to the porch, corresponds to a Greek temple portico. The adjacent two columns, with their bas-reliefs of scenes from the saint's life, were modeled on Trajan's Column in Rome. Overall, the exterior is a stunning example of the Roman Baroque with its ovate dome rising above the high drum."

Rebecca said, "Father, you have an excellent knowledge of this beautiful edifice."

"*Ja, Ja, Fräulein Quinto*. The religious order to which I belong cares for the church."

Kayne pointed to the boy's forearm.

"The Knights of the Cross with the Red Star?"

"*Natürlich*, Professor Sorenson. *Ausgezeichnete Beobachtung.*"

Hochwürden Sanger stood up as a liveried waiter from the park's café approached to gather up the remains of our picnic. With the crisp manners of a military orderly, the staffer removed the dishes and flatware. He clicked his heels and bowed as he accepted a gratuity from Kayne before retreating back up the tree-lined walkway.

The priest motioned for us to follow. "You will come this way, now, please?"

He continued his tour, explaining that the cathedral served as an architectural counterweight to the buildings of the Musikverein, home of the Vienna Symphony, and of the structures of the Vienna University of Technology, TU, Wien.

We passed the two angels that flanked the entrance and were blown away by the Baroque/Rococo interior as we entered the church.

The dome fresco displayed the intercession of Charles Borromeo, supported by the Virgin Mary. Likewise, the high altarpiece portrayed the apotheosis of the saint. Amid the diffused light reflecting from the smatterings of gold leaf and the solid, arched marble openings of the nave, Dr. Mayd motioned Kayne, Rebecca, and me into a pew.

She said, "We are in your debt, Father, for revealing the glorious history of this jewel of our city. I believe our guests would like to take this opportunity to reflect and pray, so we will say, 'Auf Wiedersehen.' Ja? And allow you to continue with your ministry."

We thanked the young priest for his gracious hospitality. Rebecca extended a hand to the delighted young man and said in a slightly husky voice, "Auf Wiedersehen, Darling." My movie queen sense kicked in – Eleanor Parker, as Baroness Elsa Schraeder, bids farewell to Christopher Plummer as Captain Georg Von Trapp in the Sound of Music.

The young priest said, "It has been a pleasure. Enjoy the theater this evening. Mutter Courage is the highlight of our theater season so far. I have only seen parts of Ms. Savic's interpretation, which is astounding. And now I will set up for Holy Mass."

***

In the very empty nave of the church, Dr. Mayed sat in the pew in front of us. She turned around and spoke in hushed tones.

"My friends, allow me to say two things for your consideration. First, the research of the scientists you mentioned to me, Dr. Sorenson, is unmatched in the field of biotechnology. These scholars have created much advancement in the field of gene editing therapy – repairing defective DNA. Their work must not be destroyed."

Kayne interjected, "Doctor, you are referring specifically to the CRISPR tools often referred to as 'genetic scissors' because they cut a patient's genome at a hopefully precise location, correct?"

"Yes, Doctor Kayne. The theory supported by these scientists is that faulty genetic sequences can be removed at the very least. At the same time, it's theoretically possible to go a step further and insert working genetic sequences after cutting out errors. And since many diseases and cancers can be characterized by genetic instability, it's not difficult to see why the case for DNA repair mechanisms is so important for medicine around the world. Their research represents a significant breakthrough for treating Duchenne Muscular Dystrophy, Sickle Cell Anemia, Cystic Fibrosis, and a host of others.

"My friends, these three have done it. They hold in their hands monumental advancements in medicine. Unfortunately, they disappeared before their research could be shared. You, of course, understand the financial issues should a profiteer decide to.... "

The professor stopped and looked around as small numbers of the faithful moved up to the front pews as services began. She was apprehensive about continuing that was clear.

In the beautiful sanctuary in front of us, our young cleric, now dressed in a long white alb and stole, welcomed attendees and began the worship prayers in German.

Dr. Mayd hurried to continue, saying, "This is all very important. *Ja.* But compounding this problem is that the cause to free professors Dudayev, Patarava, and Abkhazi at the University and in the more enlightened communities across Europe has become a *cause célèbre.* There is much protest condemning human rights abuses on a continent that every day grows more and more intolerant of gays and other marginalized people."

The tiny scientist reached out to touch her friend as a dark figure crossed the opening of a nearby side chapel. Sandra Mayd seemed to start at the movement at the periphery of our group. The observer slipped behind a column and a group of tourists. The presence seemed in no way interested in the architecture of the monument around us but rather in the makeup of our group, conferring in the central aisle's pews.

The petite professor looked Kayne in the eyes and said, "I do not want to know a lot of details of what may follow in the upcoming days of your stay here. I cannot. And I am somewhat fearful for your safety... but... you will find much opposition in your work. I have become aware that there is a turning of political thought in the country. There is a plague of evil and intolerance coming back to Eastern Europe's cities, villages, and rural communities. But many of us resist, nevertheless.

"There is an organization of death and terror behind all of this. This is a very evil turn to distrust, discrimination, and the calls for cultural purity. The agents of this movement are everywhere and will stop at nothing. Please be careful."

Our friend stood, grasped our hands, and abruptly ended with, *"Genug, ich werde nicht mehr sagen Auf Wiedersehen."* She hurried down the nave to the back of the church and the exit away from the menacing shadows in the side aisles of the cathedral.

As we stood and followed, I looked up at the service playing out on the magnificent altar. At the lectern, a dark-haired young man was proclaiming the first reading with an angelic sincerity.

Last, out of the pew, I genuflected and made the sign of the cross.

To the curious gazes of my companions, I whispered, "So, what? Italian American boy from the Bronx. I was a freaking altar boy. Deal with it, you heathens."

Kayne placed a caressing hand on my shoulder and smiled.

Chapter Eleven: Belvedere

The tall man stretched his long legs and crushed his cigarette against the slats of the bench he shared with the woman and her backpack. Tourists passed by in the bright morning sunshine that bathed the campus of the two imperial palaces set facing each other across a stunning park of formal Versailles-like gardens. The Belvedere Palace stables were less crowded than the museums at this time of the day, and it was in that courtyard that he chose to smoke.

The young woman pretended to review the emails and photos on her mobile, acting like a typical visitor and pausing from time to time to suck on her water bottle. She brought the phone up to her companion's face as if sharing some recent pictures with her tourist friend. He nodded and pushed at the screen. They both wore Ray-Bans and spoke in German.

"What shall I tell him?"

"Too early to report much at this point, Lieutenant Irena."

"Which means what?"

"Which means there are key components that have not aligned yet. This whole thing is like a clockwork movement, parts in motion that must line up. That is all His Honor needs to know. He has no choice but to wait."

"He grows anxious."

The man turned and spoke in the opposite direction, away from his companion. "My dear, I do not care or give a rat's arse. You must know that. The timeline on this is mine to control whether he likes it or not. In other words, he can go fuck himself."

"Your arrogance is troublesome as usual. You must learn respect."

The surly man said nothing. He pulled out his mobile and pretended to text. He pointed to a tiered fountain glimmering in the sunshine.

A small child, panicking his parents, ran straight at the couple on the bench, dodging and squealing behind them in an impromptu game of tag.

The man shifted his long legs and added, "In the end, he will have everything he wants."

"And you?"

The child tumbled into a pile next to them and began to fake cry.

The man stood and righted the boy. He picked up the wiggler and took a few steps to return him to his parents. He held the child away from his body as if he was avoiding some sort of contamination. The woman felt herself cringe inwardly, watching the man encounter the child. *A touch of evil.*

The adults were grateful and apologetic for their son's antics as they accepted the squirming boy. Cute but sometimes unruly children were usually allowed leeway in most social settings. The man registered no response to their smiles and thanks. He might as well have been handing them a sack of dirty laundry. The smiles on the faces of the parents froze and then faded. A bit confused, they made their way, child in tow, towards the lower palace.

As he sat back, he locked his hands behind his head. She repeated her question.

"And you, what do you want?"

He said nothing.

"Surely..."

He pulled a Murad from his pocket and lit up, blowing the smoke into the bright morning air. He sat forward and turned to her, clenching his free hand.

"The boy. I will take the ginger boy. He amuses me. He will present no danger to anyone when I am done, and I will have fun. Of this, you can assure your boss."

He examined the end of his cigarette. "He can do whatever the fuck he wants with the others."

It was the woman's turn to look away, and she did, feeling her skin crawl as the baritone voice, dripping with malice, trailed off.

"One more thing. Keep your fuckin' agents away, Irena. They interfere. I have better things to do than to neutralize our own people, as much as I like inflicting pain. Besides, my brother and his boy toy are no fools.

"We are finished here." He stood and stretched, the muscles of his body coiling and uncoiling beneath his t-shirt and jeans. He started off.

"You never smile, Mr. Garber."

He turned but continued to walk away, stepping backward. He spread his hands.

"I have been advised against it."

Thomas Severino

Chapter Twelve: The Actress Prepares

"This one came today, Madam."

"Put it with the others, Uwe. I want no distractions tonight."

"Excellent, Madam, but I will say I continue to grow concerned."

The actress began her makeup routine, her long red hair held back from her face by an encircling band. She applied the pancake. He stepped over to assist.

"How long have we been together, my boy?"

"Almost twelve years, Madam."

The dresser donned his nitrile gloves and handed tissues to the actress as she wiped her hands. She turned in the chair as he sat in front of her and began to apply her eye designs and exaggerate her face's world-weary lines. He traced and filled in a mouth that would chew on fear, heartbreak, and manic rage throughout the next two and a half hours.

"Please hand me another one of those tissues, dear boy. It seems you have given me your cold. I cannot stop the drama to blow my nose."

Mira Savic stopped for a moment and looked wistfully at her young man.

"Imagine. You were a 15-year-old outside the stage door at the Millowitsch Theater in Cologne, a pushout, an obsessed fan, and an aspiring young actor. Remember our arrangement, my dear boy, and our agreement with the state? School first, then a career on the stage."

"Have I not lived up to the bargain?"

Mira Savic appraised the young man who held the pencils and brushes that completed her transformation into Brecht's mercenary camp follower. Mother Courage was a pivotal character in what some considered the most significant play of the 20th Century, written in resistance to the rise of Fascism and Nazism in 1939. A frightful wig hung from a stand on a nearby table.

"You have, indeed. Excellent schooling, including university. You even managed a part-time career in football. For a time there, I thought you would end up choosing the stadium over the theater."

Wiping her makeup from her hands, she removed the tissues from the neck of her dress, picking up the worn work gloves that completed her costume. They prevented painful callouses caused by pulling Mother Courage's War Wagon eight performances a week.

She swept one arm above them, taking in the glory of the performing arts, and brought it down on the strong shoulder of her protégé.

The boy blushed but concentrated on completing the physiognomy of the great actress. He powdered the illusion of slight neck jowls, obscuring even more of her natural beauty.

"You are much too modest, Uwe. Your recent successful experience in the theater is rapidly bringing us to the day when you must leave me, my dear. Supporting roles will soon give over to some leads. Remember what the critics said about your last role. Magnificent portrayal. And a young man shirtless on stage always makes a big hit with your tribe. Especially if you are adorable, and you are, my son."

She added, "You are destined for greatness in this profession, my dear. Not the life of a dresser."

"I had to be here for this performance, Madam. The role you were born to play. It will put the seal on a brilliant career. Oh, and then the come-back... you'll...."

The legendary actress smiled. "No, my beauty, this is it for me. My advocacy work takes center stage now, and much is to be done. Voices must be raised to stop the hate which every day grows around us. Have you seen the crowd outside the theater?"

The young man spoke softly, saying, "Yes, Madam."

Mira and Uwe said little more as she pulled on her boots. They worked at the grey and red wig, pulling it into place and allowing a few strands of her own hair to extend below and off to the sides of the tight bun in the back. The effect was a classic interpretation of the Thirty Years' War female denizen, a rough and rugged survivor, a wild beast of the battleground.

"And speaking of your gays, my dear, how was Mass this morning?"

Uwe was used to the conversational switches of his mother, mentor, and friend. He stood behind her and bent his head so that it was next to hers in the mirror.

"It was fine. I prayed for you, Madam, as always, with gratitude and for your protection. Your opposition is growing."

He pointed to the notes.

She raised a gloved hand to his cheek, a caress with no words.

"And Father Sanger. He is well? Did he receive the ticket?"

Uwe bent to tie the actress's boots. Lifting his eyes, he searched her careworn face.

"Yes, Madam, thank you."

She looked again at her dear boy. They stopped as if frozen in a tableau, the legendary actress seated and gazing adoringly as the young man knelt and returned the look of affection.

"You are wonderful, my boy. Truly."

A knock at the dressing room door, "Five minutes, Ms. Savic."

Mira Savic stood and checked her look in the full-length mirror. *Just right.*

"Come, I have a wagon to pull, my dear."

As they exited, she stopped in the doorway to retrieve the silver cross on a chain she always wore around her neck.

"Come here, son."

She placed it around his neck and kissed both his cheeks.

"Courage!"

Thomas Severino

Chapter Thirteen: The Hyena of the Battlefield
Nick Sechi's Journal

No Eric.

"Well, children. I, for one, have been stood up by better."

Kayne shrugged, "Who knows? I suggest we go in."

The Rococo statue of the Viennese actor and dramatist Ferdinand Raimund occupied a corner just north of the Volkstheater. He was depicted on a marble bench. Whispering to him on a rock was a voluptuous muse, inspiring his genius, a glorious remnant of the age of art and empire.

Between the memorial and the grand Imperial-style theater, demonstrators had gathered. The slogans of the cultural conservatives proclaimed a populist politic, decrying those who would allow immigrants to overturn and threaten the growing spirit of nationalism. Their shouts and placards raised the fist of xenophobic and racist sentiments prominent in many European far-right-wing groups.

Kayne took my hand as we crossed the square, walking toward the theater entrance. As we stepped off the curb to Arthur Schnitzler Platz between the two armies of protesters, I pulled Kayne in for a very public and passionate kiss.

The conservatives booed, the liberals cheered, and Rebecca said, "Bravo, Darlings."

We were surrounded by four policemen. Jail? Theater? Oh, well. An exciting evening in the dungeons of the Imperial Capital....

A young, dashing member of the *Stadtpolizei* with a dark mustache spoke to Kayne, "This way, Dr. Sorenson, if you please."

I thought, *Recognized on the streets of Vienna. Impressive. So much for our undercover operations.*

Rebecca wrapped an arm around one of the members of our police escort. She said, referring to the very boisterous haters, "What I find irrational about ultra-conservative Christians is that they are all too happy keeping people in poverty and illness, uneducated and ill-housed. They are prepared to kill to protect their belongings, to kill doctors, to send troops to kill overseas, and to forego medical treatment for their children, all in the name of Jesus."

Kayne turned and added, "And they hate homosexuals. Look."

He pointed to a sign in German and translated, "Gay People Destroy the Christian Principles of Europe."

As we approached the Volkstheater and just a block from the Hofburg National Government Center, counter-demonstrators waved banners supporting more liberal immigration laws and the acceptance of migrants.

I pointed out one group waving the rainbow flag with a sign. Rebecca translated, "Austria Fails to Act Against Chechnya's Murder of Gay People." The dark-haired police officer shook his head but said nothing, securing our safe passage to the theater.

***

Yet another imperial baroque masterpiece, the Volkstheater, was built for new and traditional works in 1889 by request of the citizens of Vienna to offer a popular counterweight to the Hofburgtheater, a company known for very conventional and conservative theater offerings. In our box, we were surrounded by the ivory and gold leaf design of the auditorium, shot through with frescoes celebrating the divine Greek origins of the theater arts.

The proscenium arch was hung with a gold curtain. A Gobo light projector rippled the words *Mutter Courage und Ihre Kinder* across its surface in dripping scarlet letters.

Kayne addressed the detective, and we took three of the five seats in our loge, "Thank you, Kapitän Pichler, you have been most kind."

"Bitte genießen Sie das Spiel meine Freunde." The hunky officer kissed Rebecca's hand and smiled.

"I am sure we will enjoy the production, Dieter Darling."

Kayne and I exchanged a look. *Our girl moves super fast.*

Kayne leaned across Rebecca and said, "Nick, the play is in German. Would you like me to sit next to you for translation purposes?"

Before I could respond, I felt a hand on my arm as one of the occupants of the last two seats in the box spoke, "I would be happy to assist you, Officer Sechi."

I was surprised to see the attractive young man sitting next to me. "Father Sanger. Hey, good to see you, buddy. And it's Nick."

"*Danke*, Nick. Please allow me to introduce my friend, Uwe Müller. Uwe, I am very pleased to present Officer Nick Sechi, Ms. Rebecca Quinto, and Dr. Kayne Sorenson. I met these folks this morning and had the good fortune to give them a tour of *Dieterskirche*."

The hottie who did the first reading... hmm... yes. I see....

The priest was dressed in secular clothes, jacket, and tie, and his companion sported a similar outfit but without neckwear. Uwe's shirt collar was opened, and a delicate silver neck chain descended under his white shirt from his neck onto the planes of his smooth chest.

"How fortunate then. You will not need me."

Kayne's remark dripped with a bit of sarcasm that was missed by our guests. I leaned forward and said, "Don't make me kiss you again, Mr. I'm-So-Jealous."

Rebecca said in a stage whisper, "Lordy, you two, control your friskiness for heaven's sake. What, are you both 15? We have a priest right over there. Remain calm and do theater."

But Kayne was not looking at Rebecca or me. He was looking through a pair of opera glasses. He focused on a couple directly across the expanse in what was the twin of our box.

A dark-haired, athletic man parted the curtain at the back of the loge. He escorted a tall, older woman swathed in luxurious fabric, including a fashionable scarf obscuring her features. She wore dark glasses that announced her as a celebrity. A regal Garbo, she settled into her seat as the man gracefully folded into the place next to her. As the house lights started to come down, the man took her hand and spoke softly and lovingly to her. She smiled, looked in our direction, and took off her eyeshades as the curtain rose.

**

It was indeed the performance of a lifetime in what many regard as Brecht's masterpiece. Ms. Savic ran the gamut of Mother Courage's story with a pathos rarely seen on any stage, portraying a shrewd and resilient yet selfish and cowardly woman who profits from the war by following the troops and selling them her wares. Despite my inability to understand the dialogue, the experience was like attending a grand opera suffused with flashes of artistic lightning surrounding an exquisitely and poetically brilliant interpretation. Savic crushed.

During Intermission, the five of us discussed Brecht's ruminations on the nature of war. Uwe commented, "The author is not interested in having the audience empathize with Courage. She is a profiteer in a world that is in a constant state of war."

"Right, Darling. Brecht has written what is called a work of epic theater. This piece intends to teach the audience the horrors of war within the political climate of the late 30s, especially as connected to Fascism and Nazism, where virtuous and moral behavior are seen as deficits."

"You know quite a bit of theater, Ms. Quinto."

"Some, Darling. I co-majored in theater as an undergraduate."

Father Sanger returned with a waiter who took our drink order and disappeared. Tomás waved his phone and turned to me.

"You know you and Doctor Sorenson went viral, right? *Prost, Mein Freund!*"

The post was the man-kiss on Arthur Schnitzler Platz. We had become instant celebrities.

"Kayne?"

"Yes, my love? Sorry. Yes. Exquisite theater. Epic, yes."

I moved closer to him. He was distracted, as he usually was in large crowds, his ADHD running in ultra-high gear. However, far from a jumble of distractions, he was processing a series of seemingly significant observations.

"Are you able to follow the story?"

"Yes, I read up before, and Father Sanger has been whispering important plot elements."

"Hmm. Is that what we're calling it now?"

I softly shoved him. "Handsome, you are not even good at faking the green-eyed monster. Tomás is a Catholic priest."

"Precisely."

He did not react further, caught by movement in the balcony. I handed him a cocktail from the tray of the returning waiter and tried to read his agitation.

Taking the glass, he said, "Stay alert, Nick. Too much going on. As Holmes would say, 'The game's afoot.' Danger is very near."

The house lights came down.

***

It happened so fast. Most thought it was a variation on the dramatic ending to the play.

As Mother Courage prepares in the final scene for her parasitic following of the regiment, the actress seemed to be disoriented, stumbling over her lines and staggering as she frantically wiped her face with her apron.

Mira Savic, blood streaming from her eyes and nose, reeled against the wagon's yoke and collapsed on the stage, coughing up blood.

Kayne jumped to the balustrade of our box and dashed along its edge to the proscenium arch. He leaped, grabbed the stage curtain, and slid down to the stage. He ran across to the stricken actress. The massive curtain closed. The reaction from the audience was one of astonishment.

Uwe reached for me.

"This way. Hurry, please."

We descended to the stage right wing via a back stair on our side of the stage. Kayne was standing near the body of Mira Savic, shouting in German.

"No, no. Stay back. There may be contamination here."

I moved forward to help him keep the crowd at bay. Nevertheless, Uwe pushed forward frantically.

"Madam!"

Kayne grabbed him.

"No, Uwe, we can do nothing for her now. Go to her dressing room and secure it, but do not, by any means, go into that room. Touch nothing."

The stricken young man turned as Rebecca guided him backstage, handing him her opera gloves.

Father Sanger removed a small purple stole from his jacket pocket and knelt a moderate distance from the body. He made the sign of the cross and began to pray. The company's doctor, escorted by Kapitän Pichler, pushed through the ensemble, placed a handkerchief over his face at Kayne's recommendation, and carefully examined the body. He shook his head.

"*Nein, sie ist tot.* She is dead."

Chapter Fourteen: The First Floor

The Case Files of Kayne Sorenson, Ph.D.

The bar was a re-creation of a 1930s Vienna nightclub. I asked for a large table in the back. Everyone was very shaken from our experience of murder, most foul of just over an hour ago at the Volkstheater.

"I believe, Kapitän, your detectives will find that the cause of death was a nerve agent in her makeup, an organophosphate such as Soman. Fortunately, Mr. Müller, the late Ms. Savic's dresser and protege, used gloves to assist her with her makeup. Uwe is allergic and must use hypoallergenic grease paint when he appears on stage. I turned his gloves over to your officers.

I would say there is little to no danger of contamination to the company. Still, I am informed that you have sealed off the dressing room after the examination and have kept the young man under surveillance."

The police officer, now in mufti, nodded. His good looks had attracted the attention of many of the club patrons, drinking and conversing in the soft lighting of the club. Table lamps and background lights had the effect of casting odd illuminations from beneath the faces of the clientele and the wait staff.

Nick looked at his phone.

"Kayne, Tomás, and Uwe are on their way here. It appears the medics have given Uwe a clean bill."

Rebecca said, "Strange, I would have thought Uwe would be too...."

She did not finish her thought but handed our guest the bottle of glowing golden liquor recently delivered with a tray of glasses by a shirtless waiter in a vest and bow tie. This place was very "Cabaret."

The Austrian police officer did the honors, passing each of us a glass and saying, "*Whisky aus Österreich*, single malt."

The dark-haired, brown-eyed officer raised a glass.

"To Mira Savic, a legend and a dedicated human rights activist."

It was unclear to me whether Dieter Pichler shared any sympathy for the famous actress' cause. This was a man who played his cards close to the chest. We silently joined in the toast.

I was distracted by a random thought, as I usually was when my mind was overstimulated. The events of the murder, the panic, the grief of the theater company, and the impending public outcry specifically seemed to cause my cognition processes to fire like an overloaded circuit board.

I put the one annoying idea aside, as I had often trained myself to do. But it continued to assail me. *What is this bond that law enforcement officers have, no matter their nationality?* Nick and Dieter Pichler-- the look was unmistakably recognizable. Nick's manly beauty and gregarious personality often drew the attention of both men and women.

Rebecca must be so intrigued by the testosterone in the air. I also noted with frustration that feelings of jealousy, so very rare in my experience, had intruded a couple of times during this very chaotic evening. Strange.

I looked into Nick's rather dazzling green eyes in the glow of the table lamp as Dieter poured me another shot. Nick demurred and raised his beer to the detective's toast.

The waiter led the two young Austrians to our table. We stood at their arrival and expressed our sorrow for his tragic loss to Uwe. He seemed to be in a state of shock but managed to respond.

"Thank you. To get to the point. I seem to be contaminant-free though I have been warned to be on guard for unusual reactions. I was given atropine and thoroughly washed. Please pass me the whiskey. They indicated no precautions regarding this stuff."

This was a stunned man who wanted very much to get drunk. His young companion looked concerned but joined in tossing a drink back.

Uwe tried hard to focus on the details of the investigation despite a grief-stricken heart. "The theater has been closed for the rest of the week. The press is calling this a political assassination. It would appear that the entire European community is outraged by this senseless act."

Rebecca asked, "Why would anyone kill Mira Savic?"

Uwe reached into his jacket pocket and handed me a stack of envelopes. He said, "It appears that it is appropriate that you know of my relationship with Ms. Savic. My ..."

He stammered and choked back emotion.

"My parents were killed in Iraq by ISIS troops nine years ago. My father was a Doctor from Germany who went to that country to care for the war-injured. My mother was a Syrian national of French descent and a nurse. I was born in a village north of Bagdad. We moved where the fighting took us.

"When they were killed, I got out by tagging along with a group of refugees. In time, I was connected with my father's family in Hamburg. When I came out to them, they wanted nothing further to do with me. I wandered and eventually ended up in Cologne.

"My mother-- for that is what one calls a person who takes an abandoned child into her home and raises him, is it not? My mother, Mira Savic, was outspoken in her political views. She came to represent a movement. I am not surprised that she paid for it with her life."

I passed the death threats to the police officer. As he leafed through the series of one-page notes, he translated them for Nick and gave them to Rebecca.

"They are scripture verses justifying execution," said Father Sanger. "They reflect a distorted view of humanity and call for the death of not only the sinners but also those who aid, abet, and abide them. Most disturbing. Please note that these threats quote the Bible, and they also quote the Quran, albeit badly."

Uwe said, "Madam was outraged over the political shift of the European nations and the conservative policies regarding refugees and homosexuals. The current rise of ultra-nationalism and intolerance disturbed her greatly. She took every opportunity as a public figure to challenge the public conscience. This included the roles she chose."

He turned to the Kapitän, "In your search for suspects, I would advise the consideration of local and international politicians, religious leaders, and social reformers who despised her views. She was the object of the new 'cancel culture.' In fact, many called for her blood in this increasingly savage age, especially after her remarks condemning the boldness of the Chechen government's imprisonment and annihilation of gay people."

The Austrian actor poured himself another drink, but the priest's hand slowed his progress along the road to intoxication.

Rebecca said, "Chechnya is a predominantly Muslim, ultra-conservative society in which homophobia is intense and rampant. Homosexuality is grounds for imprisonment. Citizens are encouraged to believe that having a gay relative is a stain on the entire family. President-for-Life Kadyrov has encouraged extrajudicial killings by family members as an alternative to law enforcement. In some cases, gay men in prison have been released early specifically to enable their murder by relatives."

Nick added, "In one of the biggest allies of the United States, Saudia Arabia, homosexuality, cross-dressing, and transgenderism are punished by fines, floggings, life in prison, death, and torture."

Uwe nodded. "My mother was a founding member of *Šumarski Ljudi*, the Forest People, named for the Serbian Nazi resistance movement. Presently, the group is a political activist movement and has achieved some victories for refugees in Europe."

Father Sanger took up the narrative.

"Last year, Germany and Lithuania granted gays visas for entry to the countries based on humanitarian grounds. The Dutch government changed its policy to allow LGBTQ persons from Chechnya to gain almost automatic asylum-seeker status and entry to the Netherlands."

I added, "Thankfully, these governments are much in line with the efforts of the Rainbow Railroad in creating asylum situations to deter these atrocities."

Dieter's mobile chirped. "My friends, I must return to the office. There is a need for me to discuss this case with colleagues. I have been informed that you were given the opportunity to inspect the dressing room with my detectives, Doctor Sorenson. How obliging of them. It seems this case is destined to be a collaboration."

I was not convinced he was pleased by this.

He turned to Nick. "And so, it would be my pleasure, Nick... please excuse my familiarity, Officer Sechi... to invite you to our headquarters as an unofficial consultant. I have looked into your stellar record of bravery with law enforcement in your home of Florida. You will find Viennese police enforcement is among the best in the world."

Nick beamed and said, "Sounds good, and it's Nick, buddy. That's cool. I Air Dropped you my contact information, dude."

The captain stood, bowed, winked at Nick, and left the table.

My ADHD kicked in again, and I noted that we were being watched from a dark corner. The mysterious operative remained at a moderate distance from our group and directly across from my line of vision. The shadowy figure spoke to our waiter and made a slight gesture in our direction.

At first, I thought the observer was my brother as the man seemed to be of similar form to the tall and athletic Eric. I marked him as a person of extreme interest, and I sensed one who represented some danger.

"Kayne? Kayne Darling?" Rebecca was excited, and I knew we needed to do a tete-a-tete. Her antennae were up, absorbing the rather unusual overtures initiated by the exiting detective.

"Kayne, something tells me Vienna cop is either on the make or a huge phony, Darling. So many mixed signals. I don't trust him."

Her remarks brought my attention back to my comrades, who were staring at me. Nick's face held some questions, but he sipped his beer casually. The slightly retro and shabby orchestra played a Kurt Weill selection. A smokey-eyed chanteuse caressed the melody and lyrics of "Surabaya Johnny."

I raked back my hair and reached for Nick's hand across the table but missed. He scooped up his mobile.

He looked up at the Austrians. "Whoa, Dieter says they have a suspect."

He read aloud.

"Viennese police seek a person of interest in the on-stage murder of the internationally acclaimed actress Mira Savic, who was killed during a performance of *Mother Courage* at the Volkstheater tonight. Uwe Müller, a Syrian immigrant living in Germany and Austria since 2009, was employed by the murdered actress."

Uwe slammed the table with dramatic energy.

"This is preposterous. I am a German national. Why would I harm someone who has done me nothing but kindness? What should I do, Dr. Sorenson?"

This did not look right. I had the feeling that the current investigation was not worth a brass razoo. My first instinct was that this was a poorly constructed frame-up. The news item made little mention of additional details.

Uwe's companion was very anxious concerning the events of someone for whom he cared a great deal. Their body language suggested they were lovers.

I looked at the troubled young man and said, "Uwe, if you are innocent, and I believe you are, I will do what I can to bring the killers of your foster mother to justice.

"Holy fuck! Ahh, sorry, Father. The haters are having a field day. Holy shit." Nick all but shouted.

He scrolled his phone and began to quote various sound bites.

" ... Müller, a suspected gay man and foreign national... amid public outcry to end crimes and killings perpetrated by immigrant criminals... right-wing political leaders across Europe... Hungary, France, Poland... another vicious crime by foreign nationals taking over our lands... assassination for political motives...."

Rebecca, reviewing her news feeds, said, "It's been less than two hours since the killing. The techno-universe is on fire with this."

I looked at the handsome actor who now held the hand of the young priest. I said, "There will be much civil unrest, I am afraid. And I fear, my friend, that you are about to be arrested."

I nodded to the two police officers who were approaching our table. They addressed us in German, apologizing for the intrusion.

"Bitte entschuldigen Sie das Eindringen, Herr Doktor Sorenson. Wir sind hier, um mit Herrn Müller zu sprechen."

I said, *"Bitte fahren Sie fort, Offizier."*

The police officers turned and addressed the young man.

"Uwe Müller, Sie werden wegen der Ermordung von Mira Savic gesucht. Sie werden uns bitte folgen."

Rebecca translated, for Nick's sake, "It appears Herr Müller is indeed being arrested for the murder of Mira Savic."

The staff and the clientele of The First Floor were shooting glances our way concerning the presence of the arresting officers. I wondered how many of our fellow clubbers would not prefer to be recognized by law enforcement. Tomás and Uwe were about to panic as the cuffs made their appearance, following an order for Uwe to stand up.

It was all so Josef von Sternberg, the Austrian film director. The candle-lit glances created striking pictorial compositions of dense emotional intensity. The club had taken a gangsterish, dystopian feel reminiscent of the nefarious underworld in von Sternberg's "Greed."

Struggling to control my seemingly exploding brain – the images, the emotional, personal dynamics, I addressed the arresting officers.

"Es gibt keine Notwendigkeit für Handschellen und Fesseln, Offiziere. Herr Müller wird ruhig mitkommen."

"Oh, yes, Darlings. Put the handcuffs away. Mr. Müller will cooperate."

Rebecca touched the anxious man on the shoulder in a gesture meant to allay his fears.

I looked at my man and said, "Nick, considering the charming invitation of Kapitän Pichler, I believe it is appropriate for you and Rebecca to accompany our new friends to the *Polizeikommissariat, Margareten*. I would like you to try to obtain information regarding the suspect in an unofficial consultation. Cop to cop and all that."

I waved them off.

Nick frowned.

"Aren't you coming with us, Boss?"

"I need some time to think this through and would prefer a bit of solitude if you don't mind. There may be something I missed at the theater. I will meet you at the hotel. There's a good lad."

I heard Rebecca say in a stage whisper to Nick. "We have been dismissed, it would seem." She rose and exited with Nick.

Club patrons went back to their drinks, spirited conversation, and moody dancing, ignoring me.

My ADHD was kicking in big time. I took a deep breath and began a meditative process to control the random firing of my brain. I must regain cognitive control if I hope to pursue this case with the accuracy required. One by one, I filed my thoughts in "rooms" to be explored later.

Dieter: "Please accompany me, Nick…."

He is a strange and mysterious figure. All is not what it seems. Note: His German is accented, therefore not his native tongue.

Nick: Interested and excited… would he be looking for additional stimulation in our relationship? Jealousy, Kayne. Get rid of this feeling.

Tomás: A clerical mess of anxiety and fear… there is something he is hiding in connection to his illicit relationship with the young actor.

Uwe: Shock, grief, anger, and confusion… he has danced too close to the wildfires of death and destruction.

Rebecca: Trying to sort out a total "What the hell is going on, Kayne?" Is she truly in control of the proposed rescue attempt?

Eric: Disappeared... and his mysterious woman companion at the Volkstheater... analytically, what is the risk factor of proceeding with him in this case, given his mental condition?

And the shocking death of "Mother Courage."

In the dim candlelight, I mentally opened the door of my feelings, at once usually sparse but always overwhelming. Emotions interfered with the cognitive processes of my analytical mind. I needed to shut away some powerful urges and illogical concerns. One by one, I dismissed baseless suspicion, jealousy, anger, self-doubt, and fear– chained down like so many Frankenstein's monsters in the cold and impenetrable dungeons of my mind palace.

I admitted I was a bit knackered and surprised at my flippancy with my companions. Still, my reactions to Nick and Rebecca were driven by the way the shadows in the corner of the dark, smoky bar beckoned. I would assuage their hurt feelings later. Something was moving me to walk the tightrope of danger and destruction tonight. It was essential to remove my loves from any imminent harm posed by the lurking menace of the stalker and my own feelings of despondency.

I opened my eyes to find a mysterious note requesting my presence, accompanying the drink tab.

Thomas Severino

Chapter Fifteen: A Ghost of Gold

The Case Files of Kayne Sorenson, Ph.D.

Alone, I nursed another whiskey and watched the man across the club sitting in the shadows. He was seated at one of the only tables where the candle had been extinguished.

I stood up and began to approach. The stranger rose, did an about-face, and walked to the back of the club. I followed, noting that he was taller than average and moved with a military gate. The man pulled a newsboy cap over his head, but not before I caught a flash in the club lights of his very blond hair. He turned down the corridor of the *Herrentoilette.*

I entered the dank hallway and noticed that the exit door at the rear was ajar. Passing the men's room, I exited the club into a very dark alley. Sheets of rain descended from rumbling black skies.

As I turned to find my prey in the dark, narrow space, I was immediately apprehended and crushed into the brick wall. My assailant pressed his mouth to mine.

"You taste of expensive whiskey, and I should be licking it off your naked body as you were when last we were together, my Kayne. Mmm, so delicious."

***

I brought my arms up to break the hold, but the muscled-up tall man was adept at body-to-body combat, and I was a bit knackered. Through bruised lips, I said, "You are supposed to be dead, Ádám. I was informed in Colorado."

"The White Dragon lied. Are you surprised? There is no truth these days, *Szerető.* Umph! Sometimes, you are as gullible as you are sexy."

His hands moved with determination over my body, exploring the buttons of my shirt, unfastening them, and finding new places for his mouth and tongue. I pushed and pulled at his body and his clothing.

"Ahhh. Wait... wait. Ádá... Ohh... um, I am with someone now an... well...."

"You mean that boy inside the club who was drooling over the police officer? I could see that from where I watched. I am no fool, *Gyönyörű*. He is a ginger, muscled beauty, as the American gays like to say. That one is obviously your pet. But I can tell he merely amuses my Kayne, a toy, I surmise. Men and boys– we exceptional males use them and toss them away, *Ja*?"

His deep voice continued with a lusty huskiness. "You are a superior male, like your Ádám. We use gym boys for our pleasure, but, ultimately, you need a real man, a strong man to keep your mind stimulated and this hot body satisfied."

Now his strong hands were inside my shirt, slipping down my back and into the waistband of my slacks. He growled, "I feel how responsive you are. *Ja, dein Körper gehört mir.* Your body remembers it belongs to me."

The former member of the Hungarian Royal Guard pushed his hips and thighs against me. Any doubt about his ardor would be confirmed by the full contact of his body against mine. He kissed me again, pulling my head against his and probing my mouth and tongue with his. I responded very heatedly, finding my hands exploring his clothing and body.

He pushed back and said somewhat philosophically while adjusting his outerwear, "Is it not the custom this these times among gay men to share? Many of my gay married friends have a boyfriend or two who provide added excitement. And it is said that your brother...."

I pushed him back further bit, the rain cascading down and soaking both of us. His long blonde hair hung wet to his neck under his low-pulled newsboy cap. His black eyes glinted in the scarce light – steel-like points from under its brim. His mouth and lower jaw were wet with rain and saliva.

I mumbled between panting, "I am quite mad about him, you see. We are new to the relationship, but it is authentic and quite wonderful." I was still in shock to see the Hungarian soldier alive. I plunged my hands into my pockets to control their movements.

"No! Enough!" He persisted, "Do not speak to me of this weakness. I had you once. Possessed you. You were mine then, and you will be mine again. I will not have it otherwise." He slammed against me in protest and lust. Again, his sturdy legs propelled his upper body against mine.

I turned, brought my arms back up, and broke the hold, slipping out of his grasp. I stared through the rain and our heated breathing. I said in utter frustration, "And I left. I ran away. Ádám, I put an ocean between us. That is the truth, my Golden Hussar. We cannot go back."

As I spoke, my voice got louder and more percussive. I spit rain and saliva into the space between us.

He pulled a flask from his back pocket and took a pull. He passed it to me, and I did the same. He looked deeply into my eyes and smiled partially.

"No, my Kayne?"

"No."

We said nothing for a bit. I bent over to catch my breath. My MMA training was for shit, considering the whiskey. *What the bloody hell was in that drink I had inside the club?*

Ádám turned his back to check out the alleyway to the street. He said as he turned back to me, "This American police officer, he must be a very exceptional man."

I shot my dripping forelock, which was covering my eyes, and too late, remembered how much he liked that movement.

"He is. He definitely is."

Ádám chuckled, "Then, will you leave me with only an image of your naked *Arsch* fleeing from me on the Danube embankment?"

I said nothing. The golden soldier backed to the wall and raised the flask again to his lips. He was, indeed, a handsome man. I had fallen hard when we were both younger.

"The woman in the cab that morning, one of your table companions this evening?"

"Yes. Rebecca. My friend."

"And your rescuer that morning so many years ago."

I nodded. We stood silently for a moment.

He moved closer again, toyed with my hair, and licked raindrops from my face and neck. I panted at the erotic play pushing him away.

One does not rebuke the golden warrior prince. His tone was deadly as he drew back and said, "I would rather have you dead than have your heart owned by another, my Kayne."

"You will not prevail, Major Haagen."

"*Ja?* Perhaps not. Then, I will simply tell you that you are in the gravest of danger regarding your proposed exploit. And only I can save you. But only if you come back to me and give me your loyal obedience.

"This murder, the political climate surrounding it, and the investigation in which you and your friends are immersed – beware. Opposing forces here are extremely perilous, and they are gathering against you from every side. Listen to me carefully, my beauty. Kayne, trust no one."

He touched my mouth with his index finger.

I squinted in the darkness and shifted, stepping away from the wall. I walked further into the rain-soaked alley. If Ádám Haagen knew of the proposed rescue, who else had breached the security of this most dangerous game?

"It should come as no surprise to you now that I am operating very close to a malevolent eminence. I am speaking of a deadly dragon whose bloody talons of chaos extend across Europe and beyond, even to your adopted country and the...."

I turned with extreme anger and shouted, "Oh bugger that, ya bloody bogan!"

My frustrated ardor had turned to outrage. I walked back to the beautiful demonic confederate and stabbed the Hungarian's hard chest with my index finger.

"And why would that be, Ádám? How can that be? You are a man of honor, or you were once. Integrity and bravery, badges of your officer's commission, like your grandfather, your father, and your brothers."

I looked at him in disgust, "How far the angel warrior has fallen into hell. How can you be allied with such a dastardly oligarch? I suspected you were being seduced by some vicious evil back when we were lovers. It would seem that you have descended even further into that dark abyss. So you go on and tell me bloody why."

My pointed finger had turned to a fist pounding on his chest. I stopped and snatched the flask out of his hand and tossed back a swallow and then another. A clap of thunder followed a fork of lightning that shot light through the rain-drenched brick cavern.

I loudly accused, swaying on my feet, "I loved, and I mean really fuckin' loved, a man of honor, of loyalty, a bloody golden knight, and he turned out to be made of wax– untruthful, devious as hell, and complicit in some very dishonorable shit, Boyo."

I slammed a hard fist back into his pecs.

"Where is he? Huh? You tell me that! What happened to the soldier I loved? Answer me, you fuck!"

I smacked him in the chest again. He caught my returning arm in a vice-like grip. In a flash, he locked my arms behind my back, his face inches from mine. His hold was firm, his gaze angry and filled with the hate that comes when someone tells you that you have lied to yourself for a long time. After staring for what seemed like a long time, his face softened to an empty smile, but he spoke with a hot breath.

"One makes compromises in life, my beauty."

He released my wrists and turned away. The erotic marauder added in a soft voice, "Sometimes circumstances dictate, and you convince yourself that there is no alternative."

"Bollocks! What did he do, threaten to out you? You are a coward. Of that, there is no doubt."

As soon as I said it, I knew that it was an incendiary accusation. Ádám was a proud man. Clearly, his "owners" had more power over their errant agent than just the threat of social disgrace. His life most likely was held in the balance, then as now.

Ádám raised his arms, and I countered by assuming a wobbling martial arts stance. Again, I felt the effects of the alcohol and whatever was dulling my reflexes. His two powerful backhands sent me into the ground at the base of the opposite brick wall, scraping the right side of my face. He stood over me and continued to beat my face and head. I fought the warm darkness of unconsciousness. I rolled over and unsuccessfully attempted to rise.

I tried to cover my face, but a numb darkness would not be held off. My body felt a shift in the attack, and I braced for a resurgence of the hammering attack. Then, there was the touch of a boot against my arm.

"Drunk and brawling in the alley, my brother? You are ever as much a hoolie as your father."

Ádám had disappeared, and I was very dazed. Multiple images coalesced into a single form of a very wet man who stood over me, extending his hand.

Eric pulled me up into his arms and attempted to set me on my feet. Being unsuccessful, he propped me against the wall with one hand and leaned down to rescue the hip flask and the newsboy cap. He offered me a swig, which I pushed away, stumbling against him to rise.

"Whoa." He slapped the innocuous hat on my head and put a supporting arm around me.

"Do up your shirt and trousers, brother, and I will get you back to your buddy. He is going to love this."

His laugh in the alley was empty and mocking.

Chapter Sixteen: The Dingus

Nick Sechi's Journal

I opened the door to our suite.

"Holy shit, Kayne!"

"Have you lost something, Officer?" Eric dumped Kayne into my arms.

Rebecca jumped up and joined us at the door as I maneuvered the stumbling Kayne, attempting to seat him on the fainting couch. She rinsed a towel at the wet bar and worked to clean his face of the blood and dirt. He winced in response to her ministrations.

"Darling, what happened? You are wet through and through."

I advanced on the sarcastic brother, "Eric, if you hurt him, I fuckin' swear to God...."

Kayne was squirming under the wet towel. He took the cloth, turned down a drink, and requested an alternative, "Water, please, my dear."

Eric drew closer to me with an ice-cold leer contorting his scarred face and said, "Don't get your balls in a sling, Bloodnut. How can I be faulted if your totally blotto sweetie decides he wants to go berko in some back alleyway?"

He patted my chest with the palm of his right hand.

"Just keep ya' shirt on, Bluey. Our reckoning will come soon enough."

He plunked a grey herringbone cap on my head and took a lean against a wall, arms folded, long legs crossed at the ankles. He dripped.

God, I hated this arrogant prick.

Kayne, head in hands, did his best to clear his thoughts and throw off the effects of the liquor. He was wet, bruised, and dirty but seemed relatively unhurt.

I asked, "What happened?"

"Just in the wrong place at the wrong time, Nick. Nothing to worry about, my love. I noticed we had an observer when we were at The First Floor. I followed a suspicious character into the alley and was blindsided. Turned out to be a local tough in search of an evening of scrapping and pinchin' a bloke's wallet. I would have had a go, but I was a bit on my face, you know? Nothing broken, my love."

I said, "Fuckin' bullshit, man. You could have been killed. I mean, what the fuck?"

I felt my blood rush to my face and neck.

He tottered a bit, rising from the couch. I could smell the whiskey and could feel the drip of his rain-soaked clothing. He reached out to steady himself, attempting to calm me down. I lowered him back into the sofa.

Rebecca retrieved a towel from our bathroom and tried to dry him.

"That doesn't seem right, Kayne. Something's missing here, Darling. You were not that drunk when we left, and you are one hell of a martial arts master. You look as if you took a major ass beating."

He shrugged and eyed his brother.

Eric shifted against the wall. Shook his head and walked to the balcony. He lit a Murad and blew smoke into the sky of the glimmering city. The rain was ending as low clouds over the Danube swept a carpet of wet fog over the city. He tossed a comment in his wake.

"The 'master' seems to have taken the night off."

"As long as you are alright, Darling. It's all good."

He managed a question. "Nick, what did you find out about Uwe?"

"Dieter allowed me to watch the questioning and translated for me what was going on in the interrogation room on the other side of the glass.

"The only thing they have connecting him to the murder is his presence in Ms. Savic's dressing room before the play. Their suppositions regarding motive suck."

"Ow! Have a care, Rebecca. Crikey!"

Kayne grimaced as our friend applied some first aid to his very red right cheekbone.

She sat back and appraised him as if he were five years old.

"Such a baby! Be a man and hold still. Holy shit, Kayne. Roll up your pant leg, and let me work on that knee. Looks like steak tartar, Darling."

I switched to our meeting at the police headquarters. With measured words, I explained, "The police questioned Uwe about his whereabouts before and during the performance of *Mother Courage*. Uwe's access to the poisoned makeup is incriminating. They also interrogated him concerning his relationship with his foster mother. They were hot to uncover issues related to his sexual identity and his associations with foreign nationals.

"It looks nasty, and Father Tomás Sanger confirmed that, given the current political climate, this is most likely a frame-up. Dieter told me he is grateful for anything we may uncover in this case, but we needed to let due process take its course. Uwe is being held on suspicion of murder. His arraignment will be soon."

Kayne pulled out his mobile, "I am texting Father Sanger the contact information for the name of an *Anwalt*. The lawyer is a friend, and he is family. His legal firm is the best in Vienna."

Eric stepped into the room, "This affair is a distraction from our real purpose together. We must proceed with the plan to ransom the three scientists and do so quickly. There are three pieces yet to fall into place. The manuscript, the copy, and the exit strategy. To delay now would put the lives of the...."

He was interrupted by a knock at the door.

"Who could that be, Darlings? It is after 2 AM."

Eric gestured for silence and dropped to one knee. He pulled a small revolver from an ankle holster. Coming back up, he looked at me and communicated the following by gesture, *Open the door and step back.*

The man on the threshold was dead.

***

As the corpse fell into the room, it crushed the bouquet of flowers he held when he landed. Eric pulled the body a few feet into the suite, stepped into the hallway, returned, and closed the door. The dead man was clad in an overcoat and a slouch hat.

Kayne retrieved the bunch and handed them to Rebecca, who gasped as she unrolled the newspaper that contained the spray. Realizing that speed meant everything, she arranged the flowers in a vase on one of the tables in the suite. She slid the papers underneath a nearby stack of magazines.

"Who is he?" I asked.

Kayne shook his head. He used a pencil to move the dead man's coat. "Not an Austrian. I would say a Pole from his clothing labels. He has recently been on the Vienna River embankment, the northwest shore of the Wienfluß, in the park, to be exact." He pointed to the mud on the cuffs of the dead man's pants.

He smelled the body and the boots and, still kneeling, examined the hands and face of the dead man using a hand-held napkin to open and turn over the palms. Kayne carefully studied the facial bruises and gingerly moved the nose from side to side. Bloodstained the table linen. He paused to jot a note on a piece of hotel stationery and put it into his pocket.

"Our guest has been beaten about the head. Quite recently, to be exact. His nose is broken. We can tell his profession was an artist... he sports a variety of paints and... inks on his hands and shirt cuffs. A printer, most likely."

"Art forger, to be exact," Rebecca said. It was apparent she knew more than she was revealing at this time.

"Gun in his left coat pocket." He removed it, still using the hotel napkin, and sniffed the barrel.

"Recently fired." He carefully replaced the weapon.

He pointed to the dagger embedded in the man's back. "Death was somewhat delayed but inevitable considering the point of entry and the force involved. Most of the blood was absorbed by the coat and the shirt beneath it. There is no wallet or other identification on this unfortunate man."

Eric entered after searching the hallway.

"Nothing."

He instructed. "Contact the *Polizei*. Now."

Eric looked at me. "Pichler. Tell him hello for me. No, on second thought. I will do that myself. I leave the dead in your hands." He left the room, dropping behind the memory of his leering smile.

***

"I am not convinced that you are telling me everything, Herr Doctor." Corpses do not walk in Vienna. And they definitely do not enter hotel rooms. We do not have the "Walking Dead" in Vienna."

"My dear Kapitän, it is as we have stated. You will find a trail of blood on the carpet outside the hall, and I would venture to suggest on the rug in the lobby leading to the elevators. Due to the time of his arrival, there will be few witnesses among the hotel staff. Look for pond mud in any of the few cabs that would have arrived near the Prinzessin Louisa Hotel at this ungodly hour.

"His traveling this evening involved a walk on the mucky banks near the Mihai Eminescu Linden Tree landmark in the Stadtpark. Two linden leaves are stuck in the left shoe near the inside ankle.

"There is a small construction site near the monument where there is a large amount of iron oxide and a copious quantity of duck guano. Taxi stand 300 on the Weiskirchnerstraß is a few steps away to the northwest in front of the Hilton. You will find he was stabbed somewhere close to our hotel, however. One does not go for a cab ride with a knife in one's back."

I looked at Kayne with a quizzical expression on my face.

"So sure about the cab?"

"It is obvious, Kapitän. The mud is fresh and plentiful. It would have been sloughed off, walking the streets. Surely, you see, here and here. The deposit on the calf of the right leg is obvious."

Kayne went down on one knee, inches from the corpse.

"Also, the murder weapon … This is a Bayonet HK56142B-Tactical/Survival Knife. Supplied to official militaries and mercenaries by Schlachtross, private military contractors, a division of the multinational conglomerate, the NEO Group."

He turned back to the detective. "We have no other information to share with you, I am afraid. I hope we have been helpful."

"Your conclusions are interesting, *Herr Doktor Sorenson*, but I am not convinced of your implied coincidence regarding the dead man in your hotel room. You reveal nothing about the connection. Two murders in one evening, and you three are at the periphery, if not the epicenter.

"Furthermore, you have been in a scrape this evening that you explain as a stumble on the rainy streets of our city. Please. I am far from naïve, Sir."

"Didi," I said, "None of us have any idea why this person would have ended up on our doorstep with a knife in his back. I would say, wrong room."

"Your charms do not include being an expert liar, Nick."

Rebecca looked away, avoiding the gaze of the detective.

Pichler insisted, "He was delivering something, I believe. A delivery man, *Ja*? Transporting something that got him killed. What would you be expecting at 3 AM, eh?"

He turned to the other detectives and said, *"Durchsuche diese Räume."*

Rebecca spoke for the first time, "Not without a warrant, Officer. I believe the search and seizure laws in Austria are similar to those in the United States."

She held up her cell phone.

"I have the American Consulate on speed dial. Shall I ask them to intervene?"

"Please take the body, Didi, and go. We are exhausted and will be traveling soon."

The stretcher boys began to load it up.

"*Nein*, my friend. You three go nowhere. I want this cleared up, and it will take some time. I will be back with a warrant well before dawn."

He pointed to the hotel phone. "Order coffee."

***

Eric leaned on the balcony as the first light of dawn began to tint the roofs and towers of Vienna, burning off the evening fog. He smoked and addressed us.

"Where did you put the dingus?"

"Among my personal feminine care products. It seems men have an aversion to menstruation and feminine hygiene. The *Polizei* went through my things but steered clear of certain items."

I asked, "Is it authentic?"

"Yes. He was carrying the original and a copy. The dead man is Karl Zollner. He is an expert art forger, Darling. He masqueraded as a simple, starving artist. These days, he has been forging documents for distinguished refugees from Asia and Africa who wish to travel through Europe without complications."

Rebecca continued, "Once Eric secured the original, we were connected in Paris by certain co-conspirators in this project. I only met Zollner once to provide the treasure for copying. It was arranged that he would contact me again once he had received the folio and when the copy was completed. I expected that to be in Hermagor, but when we left for Vienna, he must have changed the details of the delivery."

Kayne asked, "Tell me again how you came by the stolen manuscript, my dear."

"So that would be me. And it's how I met the 'Count' here."

Eric picked up the narrative.

"One of my contacts had located the stolen artifact. I think I mentioned that I was able to persuade the thief to give me the manuscript. I did the handoff to Rebecca as Count Lajovic, semi-professional in the art of fencing."

Kayne said, "Yes, your superior fencing skills, my dear-- the sport and the crime, it would appear."

Rebecca mugged innocence, raising her eyes and placing an index finger to her chin.

"Surely, this was an expensive undertaking."

Eric responded to his brother, "All costs incurred were funded by someone with an avid interest in assisting the persecuted minorities, especially members of our tribe, my brother. She is a woman who moves in old European circles of nobility."

I thought of Eric's late-arriving companion at the Volkstheater, the woman of mystery.

"Our instructions to Herr Zollner were to make an undetectable copy. He worked under the supervision of one of Eric's associates."

The brooding operative added, "My associate, as you call him, kept the forger under surveillance to ensure that there were no attempts to steal the manuscript."

I asked, "And those official agencies who reached out to you, INTERPOL, the FBI, they're OK with all of this?

Eric dragged on his cigarette and smirked, "Ever hear of *Mission Impossible*, Boyo?"

Kayne quoted, "As always, should you or any of your I.M. Force be caught or killed, the Secretary will disavow any knowledge of your actions."

"Exactly, Darling."

I asked, "So Eric, your guy? Why would he let Zollner alone with the dingus?"

"While you were with the Viennese police, I attempted to find him. He is currently floating in the Stadtpark. Quite dead."

Kayne observed, "Someone who knew that our forger had the piece and tried to intercept him tonight. It is evident that Zollner fought back but did not survive the attack."

"I have no doubt, brother. Your oligarch wants all the cards. He has the hostages, the treasure, and the opportunity to create some terror by catching you both at a disadvantage. If he is who I believe him to be, he is playing for very high stakes."

Kayne looked at me. It was a name from a shared nightmare. I said, "Karadžić."

Eric did not respond to the announcement.

Kayne confirmed my suspicions. "Yes. We have dealt with him before."

Rebecca added, "I have no intention of cooling our jets here in Vienna over the murder of Zollner, Darlings. I say we get the heck outta Dodge."

Kayne nodded, "It is only a matter of time before both the manuscript and the copy come to light. Did you observe how Kapitän Pilcher examined the flowers? It must have already dawned on him that a hotel like the Kaiserin Elisabeth does not feature cheap silks. I agree we must leave Vienna."

My phone chirped.

"Mother."

"Nick Baby, we're here in Bratislava. Are you ready for us?"

Thomas Severino

Chapter Seventeen: Death and Life

The man known as "The White Dragon" turned in his chair and pressed the contact that raised the painting on the right-hand wall. *Death and Life* by Gustav Klimt rose to the ceiling, revealing a one-way window. He dimmed the lights in his office with another touch and turned on the speaker, allowing him to see and hear the meeting in the next room.

Ruslan Dudayev, Eteri Patarava, and Ioane Abkhazi sat at a large table in the plush conference room surroundings. A man and a woman sat with them as they eagerly enjoyed food and drink.

"... so this does not compare to the food we were given in prison, my friend. We owe you our thanks." The woman, Eteri Patarava, was expressing the gratitude of the group.

"The Director has gone to great expense and risk of life to bring you here from Grozny. Even with the substantial bribes paid to officials in Chechnya, there is still danger." The representative of the organization warmly smiled as she sipped her tea.

Dr. Dudayev helped himself to another portion of the savory Serbian meat dish, sarma. He said, "Before I was arrested in Gudermes, there was a story of a 20-year-old who was kidnapped taking out the trash in a safe house in St. Petersburg. He was abducted by his father and members of his family."

"Yes, families in Chechnya have been encouraged to turn in their queer children and even engage in honor killings. Quite disturbing." The Director's representative, known as the Lieutenant, made a note on her tablet and continued.

"I would like to be sent to my friends in Marseilles as soon as possible. Please tell me...."

"You must realize, Doctor Abkhazi, this will take a bit of time. The political climate in Europe is a difficult one for your people, and many would stop at nothing to do you harm."

"With respect, France, Belgium, and a few other countries have offered asylum to LGBTQ people. Canada has also led the way in championing human rights. We will simply go there and...."

"As I said, this is very difficult, and the Director is very interested in … how shall I say it … a return on his investment."

She left the last phrase hanging in the room as the conditions of their liberation became clear.

"Please explain, *Poručnik.*"

The Lieutenant smiled with cold eyes.

"The Director has gone to great lengths to bring your individual research labs, files, and equipment here to the Fortress. You will be pleased to know that you will be able to continue your research while you are our guests.

"Gene splicing is of particular interest to the Director, especially in connection to the genetic disease sickle cell anemia. You will find the laboratories here have the best scientific equipment for your work, in most cases upgrades from your previous facilities. You will be provided with test subjects, both animal and human. You are directed to focus solely on putting into place the treatment protocol you have developed.

"My colleague and I will supervise your work and the hospitality we will provide during your stay. It will be a most comfortable and productive arrangement. We have experienced medical staff who will assist you and keep records of your progress."

"So, we and our work are your prisoners?"

"Oh, my dear Dr. Patarava, you are the guests of the Director."

"Guests are free to come and go."

"I want to be clear that at this time, you will be restricted to this compound for your own safety. There will be no exception to this."

Her statement was greeted with silence.

"Please enjoy your repast. My staff will return to take you to your lab. Thank you."

The Lieutenant stood and joined her confederate in walking to the door.

The Director lowered the painting.

Thomas Severino

Chapter Eighteen: Didi
Nick Sechi's Journal

"Didi? Seriously, Didi?"

"It's his name, Kayne, the diminutive for Dieter. He and his family emigrated to Austria when he was a child. His mom's family was Viennese. What's the drama, Boss?"

"Ohhh, drama, is it? Well, I would have thought that an informal consultation on the Savic murder case would not have become that casual. Could you have been thinking with your little head again, young Sechi?"

We were on the train to the Slovakian capital in a compartment with a sliding door into the passage. The windows opposite contained an entry for access to the platform when we pulled into a station. I had drawn the curtain of the inner door.

Rebecca, as Count Lajovic, was napping as was Eric on the seat opposite. She had pulled the herringbone newsboy cap over her face to keep out the light. None of us had much sleep in the last 24 hours.

I stopped a very strange cuddle up with him as we semi-reclined. I tried to be careful of his tender face scrapes and injured knee. He was not in a likable frame of mind.

"I cannot believe this. Kayne, you *are* jealous. Amazing."

His gaze was direct, as if he was examining a bit of evidence. He cocked his head from side to side and swept his forelock.

"When we got to the police station for the interrogation of Uwe, Didi – OK, Kapitän Pichler, OK? Well, he was very casual and friendly, insisting that we not stick to formalities. I am capable of keeping my libido in check no matter what others say. And I resent the suggestion that I am some sort of walking hard-on."

"Please lower your voice." He indicated the stretched-out form of his brother, Rebecca's head on his shoulder. "He is not sleeping."

Eric opened his eyes and stared. Without looking at the sleeping woman who was using his shoulder as a pillow, he stood and gently lowered her head to the seat.

He turned away, removed a small container from his pocket, tossed his head back, and took a pill. Replacing the packet, he pulled out his cigarettes, turning back around to the compartment exit. As he passed his brother and me, he touched Kayne's exposed collarbone.

"Try nuzzling him there, Boyo. It always gets him frisky."

Kayne's grab of the invading finger was lightning fast.

"Don't you have some espionage to attend to, brother dear, a bridge to blow up, an assassination, or a government to overthrow? No? Then how about a diplomat's son to deflower?"

He released Eric like he was tossing away a piece of trash. The spy's silver-irised eye seemed to grow even colder as he looked us both over. He stepped back.

"Well, I shall choose another time to insert myself in your play, eh?"

He sauntered to the inside door and exited, turning down the car and heading for the outdoor platform to have a smoke. Before he stepped from view, I noticed that he had his mobile out for a call.

"I must confess I do not like your brother, and that is an understatement."

Kayne's ice-blues caught me in a dream-like gaze with one cocked eyebrow. "But you do like Didi. Remember, I can read the heart. Or, in this case, the...."

I covered his mouth with mine, and we kissed up for a good interval. "Stop this nonsense. Shall I do you right here, or will we awaken our friend?"

"Ha! She has more than once indicated her willingness to watch. Our Darling girl loves gay porn, especially live-action."

He pulled me back into the kiss, his hands moving over my eager body.

A sleepy voice said, "Just how long is this foreplay or whatever it is going to take, Darlings? I am not quite sure if you two are angry with each other or…. Kindly advance to the main event, and I will form my conclusions." Rebecca yawned and stretched.

We pulled into Bratislava.

Thomas Severino

Chapter Nineteen: A Call from the Train

"Yes, you have no worries. Not only are they not going very far, but they are not responsible for the death of Zollner, and you fuckin' know that."

The tall man clenched and unclenched his free hand as he spoke to the man at the other end of the call.

"Stop! You are babbling. Listen carefully to me. In that case, I will get them back to Vienna. Fuck extradition! Listen to what I am bloody telling you. They are not going to bolt. I have this under control, boy. Do not question...

"You know what? Fuck you. You threaten like coming after me will get your hot arse nailed faster than you can drop a cake of soap in a prison shower.

"*Nein*! At this point, you have no choice if you want this to fall out the way we discussed. Oh, and Officer Fucko, you know that actor boy is not guilty. You are just keeping him on ice for political reasons. Or perhaps you have more carnal intentions there. Just remember, he is in love with a priest.

"What? Well, start looking for other suspects, Mate, some credible ones. Act like a bloody police officer instead of a...

"Yes... my brother would be happy to provide you with more consult. He loves showing off his logical bullshit.

"Good.

"Now, you are making sense.

"No. I am not sure when I will see you. Our last session was not as intense as I intended. You got one deadly vibe going on when we rut, *Schlampe Junge,* and you bed like a person with an addiction, but you are losing your unique ability to service my needs as savage as they may be. Kill me or satisfy my lust, you decide.

"No, I will not see you for a while. Stop! Your begging is amusing but useless. This project is incredibly complex, and our encounters only fuck up your thinking. Find other enjoyments.

"Oh yeah. Your little muscle boy is apparently quite hot for his *Polizei* buddy. He actually refers to you as 'Didi,' mate. Drives my brother crazy, and I fuckin' love it."

He ended the call.

Chapter Twenty: The Theatrical Team
The Case Files of Kayne Sorenson, Ph.D.

Nick's mother was an attractive woman in her fifties with an assertive but kindly style and an instantly perceived love for her only son. Her reputation as an eminent educator and internationally known Shakespearian scholar had no effect on her very personable manner. Professors tend to be such eggheads, and I am no exception, I realize.

Dr. Viola Sechi and Ms. Portia Sechi sat with us for refreshments in our rooms on the fifth floor of the Hotel Devin, Bratislava, on the banks of the Danube. Nick's sister was a very focused young businesswoman under whose gaze I was the subject of inspection. Her talents for organization and leadership of a significant international arts program were easily discerned. As I have always found women intellectually fascinating, these two were no exception-- one the consummate scholar, the other the entrepreneur and CEO.

Both women were dark-haired and dark-eyed, indicating that Nick's ginger coloration came from his father. He delighted in their attention and was eager for them to take a liking to his former educator and current love interest.

"We are around the corner at the Radisson. We do not have such a stunning view of the Danube. Nick, you are so thin. I need to cook for you."

"I am fine, Mother. The last thing you need to do is be harnessed to a kitchen on this trip."

Viola pursed her lips and pulled at her son's cheek with the thumb and forefinger of one hand.

"Dr. Sorenson, see that he gets some good Italian food. And what's all this about the killer in Ft. Lauderdale and that scandal in Aspen? Nick, you are dancing on the edge of the volcano. This is all I need."

Dr. Sechi looked at me with one of those friendly but seriously-I-want-to-know-who-you-are looks that are a mother's stock in trade.

She continued as she sought to examine my soul, "He always has been a risk-taker-- the family superhero, Dr. Sorenson. Has he told you about running away to join the circus when he was a boy? All the way to Montreal. May I call you Kanye?"

I struggled with my coffee to hide a spit take.

Portia and Nick jumped into the conversation simultaneously.

"Kayne."

"Kayne, Kayne, mother, Remember?"

"Yes, yes. I do apologize. Kayne. Of course."

I smiled.

"See, I even have the mark of divine punishment and paradisiacal exile." I raised my pesky forelock to show the scar near my hairline.

Portia joined her mother in scrutinizing my face.

"And, while I will admit that I enjoy singing on occasion, rap is beyond my meager talents."

Portia smiled, "You are much too modest. I saw the videos on Nick's Facebook page. Let me just say, if neither of these gigs works out for us, I will so manage your singing career."

Nick said, "So, what is the schedule for your Ars Europa program?"

"Quick in and quick out, so to speak. Funding for the multinational project has been cut to the bone. We are in rehearsal to the end of the week for 'King Lear.' We open Thursday night and go for four nights at the Old Slovak National Theater."

"Wow, Portia. That seems fast!"

Viola said, "Tell me about it, Nick Baby. Actually, Portia arranged for the company to rehearse our program offerings last May, and when we left Brussels, the production was in excellent shape."

"Mom is a master of her craft. She has a comprehensive understanding of the play and nuances the interpretations for a 21st-century audience."

"Thank you, Portia. We are an excellent production and direction team, and Ars Europa is such a fine organization. Each summer, they mount productions throughout Europe and the Mediterranean. So, there are cycles of traditional offerings from Reykjavik to Istanbul."

Portia added, "From here, we go to Budapest and then Ljubljana in Slovenia. Ars Europa wants to hit a variety of European communities with the power of theater. So we contracted four performances, each city, a real "bus and truck" gig."

I said, "I hope we can spend some time with you and enjoy each other's company. Bratislava has much historical beauty and a proud Czech culture going back thousands of years."

Portia looked at me over her coffee cup with a somewhat piercing gaze. I wondered: *Is it a family trademark to mentally undress persons of salacious interest?* Nick was a master at it. The visual sense was strong in this family.

Viola said, "Kayne, I hope we will be able to tour the famous Bratislava Castle and the Sigismund Gate."

"I would be happy to arrange a tour, Doctor."

"I would love to get some running in," Portia said. "The Promenade along the Danube looks especially inviting."

Nick responded, "Great. Kayne and I have just been talking about getting back to training. Nothing has been going on in that department since we left Hermagor. We'll make it happen."

The door to the suite opened.

I announced, "Dr. Sechi, Ms. Sechi. Allow me to present His Excellency Count Krisztian Lajovic." The Count removed and placed a hat on a table, shook her bobbed hair, strode forward, hand extended – million-dollar smile.

"Welcome, Darlings. I am Rebecca."

Thomas Severino

Chapter Twenty-One: Karadžić

Notes from Rebecca Quinto

Nick asked that I keep notes of the case for the historical record. I continue to be a lead player in the attempt to rescue the three scientists from their captivity. This adventure has come solely through my initiative. I accept the consequences of the project and its implementation completely. It is important to say that should anything go wrong, it's entirely on me. And that, Darlings, is saying a lot considering the cast of characters.

I felt it was essential to be proactive. Kayne and Nick were excellent backups, but, as you have realized, our team's chemistry was incredibly complicated. We were not coming together. We seemed to be held back by family rivalries, sexual tension, and a casual familiarity that comes with being close friends. But, let me just say, men can be a lot of work sometimes.

When we arrived in the Slovakian capital, Eric and I disappeared for a few hours. I sported a very drab Eastern European look, slightly Sally Bowles (the hair) and partly Julie Andrews in "Topaz" (the trench coat). We met with an operative associated with INTERPOL a few blocks from our hotel at the Soldier Monument, the *Pamätník padlým vojakom.* I pulled my cap down and sat next to a woman who, from time to time, rocked an empty baby carriage.

Eric stood with his back to us, leaning on a wrought iron, waist-high fence, watching the waters of the Danube. Even from the rear, Eric Sorenson was an impressive male, his body stretching the confines of his t-shirt and jeans. From the front, it was apparent he was going commando. Lovely... The middle Sorenson used his body and choice of clothing as carnal temptation, inviting extreme and intense physical encounters.

He smoked. I knew he was instinctively aware of everyone around us without turning his head.

The woman said, "We understand that the "Director" has successfully removed Patarava, Abkhazi, and Dudayev and is holding them somewhere in the mountains southwest of Zagreb."

Eric spoke in the direction of the river.

"So, mate, we make the exchange and take possession."

"Not that simple, Mr... um... Garber. Please do not be hasty. The Director is stalling for a reason. It should be obvious to you both that he wants the research. It is worth billions. And this may take time or, then again, it may not."

"I'm gonna need you to go all-in on this, Agent Kalis. There is more going on here than the rescue, yes?"

"True. The neutralizing of General Raheb Karadžić, aka 'The Director,' is the prime objective here. He has been instrumental in creating instability among nations across the globe. He arranges and funds a murder, terror, assassination, corruption, and election interference program. His services are for hire. Many of the ultra-conservative regimes are either availing themselves of his expertise or adopting his philosophy of extreme nationalism – fascism, pure and simple."

I said, "So, you led us to believe we were going to waltz into his lair and do a rare-art-for-people swap, and that was it."

"My dear, Ms. Quinto, there is no way Karadžić is going to let these researchers go. The finale he intends is that he gets the manuscript, the researchers, the two of you, and any associates you may bring into this affair. You do not want to end up his captives. If they aren't ransomed, his prisoners do not last long."

Eric said nothing. I was beginning to think this lesson was for my edification and that he was well aware of the end game.

"That is where you come in, Mr. Garber. We understand you have the manuscript and the copy for the switch."

I answered. "Yes. And at a very great and dangerous expense. Zollner is dead."

"Here again is the hand of the General, most likely eager to shortcut the plan or to inspire terror in you or your confederates. He is also behind the death of Mira Savic, I have no doubt.

She paused to rock her invisible baby. She continued, "We require that you turn the original over to me for restoration to the London Museum."

"I'll think about it."

"Your hesitation in this matter is disturbing, Ms. Quinto. I strongly advise you to acquiesce."

The agent switched gears. "Mr. Garber, with your unique field operative experience, we depend on you to secure the General and deliver him into our hands. Do whatever needs to be done. Are we clear?"

"So, what I am hearing is that the rest of us, the academics, Dr. Sorenson, Officer Sechi, and whoever are collateral. Expendable."

"I am sure that it will all work out, Ms. Quinto. Your colleague here is one of the most lethal agents ever to stand on European soil. Excellent strategy on our part, eh? The most highly trained mercenary on the continent against a beast of legendary proportions."

Agent Kalis waved a dismissing hand. "Thank you, and we will be in touch."

Eric sniffed and blew smoke into the air.

"One last thing."

We turned from our exiting to view the speaker.

"Dead, Karadžić is of no use to us."

Thomas Severino

Chapter Twenty-Two: The Promenade

Nick Sechi's Journal

"So, I need to know your secret for snagging the hottest men on the planet, little brother. I am so jealous. The man is a god. Oh yeah, and the only other hot man I have met in Bratis-fuckin'-slava turns out to be a woman."

I raised and lowered my eyebrows a few times and said, "Not my fault that you were not born a gay man, Por. Straights are way too much work. The secrets of my people take years of practice and experimentation, hence the appellation, 'practicing homosexual.' I cannot reveal more on pain of having my gay card revoked."

She smacked me on the back of my head as we ran.

"I know you, Nicky. You hardly need any practice after nabbing all of that."

She gestured at the sweating Kayne in his nylon running shorts and running shoes. He stopped and spoke to another runner on the trail ahead of us. Squatting, he examined the jock's lower leg and ankle. We ran past them, but he caught up and alternated his facing front and then back as he ran ahead of us.

He was indeed a glorious specimen of a man, sweat glistening on hard muscles in the hot July sun. He had unleashed his black mane, which reached to his shoulders like the tresses of a heroic barbarian. The inked panther on his rear deltoid coiling as he flexed and twisted in the run. It would be overly poetic of me to say that his eyes were bluer than the Danube. So, I won't say it.

LOL

"Hey, Boss, that's so wrong you hitting on the hot jocks right in front of my sister. Wassup with that?"

Kayne laughed, checked over his shoulder, and turned his head back. He reached up with one hand to pull up his jet-black hair, plastered to his head and neck, a visual I so enjoyed when we made steamy love. He flashed a lascivious smile.

"Just getting contact information... whoa!... ohhh, baybee." He flashed a shit-eating grin.

"See how you are?"

He looked again over his shoulder and swerved to avoid a pair of runners we were passing.

"Nick, he was doing it wrong. I offered to send him my monograph on low-impact running. My love, I am innocent of all charges, and I am yours devotedly."

I winked.

"Catch me, hot boy."

He turned forward and sprinted down the promenade. As I accepted the challenge and pulled away from my sister, I heard her say, "Jesus, I am so in lust for that man!"

***

Kayne and I were pounding out push-ups on the grass when Portia caught up. We held each other's feet for the ab work-- sit-ups in various positions. Finally, Kayne sat against a tree as I stretched out with my head in his lap. He automatically and casually caressed my head, tickling it with leaves of grass.

Portia crossed her legs and sat next to us. She pulled out three protein bars from her running pack and distributed them.

"OK. The murder of Mira Savic. Who wants to go first?"

"Wow! Total key change, girl. Where's this coming from?"

"Mother, of course. She knows you were there, and from what I know of both you and the renowned consulting detective here, I am sure you are up to your asses in this."

Kayne waited for my response.

"Yeah. It was horrific. Right at the end of the performance, on stage and everything. A lot of blood. We hoped to help the Viennese police to bring the killer to justice, but they have the wrong guy. So, we are sorta on the lamb."

"Sometimes you sound like dialogue from a film noir, Nick. Come on, come on, spill it, little brother."

A voice just above my head said, "Yes, Nick Baby, tell us." I sat up to swat Kayne, but he pulled me down and kissed the top of my head, patting me like a favorite puppy dog.

Portia giggled.

"I so am enjoying the infantilization of Nick Sechi. Not." I protested. "Is this to be a continuous performance, or can I expect to somehow regain my manhood at some point."

Kayne shifted his lower body beneath me and said, "Let's not bring manhood into this, Officer."

"So, the three of you are suspects and are fleeing the law?"

I looked seriously at my sister.

"Portia, you need to keep this from Mom. No, I mean it."

"Nick, Mother realizes that in your profession of law enforcement, you must take risks. She is very proud of you."

"And she is fearful."

"From what I hear, you do take a lot of risks. He has always been headstrong and daring, Kayne, a real daredevil when we were kids. Mom called you out on that time you ran away and joined the circus."

"Total BS, doll. First, not just any circus-- Cirque du Soleil, Montreal. And I did not run away. I had a scholarship from high school. I just didn't tell a lot of people."

Portia addressed Kayne, "Father was wild. 'I did not raise my only son and namesake to be a circus clown.' Dad had a fierce temper. Went with his northern Italian coloring. They used to call him the 'Red Devil,' a total hothead. Nick is so like him in that."

"Oh, really." I could tell Kayne was rolling his eyes. I softly punched his arm.

"Blah, blah, blah– family histories are such a bore." I did my best Katherine Hepburn, from "The Lion in Winter."

"Well, what family doesn't have its ups and downs?"

"So...?"

"I hesitate to say too much. We have a case that involves some stolen property, and we were taking delivery. The messenger arrived on our doorstep dead. The Viennese police would like us to be more cooperative, is all."

"Holy shit! What...?"

Kayne said, "Portia, I am sure you can appreciate the delicacy of this case. There is much we are not at liberty to divulge because to do so would put innocent lives at risk. Please know that your brother is safe because of the strength of our team and his own expertise in fighting crime, mentally and physically. I mean, who is gonna mess with all this muscle and smarts?"

He tickled my abs.

"Yeah." I flexed and added, "And Rebecca is one kickass woman."

Kayne said, "Our friend seems to have made that apparent."

Portia continued, "Nick, let me give you some advice from the home front. Do not underestimate Viola. Mom raised six amazing children and one orphan cousin, buried a beloved husband who died at an early age, and then proceeded to rise to the top of her field as an academic and a cutting-edge artist in the theater. I have learned so much from working with her, professional to professional. Protecting her from what's going on is infantilizing her. It's like Mom calling you 'Nick Baby' and the cheek tweaking, which reduces you to that little boy from St. Raymond's Parish in the Bronx."

Ah, family memories.

"How is Cousin Nolo?"

"A fuckin' mess. Killer good looks and a real lady's man. Breaking hearts all over the City. Needs to keep his penis from making all his decisions."

Kayne roared. Yet another family characteristic on which he frequently called me out was just confirmed by my sister's gossip. We are a frisky brood, we Sechis. So, shoot me. I really, really like sex.

He chuckled, "I hate it when I am right."

Still, head on his lap, I folded my arms and tried to pout like a man and not a spoiled child.

Totally getting it, Portia's eyes flashed as she smiled.

She checked her watch and announced, "I need to get cleaned up and go to the National. We are doing the tech run-through tonight."

She threw her head back and groaned, "This is going to be a long evening. First off, the play goes on forever. Second, the National was built in 1886 during the Austrian Hungarian Empire's golden days. I find these ancient relics, although claiming state-of-the-art, are far from modern."

Kayne said, "We are looking forward to a spectacular Sechi and Company production of a work 'that transcends the bounds of literature announcing the beginning and end of human destiny.' So said the noted Shakespearean scholar Harold Bloom. It's family love gone horribly wrong."

Oh, brother. His scholarly swag is showing.

I chuckled. Portia was spellbound as he launched into Shakespearian theatrics.

"Reason is madness."

Thomas Severino

Chapter Twenty-Three: Suddenly
Nick Sechi's Journal

The singer, one hand on hip, stretched out the syllables of one word into the microphone.

" ... an-tis-a ... (Audience shouts: Say it!) ... pa-shun."

The crowd cheered as he completed the last two lines of "Sweet Transvestite" with a sexy eye roll, a sensual strut, and an erotic pucker.

Portia leaned in and said, "Mike crushed as Dr. Frank-N-Furter in our production of "The Rocky Horror Show" in Milwaukee. The boy was born for that part. Rave reviews."

The young actor stepped from the small stage and brought the mic into the audience.

Portia added, "His Edmund, in our 'King Lear,' is also quite good, a hateful beauty filled with lust and craving power. He has an exceptional career ahead of him."

"We hope that our company brings the opportunity for our actors and technicians to hone their craft and advance their careers in the profession." Viola was beaming as the applause ended.

"Spoken like a true educator, Mom."

After a very smooth rehearsal, we took over the lounge at the hipster cocktail bar "Koktejl" near Bratislava's Old Town. The hour was late, but the company was jazzed. We provided the entertainment, and the proprietor kept sending complimentary drinks. Bar patrons were three deep at the rear of the club.

Dr. Frank-N-Furter/Edmund/Mike stopped at our table and planted a kiss on my cheek. His impromptu slash of bright red lipstick left a perfect lip print. The crowd went nuts.

He teased with the microphone and appeared to offer it back and forth to the members of our table, finally settling on Kayne. Portia was freaking.

Kayne did an oh-my-gosh-no and not-me bit before accepting the offer and bounding to the stage. He consulted with the pianist, the stage manager for "Lear," and a familiar melody began.

Someone handed him a pair of geek glasses. His baritone started soft and built with warmth and passion as he took on the role of Seymour Krelborn, the nerdy and timid young florist in "Little Shop of Horrors." The love ballad "Suddenly Seymour" needed an Audrey, Seymour's ditzy lady love.

As Kayne ended his verses in the duet, he extended his hand toward our table. My sister practically propelled me on stage as the accompaniment vamped. I launched my tenor into Audrey's songlines to praise the transformative power of true love.

As we raised the last chorus to the rafters, I ended in his arms. The pianist was standing before the keyboard and pounding out the final lines as the adulation of the spectators washed over the room.

He turned me and kissed me as the applause ramped up for the last time. We reached our table just as a group of six women began "He Had It Coming" from Chicago. The lead singer was wearing a t-shirt with an image of Mira Savic on the front with a broken heart. Damn, commercialization was swift. The actress had been dead for less than a week.

Portia congratulated us and cried out, "Somebody bring me a couple of contracts!"

Viola gathered me into her arms and said between kisses, "He is marvelous, Nicky. I am so glad you are happy."

***

The audience had thinned out as the hour approached dawn. We were tired and very tipsy or "on my face," as Kayne would say.

"What time tomorrow, dear?"

Stage Blood

Portia replied, "Dress is at 2 PM, Mom. I think some local high school kids are coming. Then five performances, and we are outta here on Sunday night."

Outside, it was dawn. We decided to walk to our respective hotels.

Portia said, "Kayne, what's up with your brother? Still can't believe there are two of you looking all so…" She weaved a bit on the sidewalk, and Kayne took her arm.

"He is quite antisocial, but Rebecca is not. I would venture that he cornered her at that back table with plans and details of our current project."

"We need them both to cut loose. Rebecca's song was beautiful. I would love to see your bro get his groove on."

She drew the single rose from Kayne's shirt pocket and put it into her teeth. She did an inebriated flamenco on the pavement, clapping her hands above her head. Kayne smiled. I reached to steady her.

"Easy there, Wild Girl. Eric is a huge mess in many respects. Sorry, Kayne."

Kayne nodded.

"Ohhh yeah, sexy bad boy vibe. I just want to climb on that muscled back of his and…." She waved the rose in one outstretched arm.

"Portia!" Moms Sechi was not amused.

My mother added, "He is a bit intense, and I mean no offense."

Kayne spoke, "Also, my brother shares my… how shall I put it?…."

I interrupted, cutting to the chase, "He's gay, Portia. Sings in our choir. Big 'mo. Runs in the family."

Portia stopped and did a very drunk, hands on hips pose, "Ya, know, they're all married or as gay as a goose. What's an energetic straight girl to do?"

"Well, I would say, for now, take a cold shower and a long snooze, sister. Here's your hotel. Goodnight, Mom. We'll see you guys tomorrow. Good dress – I mean bad."

131

"Right, bad dress rehearsal, good show."

My mother embraced my handsome man and added to her departing kiss, "Take care of him, Kayne."

I thought, *Cheers, she got it right.*

As they left us and we started down the block to our hotel, I took hold of his arm.

"Come on, Aussie studly. I got some gay stuff I want us to do."

Chapter Twenty-Four: Earlier
Notes from Rebecca Quinto

Koktejl rocked out big time, starting with our arrival and continuing well into the early morning. Nick and Kayne were fantastic and loved by the group of performers and regulars. I longed for a chance to perform with them. Eric and I sat in the back, in a dark corner, and discussed the progress of the rescue project.

" ... and I do not trust that disaster, Agent Kalis, Darling. We turn over the 'Booke,' and we get dick regarding a connection to the Good Guys. I get the feeling they don't give a flying rat's ass about Karadžić's hostages. "

Eric lit a Murad and blew me off, saying, "Two things, Rebecca. We need the exit strategy, and I'd say we are looking at it."

I waited, then the creepy spy pressed ahead.

"Second, the Director has no intention of moving forward until he is sure that he has the research of the captive scientists. Our contact is saying at least another week. Seems they had reliable trials even before they were imprisoned. Do you still have the documents secured?"

He blew smoke into the overhead beam of the spotlight.

"In reverse order: The decision to embed our quarry in the theater company to get them out of Europe is going to need to be planned delicately. Nick is determined to leave his family out of this, and frankly, I can see why. Karadžić is a maniac, and there is a real chance that the death toll in this assignment could be significant unless we are careful. But I have an idea."

"Go on."

"The delay of the operation may work to our advantage. Portia and Viola need to be preached up on the mission. They are good people, and I have a feeling they would be sympathetic to our cause. If they say they want to help, I believe Nick will back down."

"How about Kayne?"

"Yeah, see. There's the key, Darling. Kayne needs to be the preacher in this. He is a first-class educator and possibly the brightest man on the planet. Somehow, we need to encourage him to do what he does best."

"And what's that, Your Excellency, look shagable?"

I smacked him lightly and immediately thought, Wrong move, girl. Do not touch this guy. His diamond-colored eye looked coldly at me.

"Your slightly lewd comments leave me more than a little bit scared, Darling. You know, sometimes I wonder if you are all there." I pointed to his head.

"Will be in a minute." He popped a pill with a swallow of soda water and checked his SmartWatch.

I continued, "I mean, I will get him into pontificating on the rise of fascism in Europe and/or the persecution of the LGBTQ community. I believe they will offer to help us following his exposé. My Mark would say, 'the power of the spoken word.' How's that?"

"Not the way I would do it."

"And what would you do?"

"Make them an offer and tell the red-headed muscle boy to go fuck himself."

"You know… why are you not dead? This smash-and-grab diplomacy of yours must have resulted in more than one bullseye on your back."

He leaned over and grabbed the opposite edge of the cocktail table. Eric pulled his upper body into a muscle-rippling stretch like an uncoiling cat.

"I am so fuckin' bored with this nonsense." He indicated the stage. "Never was a team player—should have done this solo. Damn, I need some intense amusement, a distraction."

"Well, before you take off, let me summarize my response to your first point. Delaying is fine at this point. It will allow us to get the production company on board and strengthen our team. Let me just make this other point. You guys have so much damn emotional baggage. I really fear a total screw-up unless we can get this shit together. Can you put together some team-building experiences?"

"Yes. Here, we agree. We may have to fight our way out of a close situation, and I fear that it could be a bloody mashup without a serious bout of training led by me."

"Set it up, Darling."

"Let me call in a few favors."

I added, "And, yes, the documents are rarely out of my sight. Do not concern yourself."

"Right. Well, I am heading out. There's a rough sex club on the wild side of town I need to check out. How many leather boys would you like me to annihilate before you see me again?"

"Jesus, you are a horror. Remind me again of why I have you in on this?"

"Because, and you need to realize this, you are going to require deadly force before too long, and I am prime Project Bad Ass."

I said nothing and let his words trickle down my unconscious like a deadly poison.

I stood up. "I am going to go sing, and I will be amazing, Darling. I will talk to you soon."

I walked to the stage and removed a single rose from the vase on the bar. I spoke to the pianist and hung my cap on the edge of his music stand as the opening chords of a song from "Victor/Victoria" began.

I took the mic and began to sing Henry Mancini's "Crazy World."

Thomas Severino

Chapter Twenty-Five: Return

From the Case Files of Kayne Sorenson, Ph.D.

"Thanks, Scott. This is exactly what I need. Best to you and Gints."

My web researcher in Colorado rang off after promising to send the link to his report by secured email.

"Our family and friends in the American Rockies send their love, Sleepyhead."

Nick grunted and hugged his pillow, mumbling incoherently. I kissed his shoulder and pulled the covers up to his neck as I exited our bed and headed to the bathroom, thinking, *He'll be fine. I will text Eric to be on his best behavior. I will be gone 10 to 12 hours at the most. Nothing will happen.*

As energetic as he was when we got back to the room, we both had decided on sleeping rather than lovemaking. He was drifting before I could get his clothes off. I lowered him onto the bed and tumbled in next to him, but struggled with sleep throughout the morning. It was now just before the noon hour, and I needed to finish my morning wash and head to the airport.

I was blow-drying my locks when he stumbled into the bathroom. Stepping up for a morning whizzer, he scratched his head with one hand and his sweet, naked arse with the other.

"I'll catch up, Boss. You hungry at all?"

"I ordered your breakfast, Boyo. I will eat at the airport."

He opened one eye and looked at me in the mirror.

"Airport? Where are we going, Kayne?"

"Back to Vienna. Scott came up with the conclusive data that will free Uwe from suspicion, and I venture to say, will point to the true killer of Mira Savic. I need to think this through and will take the time to do that on the plane. There are no direct flights, so I hired a private jet. I sent you an encrypted email to bring you up to snuff on my strategy."

He yawned, finished chucking a piss, and said, "Right, Boss. I'll get dressed quickly."

"Hey, Nick, I need you to do me a favor. Stay here and watch out for your mother and sister. I am having one of my premonitions again. Kept me sleepless last night. This whole thing could go arse up at any minute, I fear."

"But, Kayne..."

"Naw, my love. Gotta do this my way. We get there, and you'd be all nutso about Viola and Portia back here. The Big Bads are on the make, Nick, circling, and we need to take every precaution."

He did not like this and pulled a face, expressing his displeasure.

"So, I stay here and worry about you getting mugged in an alley again."

I hit a fighter's stance and smiled. I did my best imitation of a Bronx-born cop.

"Dude. I say bring it, fuckers."

"Seriously, promise me you will take care of all of this beauty. Also, that you won't ever impersonate a New Yorker." He pulled against me in expectation of recovering last night's lost round of man sexin'.

"Easy there, spunky man."

I bent to pull on my knickers, socks, and pants.

"I'll also speak to Rebecca and Eric to make sure they are aware of my plan. I know Eric annoys you, but he can be a true ally when the fists fly."

"Your brother needs to stay out of my way, Kayne. I am not going to put up with his condescension and harassment much more."

"Nick, chill. I mean it. He is a formidable enemy if we allow a rift. Eric is most likely recovering from a night of unspeakably fierce debauchery at the 'Gates of Hell Club.' By the time he fully returns to his Dr. Jekyll persona, I will be back."

To referee, I thought.

I finished dressing, grabbed my mobile and wallet, and then slipped my arm around my Nicko.

"All will be well, my love, so give us a pash. I will see you soon."

I kissed him, and he said, "Text me when you land."

***

"It is quite straightforward. A matter of chemistry. Here is the research supporting my conclusion."

I passed the report to his mobile using AirDrop. Kapitän Pilcher's phone pinged.

He pushed through Scott Iverson's summary as I continued.

"First, your forensics identified the organophosphate in the late Ms. Savic's makeup as Rorlan, a nerve agent. But they missed quite a bit. Rorlan acts immediately and is highly contaminating. She would have been dead before she crossed the threshold of the dressing room, the space and its objects made highly lethal.

"This report proves that when the deadly chemical is introduced into pancake makeup, it reacts with a formaldehyde-releasing preservative, Quaternium-15, which contains its effects temporarily. It slows down the outcome for approximately 2 to 3 hours. The killer intended that the victim would succumb during the performance of *Mutter Courage* and not before.

"Logically, this scenario points to terror, i.e., the public execution of an outspoken liberal advocate, as the killer's motive. I knew the murder weapon was her makeup as soon as I reached her body. The swelling, profusion of blood from the eyes, nose, mouth, and ears, the inability to breathe, and the odor of the concoction itself, destruction that could be seen from the uppermost balcony.

"The killer wanted theater, an audience, a public reaction raising the murder to a terrorist assassination. You will be hard-pressed to prove that Mr. Müller acted with such a motivation."

"Dr. Sorenson…"

"Why would he want a Grand Guignol-like spectacle surrounding the death if money were his motive? Your accusations are flimsy, and you know it.

"Also, my researchers have compiled a credit report for Mr. Müller. He has substantial assets and little to no debt."

I also sent the report to the police officer by AirDrop.

"Dr. Sorenson…"

"Please call me Kayne."

"And you will call me Dieter, yes?"

Not Didi? Interesting.

"Kayne, how does this prove the innocence of Uwe Müller? He had access."

"But no motive for matricide. You see, that's the thing."

I continued, "Uwe Müller is an out gay man who has been active in his foster mother's human rights organization. He is a member of the Board of the activist group Šumarski Ljudi, and in 2017 staged a very provocative theater flash mob at the Hague protesting the internment and murder of gays in Chechnya. The action went viral."

I handed him my mobile and played a short clip. In the piece, Uwe was prominent as a leader of the resistance against the illiberal forces that have invaded Europe like a disease.

"So, according to your office, the Austrian Government's case is built on Müller's guilt because he wanted the estate. Given what I have just shown you, your conclusions are preposterous. He and the institution he represented held Mira Savic as the public face of the tolerance movement. Just two days before the murder, he and his mother had a text conversation wherein he asked her to consider a bodyguard, which she unfortunately refused. You have that also."

I became more cavalier in my arguments. "The threatening notes to Ms. Savic can in no way be linked to Mr. Müller. He offered them to you willingly when we were at The First Floor, an odd thing for a killer to do.

"Any first-year legal student acting as a defense lawyer will have the public prosecutors and your detective bureau for lunch. Not going to please the Federal Minister of Justice, my man."

I was enjoying my attempts to wound his pride.

"For this next part, we need to continue the questioning of the suspect together. If I am right, you will be convinced of his innocence."

***

The prisoner looked distraught. Dark circles under his eyes indicated sleep deprivation. I suspected his fatigue was due to his own worries and not the result of his treatment. The Viennese were not barbarians.

He shook my hand. "Dr. Sorenson, thank you so much for referring me to Herr Von Gessen. I am hopeful. As you advised, Fr. Sanger has been asked to attend this meeting."

The priest and the lawyer took a seat at the table. Serving as a private investigator for the case, I had forwarded Fritz von Gessen a copy of Scott's chemical report, Uwe's bank files, and records of his leadership in Šumarski Ljudi with my annotations.

The Rev. Tomás Sanger looked worse than the prisoner. The seemingly shy priest could not look anyone in the face, visibly overcome by the entire affair.

"Yes, I was just visiting and...."

I began my questioning, "My young friend, theater security places you in Ms. Savic's dressing room at 5:00 PM. Why so early? Surely, Ms. Savic, nearing the end of the play's run, did not require more than an hour to get into costume and make-up."

Uwe looked at the faces around him, glanced to the left, and said, "It is like I told the police. I wanted to get her things in order."

He looked down at the table.

"It was our last performance."

I stared at the young man. His life was at stake, and he continued to be secretive-- the liar's "tell"-- he looked left before responding.

"Herr Müller, when the police examined the dressing room, they found that Ms. Savic's personal properties were few. The costume department was charged with all her performance-related belongings."

Dieter said nothing. I pressed, "Reverend Sanger, I understand that you also were in the house well before the performance."

The priest came to attention and responded, "Yes. I told them. I was in the habit of …."

Uwe interrupted, "The Father often prayed with cast members before the performance."

He became agitated. "We have gone over this. Why are we speaking of this again?"

"Herr Müller, I have an instinct about people, and my instincts tell me you are pretending. I have no patience for evasion and less for untruthfulness. As grave as these charges are, you have decided to protect Father Sanger."

No one said anything.

I turned to the priest and probed. "Does Uwe, like most males, experience *post-coital somnus*?"

"I beg your pardon. I am not sure what you mean?"

"No familiarity with Latin, Father?" I raised my voice. "We are looking at a possible death sentence conviction. Stop immediately with the evasions, gentlemen."

I slapped the table, hoping to shock the two of them into, as Nick would say, "coming clean."

Fritz von Gessen said calmly, "Father Sanger, Dr. Sorenson is asking you if Mr. Müller falls asleep after sexual intercourse."

Uwe clenched his fists and was visibly uncomfortable. He jumped up and attempted to reach for me, but Dieter stopped him.

Tomás Sanger said, "I understand that Herr Von Gessen, but why ask me?"

"Because you are his lover," I said, "And the two of you met before this and other performances to make love on the couch in the dressing room. Passion often leaves a residue, gentlemen."

The others in the room made no sound.

"When we met at the Rektoratskirche St. Karl Borromäus, you indicated that you never attended an entire performance of the play. Friends with Ms. Savic's dresser, the company's chaplain, and never had seen this remarkable production? Preposterous!

"I suggest that your lovemaking was assuredly private in the dressing room during performances. It provided the confidentiality required yet prevented your full attendance of the play. On the night in question, the two of you scheduled your rendezvous for before the performance, allowing you to attend what was literally the last performance of a great star."

I was tired of the shame game. There was no need to tiptoe around the facts of their relationship and their sexual liaisons. There was much at stake here.

It was not to our advantage that young Müller could resort to violence, so angry was his look at me. He started out of his chair a second time, again to be restrained by Dieter.

"Shall I call for the shackles, Herr Müller?"

He raised his voice, "This is of no consequence to the matter at hand. Our relationship is private and has nothing to do with the murder."

"You are very wrong, Sir. As you drifted into the arms of Morpheus, your partner left but deliberately left the dressing room open to the killer, who mixed the poison with the makeup while you were sleeping. This happened between 6:00 PM and 6:30 PM. The killer wanted the actress to die on stage, and the timing of the chemical reaction of the nerve agent with the preservatives in the makeup was critical to his purpose. He made possible a very brutal finale. A warning to the leaders of Europe."

Uwe shifted in his seat and looked at Tomás, bewildered and exasperated.

The priest spoke with panic in his voice.

"I met with him at the Church in the confessional. He told me he wanted a souvenir of the great actress connected to her last performance. At a specific time, I was to leave the door unlocked and go. I was petrified for Uwe, but the man told me that no harm would come to him."

Astonished, Dieter asked the priest, "Tomi, why would you do this?"

Tomás Sanger swallowed hard. He could not meet the gaze of the man he loved.

"He had pictures, Uwe. He threatened to destroy us."

"Destroy you, you mean. I am an out gay man, Tomás. Your Superior General would toss your ass out of the Order if our relationship were made public. That was the coercion here, your disgustingly closeted status quo, and the protection of the Church."

Uwe was shouting.

"No. No. The man suggested that you would be ruined professionally, given the times in Austria, especially among the conservatives. He told me that because of your association with the Forest People, your life would be endangered as well. He said he was capable of causing trouble."

In defending his behavior, the young cleric continued to be highly emotional.

"So, you let the murderer in. What happened next?"

"I went outside the theater and saw all the demonstrations and became even more fearful. I saw the hatred. I feared for my Uwe, the violence boiling over the edge of a crazed crowd. I returned and met Uwe in the corridor behind the loge."

Tears streamed down his cheeks. He was lost completely.

I reached across the table and took his hand. He pulled back at first but finally allowed the touch.

"My young friend, look at me right here." I gestured to my eyes. "That you are a man who sincerely loves another man is nothing to be shameful about and cannot remain hidden. Your own scriptures tell us that love is the greatest of all virtues. Believe what you preach, Reverend. But your commitment to Uwe demands the honesty of a life lived with authenticity."

I paused.

"But these are issues you must work out with Uwe. Your love is strong and will prevail. You cannot be motivated out of fear."

"*Miene Herren*, I believe I have just undertaken a new client."

"Accessory to murder," Dieter said.

I turned and addressed the detective, "Herr Kapitän Pilcher, I have another bombshell to drop, I am afraid.

"The man you seek is this man. I showed him a shot from my picture archive. He is Ádám Haagen, a former Major in the Royal Hungarian Guards. He is an agent for the Serbian oligarch, General Ragheb Karadžić."

I showed Tomás Sanger the picture. He said, "I cannot be sure, Dr. Sorenson. The confessional was dark."

"The death of Mira Savic was politically motivated and for no other reason. She represented the liberal left's resistance to the covert fascist political aims of the General."

Fritz von Gessen stated, "If what you say is true, Dr. Sorenson, the case against Fr. Sanger is very weak. He was being blackmailed and was unaware of the murderous intentions of Major Haagen or of Haagen's master."

I nodded but looked at Dieter.

A very peeved detective said, "This is somewhat preposterous. Where is the hard evidence to back up your claims linking Haagen to the murder? You deal in mere speculation and theories, Professor."

I opened my backpack and placed a large, sealed plastic bag on the table.

"This is a dress uniform cravat, more of a scarf, actually, of an officer in the Royal Hungarian Guard. There is also a sealed glass vial that is empty. The container, of course, held the Rorlan. The scarf will be found to contain the DNA of the murdered actress. He used it to wipe his fingerprints from the surface of the dressing room table. Hair is easily attracted to silk."

"How did you come by these, Dr. Sorenson."

"I removed them from the coat pocket of Major Haagen in an alley outside The First Floor bar three nights ago."

***

"They will require police protection, Dieter."

"I am aware of that. Please do not continue to tell me how to do my job."

"You are embarrassed by my revelations in the case. You must admit that, Kapitän. This is not a reflection of your competence. The Müller investigation was going nowhere. The suspect was totally resigned to his plight even though he was falsely charged. His grief was too great for him to realize that he was trapped."

I stabbed his chest with my left forefinger.

"And you knew there was more to it. I merely broke the logjam, my friend. I sense that you are hiding something."

The dark, handsome man looked away, across the café, where we waited for my train.

"I have one more revelation for you. Examine the entry direction of the knife blow in the body of the deceased Herr Zollner."

He waved me away, "You conceited man. Do you think we are boys in this? *Ja, Ja,* Zollner's killer, was left-handed. So am I. So are you and your brother, but not your hot boy who is simply charming. On that matter, I think he is easily led astray."

He laughed, "*Ja?*"

The police officer's stare was quite disconcerting. It was as if he was searching my face for something that was lost – not there at all. I ignored his last remark and continued my revelation.

"You will find in the bruises on the face of the deceased Zollner a unique feature. He was backhanded by a left hand sinking into his flesh the impression of a large and weighty signet ring, an impression identical to this one."

I turned the left side of my face and showed him the bruise below my cheekbone and above my jawline. One could just see a double-headed eagle. I also referred him to my sketch of Zoller's injuries.

"Haagen's?"

"Yes."

"You Sorensons play rough and quite deadly."

That is an extremely curious thing to say. This man is not who he seems.

"You have it all wrapped up, and yet I have so many questions, Kayne."

"Just send out an international search for Haagen, but beware of the machinations of Karadžić. He is..."

He would not let me finish. "As I said, I have many questions for you, Kayne, starting with the actions of your brother. He is a figure we have attempted to watch for a long time now. So frightfully unbalanced."

"What are you saying, Dieter?"

"I want you to arrange a meeting. Just Herr Eric Sorenson and me at a place I will stipulate. I do not want to scare him away. I will take him into custody myself. In the death of Mira Savic, he is more than just a person of interest. Word is he is no stranger to the assassination game."

"I just gave you the hard evidence on Haagen. What is this all about?"

His look was secretive. He picked up my mobile and handed it to me.

"There are other circumstances that tie Herr Sorrenson to the murder. Text your brother and say you need to meet him in Vienna. Tell him that there are complications in the murder case that need to be... um... pounded out, shall we say?"

"Bloody hell, man. I am under the impression that your combined dalliances have brought the two of you together in more than one den of iniquity. You saw him at the Prinzessin Louisa Hotel not two days ago. You are a frightful liar, Kapitän, but for the life of me, I cannot understand why."

"I am not a man who is used to being turned down, Dr. Sorenson. I give a command to my men, and it is followed unquestionably."

His steely gaze held my eyes as he added, "It is imperative that your brother meets with me. Do as I ask."

My train pulled into the station, and I rose to depart.

"Until you, as Nick would say, 'turn state's evidence' on this, I will leave you to your police work without my further assistance. I can do nothing for you. Herr Von Gessen will keep me informed on your progress in this case."

As we approached the train, he said, "As you insist. But know this, Dr. Sorenson, the day is coming when your brother and I will have our reckoning.

He paused, "Please, allow me to give you this."

Dieter Pichler gave me a chaste kiss, brushing my lips with his.

"That is for your Nicky. I will increase the ardor at another time."

He continued, "This is for your Satanic brother." His second kiss was deep and passionate, a Judas Kiss filled with hate and betrayal.

Completing the trilogy, he said, "And this is for you."

I was unable to catch my breath as he turned and left. The intensity of mouth and tongue against mine in the crush of his strong young arms was urgent and almost overpowering.

Why was I such a fool for lust? I cannot understand the sinister come-ons of two hyper-sexual, very sketchy men in as many days. Highly illogical.

In my head, I heard Nick asking, "WTF?"

Thomas Severino

Chapter Twenty-Six: One-hundred Kisses

Nick Sechi's Journal

Getting in at 10:35. Taking the tram to City Center. I missed you, my love.

We are at Ristorante Cento Baci. Want me to meet you at the tram station, Boss?

No. I will find you at the restaurant.

OK. Text me when you get here. Did you eat? Are you hungry?

I will. No. Yes, I am hungry, but primarily for you.

LMAO. Moma Sechi will see that you eat. The food, I mean, not me.

LOL. Ciao, ciao, Bello.

***

I waved Kayne over and kissed him. My mother placed before him an assortment: *Spaghetti alla carbonara, Bistecca con Pomodori Secchi Marinade,* and *Peperoni e Patate*

"Kayne, you are so thin! Mangia, *mio bellissimo uomo.*"

Viola was in her Super Italian American Mom persona, complete with a red and white kitchen towel around her waist and the requisite cheek tweaking.

"Grazie, mamma, ma cos'è questo?"

I helped to let Kayne understand the menu as my mother beamed and patted Kayne's head.

"Primo piatto: Spaghetti carbonara. And that other dish is peppers and potatoes. Secondo piatto: *Bistecca con Pomodori Secchi Marinade,* which means, `London Broil Steak with Sun-dried Tomatoes' and...."

"Wait. *Pomodoro Secchi*? Sechi like...."

He pointed at mom, Portia, and me.

Portia said, "It means 'sun-dried' in this dish, handsome. Literally, it means 'trouble'-- as in this dish."

She pointed to me and smacked the back of my head.

"Ehhh! *Mannaggia America*. I'm so gonna getcha, girl."

I reached for my giggling sister.

Kayne roared. Mom separated her children. I noticed, despite his delight, my Bossman looked drained and on edge. Something happened, but what?

I filled his glass with red wine and pointed to a green, white, and red dish.

"There is *Insalata Caprese* if you want to start with that, and the sweet, for after, is *Tiramisù al Limoncello*," Mom finished.

She gently smacked his invading hand and handed him flatware while stuffing a linen napkin in his open collar.

"Do not pick. Eat, eat."

The *illustre professore* filled up and dug in.

***

Rebecca was holding court nearby with a remarkably talkative Eric. The audience of theater folks was rapt with attention.

"In Poland and Hungary, you can see the emergence of conservative forces with views that include homophobia, hostility to immigration, anti-Islamic rhetoric, and Euroscepticism. They claim that their people have had enough in the wake of the 2008 financial disaster and the migrant crises. Still, the wave of discontent also taps into long-standing fears of the dilution of their national identity."

Eric added, "There are similar movements in just about every European nation from France to Bulgaria. France has the National Front. In Germany, the far-right Alternative for Germany, discontented with Chancellor Angela Merkel's open-door policy for refugees, has pushed for strict anti-immigrant policies and tapped into anxieties over the influence of Islam. Those blokes have actually downplayed the Nazi atrocities."

Rebecca took her turn, "Hungary and Slovakia also oppose EU plans to compel countries to accept migrants under a quota system. Nationalism is strong, as is the rise of populism. The anti-immigrant Slovenian Democratic Party's leader, former Prime Minister Janez Jansa, has said he wants Slovenia to become a country that will put the wellbeing and security of Slovenians first."

One of the actresses, Elena Janescue, jumped in, "Viktor Orban, leader of the conservatives, courts a far-right that yearns for the fascist days of the 1930s. He calls Hungarians to reject diversity, saying that Hungarians do not want their race, traditions, and national culture to be mixed with those of others."

Kayne pulled me closer and whispered, "How was the performance?"

I gave him a "thumbs up" as he opened for a rolled fork full of pasta.

Rebecca said, "I said, 'Right, Kayne?'"

We both looked at Rebecca and everyone else who was, it appeared, looking our way. Kayne had a strand of spaghetti dangling from his lips, which had not yet made its way inside. He swallowed, dragging in the stray.

"Folks, may I present the eminent Kayne J. Sorenson, Psycho-criminologist extraordinaire." She raised her glass.

"I beg your pardon, my dear. Your capture of the right-wing tenor of Europe, especially Eastern Europe, where there is a rejection of geopolitics, a growth of pseudo-national pride, and the distrust and ostracization of minority groups like the Romany, the gays, and immigrants is exceptionally well stated. The extreme violence in the east has sent asylum-seekers into all areas of Europe in hopes of freedom from persecution and death. But, allow me to turn back to one of the points you and my brother alluded to in your current political analysis."

He speared another forkful of dinner.

153

There was the shadow of a faint smile appearing on Rebecca's face. She looked to see if my mother and sister had stopped serving and were paying attention. They sank into seats as Kayne ate and elaborated, paying very close attention. However, he was interrupted by Eric standing behind his brother and placing a cool hand on his shoulder.

His sonorous baritone announced somewhat uncharacteristically, "Glad you could join us, my brother."

Kayne swallowed as his brother held forth.

"So, to summarize, from Putinism in Russia to the rise of right-wing, mainstream parties throughout Western Europe, and even to the USA with Trumpism, the fascist impulse is everywhere. After the Cold War, this current wave of nationalistic and xenophobic political parties has become the offspring of the demagogic populism and the fascism of the 1930s. As usual, the gays are at the center of the conflict."

He was aping his brother's lecture style in a slightly mocking tone. Kayne looked up into his sibling's face and placed a hand on the hand on his shoulder. He took back "the mic."

"Yes. The German-born American philosopher and political theorist Hannah Arendt has written that the evils of the Nazis so defied comprehension by traditional norms of language and morality that we see the eclipse of three thousand years of Western civilization."

Eric refreshed Kayne's wine, which he quaffed before continuing.

He gestured with his fork, saying, "What is interesting is that this trauma of world war in the Mid-Twentieth Century has devolved in the Twenty-first Century, a mere seventy years later, to a condition of collective amnesia. What I mean is that faced with unprecedented forms of human evil and novel crimes that included genocide, collaboration, or an inexplicably profound apathy and disregard for the plight of victims, many Europeans are, in fact, willing to forget."

He did not stop.

"Look at the political bullshit so prevalent in Austria now. The sanitized version of history consists of whitewashing that country's role during the Nazi period. The extreme right claims there were "good Nazis," and the concentration camps that exterminated millions of

Jews, gays, gypsies, and others were 'punishment camps.' The claim that these places of death kept minorities safe from public harm was and is an outright lie."

He became somewhat agitated as he lowered Eric's hand, stood, and said, "What is inconceivable is the shadowy deep state network at work, predominately in Eastern Europe, selling this political pathology to the highest bidder. This neo-fascist, Europe-wide conglomerate operates to promote an extremist Pan-European nationalism.

"These are mercenaries selling the 'theology' of a new European order. They are providing the technology to interfere with national elections as well as distributing the resources and funds to build border barriers and construct and staff internment camps. These are the great weaponizers of modern political terrorism, havoc, instability, and destruction. They deal in fear, betrayal, murder, and corruption. It is a despicable secret organization that, not too far from where we sit…."

He stopped, realizing that he had stepped publicly into an area that perhaps could bring harm to his listeners. He was agitated and very passionate.

What lurks in the shadows?

I reached across to take his hand, "Kayne…."

My mother jumped up. The consummate director and earth mother, she shouted,

"*Basta*. No more politics. Tonight, we eat and drink. Tomorrow, we play, accept the applause, and get the hell out of here. In the meantime, *tutti vengono al tavolo per mangiare*."

She held up a plate of food.

Rebecca came over and spoke softly to Kayne as his florid orator's appearance began to diminish. He said, "I seem to have gotten carried away. I apologize. The burdens of the day seem to have taken their toll."

Eric said, somewhat mysteriously, "You were just what we needed, my brother. No need to apologize. The cause is what is important. Keep your balls in a knot."

I had become an even more acute Eric observer as of late. This evening, the uber-spy's remarks had been coherent, inciteful, and logically stated. But, in the last few days, I noticed moments when Eric's speech seemed off. More disturbingly, he was talking or slightly moving his lips as if singing to his favorite songs on his mobile.

But he never wore earphones.

Chapter Twenty-Seven: Confiteor
From the Case Files of Kayne Sorenson, Ph.D.

Our lovemaking was one of our more intense, long-playing sessions. I was tired and somewhat soporific from the wine, but my body and mind craved Nick's like a person with an addiction. We trashed our bedroom and bathroom of the suite, living up to the stereotype of the sexually badass couple whose love was not confined to the bed but prevailed and used every available surface and position.

Well past 2 AM, Nick reached for the vial of bath oil and settled back against my chest. He poured the scented gold liquid into the steaming water that surrounded us. Most European hotel spa tubs are made for one guest under four feet tall. This model was an exception, generously providing two males, each taller than 6' with lean athletic builds.

"I thought you would be too tired to play tonight, but your performance was award-winning – like you invented sexin', Boss."

"Invented, no, my love. Perfected, absolutely."

I let my remark sink in and then added, "As our buddy Gints would say…."

We said together with a Latvian accent, "Is no brag, just fact," and laughed.

When I met Nick, I was "seeing" a tall, muscled-up gymbot and bartender, Gints Bergovic. We became fast and furious sex buds. Nick was in the last stages of a two-year relationship. When we fell in love, Gints stayed a good friend and was a crucial ally in our adventures in Colorado a few months back.

The remembrance of my sexual escapades of the recent past encouraged me to turn state's evidence regarding the Vienna interlude.

"Nick, I have a confession to make, Boyo." He remained in my arms but twisted his head, attempting to look into my eyes.

"I kinda saw this coming. And just how is Didi?"

I proceeded to provide Nick with the details of the meeting with Uwe, Tomás, Kapitän Pichler, and Lawyer von Gessen and the evidence against Major Haagen.

"Yeah, so. Umm... yeah, the captain is good. Weird as kanga shit, but... ah... good." I stammered like an Aussie lad caught with his hand in the biscuit jar.

Nick sat forward and managed to reposition to the opposite end of the tub, facing me.

He looked down at the swirling, bubbly water.

"So, is the hot detective a top or a bottom. My money is on the latter, although he could be versatile also."

"I have no idea."

He looked up.

"He is, however, an amazing kisser. And... um... I was not able to fend him off."

"Gee Kayne, big strong you? Please, Boss." Nick mocked with animated hands, "Ohhh nooo, Officer. Don't! Stop! Don't stop."

He panted to highlight his mime.

I tossed a washrag at him.

"Lad, it was only one... OK, three, but they were erotic enough to sit uncomfortably on my conscience and be the subject of this cleansing of my soul."

I wrung another wet cloth over my head, cascading the waters like a purifying absolution.

"Why three?"

Now, here I was, not beyond a white lie. *Kayne lad, it is a mortal sin to make a false confession. Oh, bollocks.*

"One for Eric, confirming a past dalliance and an interest I cannot quite figure out. *Quelle surprise!* I am amazed our Vienna boy is not scared somewhere by that connection. I half expected him to bite my lip on that one."

I looked to the left.

"A chaste peck for yours truly. Polite and very *pro forma,* indicating a total lack of carnal interest. You know, the Euro greeting/goodbye thing."

I could imagine Rebecca crying, *"Kayne, Darling, you are such a liar."*

"And the third?"

I smiled like a mad dingo and crawled over to him.

"Why, for you, ya bloke. And the intensity, well... but please allow me to demonstrate, like this."

I pulled his head to mine and had a go at a stellar face suck that left us both gasping for breath. Near the end, he reached up and, wrapped his arms around my neck and reciprocated.

We settled back, his face flushed with passion.

"So, I guess he pretty much demonstrated he was not interested at all in me."

I sputtered.

"He's quite stuck on you, lad." I stroked his ego.

Nick grinned like a shit-eating dog.

I splashed a wallop of bathwater into his giggling face.

"Ya mug!"

We had a good laugh, and he slid back to my side of the tub and into my arms.

"Ready for bed?"

"Not until you finish your confession, Kayne, my son." Mock self-righteousness dripped from his words.

"Is there more for which I am guilty? I half expected you to confess a round of making out when you were alone with your Didi after you both left The First Floor Bar. His office, perhaps?"

"My dear Dr. Sorenson, we must have that long-delayed discussion regarding your hyper-sexual activity, sometimes breaching professional behavior. How is it that you struggle with articulating emotions and yet release a ton of mindless passion when you are horned up and doing the nasty? Case in point: The scandalous seduction and bedding of the young, innocent, and very nubile Nicola Sechi, graduate student and model officer on the Wilton Manors police force. Ravished, ruined, and never to be the same."

He raised the back of his hand to his forehead, rolling his hazel eyes upward, "Ahh, the tragedy of the descent of the pure and unsullied hero of the streets into the depths of lust and homosexual depravity...."

"Before this melodramatic bullshit goes any further, let's analyze your choice of words, Officer. Starting with 'innocent.' Eh?"

I felt him smile.

"Kapitän Pichler and I behaved with the utmost decorum, Boss."

"Whenever you use big and archaic words, I know you are mocking me, ya mug." I bit softly into his hard trapezius at the base of his neck. The wet, muscled boy was delectable.

"Do not put me off with your manly ways. Tell me about Ádám Haagen in the alley. Surely, you and your 'Golden Hussar' were not discussing great books and nihilist philosophy in the driving rain. Just how vigorous was the encounter."

"My bloody big-mouthed brother! Eric, the sower of discord."

"Nope. All on me. I know your in inductive methods. Your telling of the presentation of the scarf and the vial to the police in Vienna completed the puzzle of why your clothes and mental state were so fucked up after your tryst in the alley. Had to be some sexin-up going on there, Professor. The facts do not lie. And I know you, Boss. You got yourself into some of his private places."

I was impressed.

"So, my question is, did you...?"

I smooched him.

"Nah, my love. Only got close enough to get my hands in his coat pockets. Both of us– KPIP. My hand to God."

"You know your 'strine is going full steam tonight, Boss. KPIP?"

"We Kept Penises in Pants." He roared again and began to exit the bath.

I followed, and we toweled each other off.

I stretched and said, "I am going to sleep so late tomorrow morning."

We strolled into the bedroom, dropping the towels.

Nick said with holy solemnity, "And still, we are not through, my son."

"Beg pardon?"

"Confessions are not complete without the penance and the absolution."

I folded my arms and widened my stance.

"Go on."

He struggled to contain a grin as he announced, "For your penance...."

"Hmm?"

He pointed to the messy bed.

"Facedown and butt up."

I guffawed and jumped into the sack, assuming the position.

"Ohhh nooo, Officer. Don't! Stop! Don't stop."

As we came together, he began, "*Ego... te... absolvo....*"

Chapter Twenty-Eight: City of Night

Notes from Rebecca Quinto

From the balcony of the darkened, sixth-floor hotel room, I looked out onto the sleeping city of Bratislava and the sparkling river. I sipped *Strekov 1075*, a Slovakian pinot noir. I raised the glass to the lights of the metropolis, enjoying the vibrant garnet color of the shimmering varietal.

On the street below, I thought I saw someone watching my window from a park across the street. My blood ran cold. I kept the lights out and remained in the shadows, the soft sounds of the slumbering city rising to my room.

I walked to the desk and retrieved the newsboy cap. Turning it over, I extracted the plastic packet containing the two small folios of *The Booke of Sir Thomas Moore*. I did not remove the folded parchment from the protective covering but looked around for an alternative hiding place. If I was going to have visitors in the night, I needed to protect this guarantee of the freedom of three innocent people.

Gazing at the treasure, I began to have my doubts about how this all would end. Had I stepped in boldly where saner minds would have prevailed? Eric said the Sechis would come around to the only exit plan possible. Still, I felt duplicitous pumping up Kayne and defying Nick.

Was I doing the right thing?

I tipped the glass and said aloud, "It's the only way, doing this together. Then, everyone comes home."

A shout instantly muffled from the street below brought me back to the shadows of the balcony doors after placing the manuscript and its copy back in the cap.

Nothing. I drank more but nearly dropped the glass when someone knocked at the door.

I went to the spy hole. Portia.

"Can't sleep, either? Come on in, Darling."

"Sitting alone in the dark? Girl, dark night of the soul or too much Italian food?"

"Oh, I'd say the former. Nothing compares to fine Italian food or a fine Italian. Know what I mean? You need wine."

I filled a glass, and we sat, feeling the crisp river air rise over the city.

"Ever get super homesick, Darling?"

"Yes. Wait, wait. The kind that feels like no one cares where I am, and I am at the very end of the world, so very far from home, and everyone is a stranger? Yes. That's the one thing I hate about travel."

"Quite that. I miss the burning home fires or, to be honest, the paradise of South Florida. Oh, Darling, Hunter's, a dance bar in Wilton Manors... Kayne, Nick, and I have danced our asses off with the hottest men. Sunday Night Tea Dance... so Studio 54."

We clinked glasses.

We were interrupted by the "wa-wa," two-tone bawl of a police siren screaming up the street below, a familiar audio meme of every 20th-century film of Europe under the Nazis.

"Every time I hear that sound, I think they're coming for the hidden Jews. My blood runs cold. It's so iconic."

Portia sipped her wine in the dark.

"So how did you come to be Kayne Sorenson's best gal pal? I am so jealous, girl, and not quite sure of whom to be jealous, you or my brother."

I laughed and said, "I was a graduate student studying at the Universidad de Salamanca and traveling around Europe doing research in the fine arts. Kayne was this baby Ph.D., lecturing at Sorbonne Nouvelle University. 'Murder, Psycho-criminology and Art.' He was a sex bomb then at 26 and still is. His female and male fandom was huge. I still remember his lectures, his Australian accent, and how he swept his forelock when confused, alarmed, or excited about an academic point or some hot guy.

"He stopped me after as we were leaving one of his presentations and suggested we hit Le Marais for drinkies. We hit it off instantly, Darling, and have never looked back."

I swigged the delicious wine sparkling in the dim ambient light of the night city.

"He really is an exceptional man. How many languages? A hyper-analytical mind and a passion for the underdog and critical social causes."

"Yes, he is really quite a man. So, the sex, eh?"

"Both of us were, at 26, the friskiest of creatures. Turns out, we both... oh, how shall I put it?... one needs to be so delicate in these cases... fucked the same football player."

Portia laughed at my attempt at comic discretion and decorum, and I realized that we needed more wine for this one."

I poured and continued.

"Futbol Club Barcelona-- known as 'Barça.' A gorgeous and very massive goal man, Luis Coutinho, aka Guicho. The jock plays for several teams, if you understand, Darling. We both found heaven in his... um... his embrace, but not at the same time. I remember because the man has a very distinct anatomical feature that we both recognized.

"Kayne used to joke, 'Were those your scratch marks I noticed on Guicho's back, my girl?' Turns out, they most likely were his wife's."

"Rebecca, are you in love with Kayne?"

"Totally and insanely. My love for Kayne had been a love-at-first-sight joining of souls, I think. But Darling, I have to say you are not looking at Grace Adler here, pining for her Will Truman a la *Will and Grace* so that no other male found his way to my heart. When it came to love and sex, I was comfortably realistic and satisfied with my men – for the most part. Kayne is my beloved friend."

"Sounds wonderful."

"Your brother, Nick, was also an instant attraction, bright, gorgeous, and willing to do whatever it takes to make things better. They were extraordinarily *simpatico* from the start. Your brother is an all-in, passionate type of guy, and his love for Kayne is epic. I adore spending time with them and facing off with the 'Big Bads,' as Nick calls them."

The sirens in the street did a second pass. A ship on the river lowed like a bovine, a car backfired, and a few shouts broke through the curtain of night below. Then silence.

"So, what's your story, Portia. How did you get to be this arts entrepreneur?"

"Did some theater in high school and college. Received a degree from NYU in the business of the arts. Then, a bit of a setback in my wanton years. Married too young. Both he and I were fools. No kids, so an annulment was a workable option. Gotta keep the semblance of a good Catholic family. No bad guys in the breakup. We talk occasionally. Seems like we are better friends now.

"Lately, I've been seeing a professor of *Parsons Paris*, the European campus of The New School, NYC. He is the chair of their design program. Fashion, management, digital innovation, and curatorial practice, that sort of thing."

"How exciting, Darling. For how long?"

"Almost two years. Taking a bit of a break, to be honest. It's complicated. I need to be in a relationship that enables both people to grow, and I am realizing that this is not it. He is a bit confining. And you?"

I did a bit of a layback with my wine glass, sinking against the couch cushions.

"I am currently under the spell of one crazy hot Welsh-American, Mark Gadarn, a world reporter for CBN. He is also an extreme risk-taker like 'the dynamic duo.' Iraq, Afghanistan, Syria. He is currently in Turkey."

I missed Mark.

We were interrupted by another rap at the door.

I opened the door to Eric Sorenson. His dirty t-shirt was torn, exposing half of his chest and most of his abs. He attempted to hold it closed.

"Is everything OK? Any visitors?... lights out, good. Stay away from the glass doors."

He stepped to the balcony and took in the street below from the side.

"No. Just Portia and me, Darling. Is there a problem?"

"Not anymore. It is of no consequence now. Where is your mother, Ms. Sechi?"

"She is next door, sleeping, Eric."

He paused and lit a Murad. His right hand clenched and unclenched.

I broke the silence.

"Wine, Darling."

"Water."

He squashed pills into his mouth as he turned away, setting the water carafe down.

"Thanks."

His dark eyes pierced the shadows near the open balcony. The silver iris glinted in the dim light and smoke. He said, "I need you to return to your room, Ms. Sechi. Open the door to no one until the morning. Please try to get some sleep. Thank you."

Portia exited, a bit confused.

"Tomorrow, then, kid. Thanks for the wine and the chat."

"Good night, Darling."

I turned. "Eric, is there trouble?"

He trembled and responded from an agitated state.

"Talk. No more talk. Do not ask. Questions? Answers? There is no fuckin' need. Go to bed, Rebecca."

He softened. "I will stay here. I will smoke. Then, I will leave. All danger is past."

I remember the rhythmic glow of his cigarette as he sat in the darkness, silently watching and listening.

In the morning, he was gone.

Chapter Twenty-Nine: Restaged
Nick Sechi's Journal

"I have found the end of this scene awkward since we opened. It is critical to moving the primary relationships of the principals forward. We need clearer visual imagery to accompany the lines. Let's re-block it just a bit."

My mother had assembled the King of France, the King of Britain, his three daughters, and the royal attendants on stage. As she gave directions, the actors followed.

"Lear, more slump of the shoulders as you leave. And attendants-- hold him up more as he walks. Your king is in his eighties, and his guts have been ripped out by his unrealistic expectations of his family.

"Cordelia, come downstage a bit more. You are pivotal to the image. Give your farewell by slightly turning stage right to your sisters.

"Too much, Elena. Turn your head and not your body. Say the lines to the audience with a slow turn back... yes... good. And emphasize by... that's it... just a look at Goneril and Regan, and the audience will know to whom you are speaking.

"Say the line, please... Nice. Thank you.

"France, come up behind her and put your right hand on her right shoulder. Closer, Marc. You just agreed to marry this woman without a dowry. Make me feel that she is your 'fair Cordelia.' Loving her is the only thing that matters.

"Now take her left hand and draw it out as she speaks and hover over it... no, Marc. Bring your lips to her hand, not the other way around. Yes... good. I love it. Very sweet.

"Goneril, I want that folded-up look with your right elbow supported by your crossed left arm. Beautiful, Mia. Correct... chin up... yes... show that defiance of your sister's warning. Yes, that's it... much better. Give me the evil queen, already plotting her heinous crimes... freeze my blood.

"Gretchen, more insolence with that mock curtsey. Give me that 'up yours, sister' look... No. Regan is more of a brat than that... Yes, better, thanks."

Viola walked to the steps and descended into the house, proceeding up to rows in the middle of the orchestra. She spoke into her head mic as she climbed.

"Mara, did you make those lighting changes we discussed for this scene? I want the company to freeze just before the blackout... right. Yes, bring up the up-stage lights... and go down on the... perfect. I want that silhouette shot. Rob, swell the music just a bit earlier, but do not step on the lines."

She turned and addressed the actors on stage and spoke to the technicians, "OK, from Marc's line, 'Fairest Cordelia, that art most rich....' Thank you."

She asked them to do the action one more time before sending them off to their dressing rooms and wishing them, "Good show."

***

"So, Zeus, full of lust for this prince of Troy, who Homer describes as 'the loveliest born of the race of mortals,' turns himself into an eagle and abducts the lad to be his own. The king of the gods gives his lover boy eternal youth and immortality."

Kayne was relating the myth of Ganymede as we sat at the foot of the eponymous fountain, a centerpiece of the arts plaza. The sculpture bore the statue of the desirable young man, his robes caught by the updrafts of the lofting eagle who carried the boy on his back. We were people-watching the strollers in Hviezdoslav Square before the Neo-Renaissance facade of the Slovak National Theater.

"Holy pederasty, Batman!"

"Plato thought so, my love. He connects the story to the socially acceptable romantic relationship between an adult male and an adolescent male. Socrates, however, disputes. He claims that the King of the Gods loved the shepherd boy for his mind. On that point, I will admit I have never seen Ganymede depicted as a geek."

The summer evening was coming on. We had dined in Old Town and were waiting for Rebecca and Eric before attending the final Ars Europa production of the "Tragedy of King Lear" in Bratislava. A liveried waiter brought flutes of champagne to waiting theatergoers.

Pointing up to the bronze group atop the fountain, Kayne continued, "Shakespeare, whose actors were all males, uses this well-known image in his gender-bending comedy of mistaken identity, 'As You Like It.' The disguised Rosalind actually seduces both Orlando and Phoebe. Rosalind's male alter ego is called Ganymede."

"Males playing females playing males falling in love. Sensational."

"And speaking of our own gender-nonconformist, here's our divine Rebecca."

Black seemed to be the fashion standard for our theater group. Kayne and I were in black suits and shirts. He wore a leather tie, and I was open-collared. Kayne had used about a pound of product to slick back his hair and to pull it into a man bun, giving him a very mysterious Euro-trash look. He had no need to fuss with his forelock as it was plastered back, exposing the mark of Cain near his left hairline.

"You look super tough, Boss. Grrr!"

Smiling and looking every bit the powerful woman she was, Rebecca did a twirl in her drop-dead outfit.

"Top to bottom or bottom to top?"

"Oh, girl, start with the shoes."

I caught the server and snagged three more flutes of the bubbly, placing them deftly on the edge of the fountain before passing them out.

"OK. First of all, this is all local couture. The Slovaks are divine darlings when it comes to fashion.

"So, the desert boots are black suede with silver lame heels. I am wearing a black cut-out crepe mini dress. This gorgeous number is a velvet jacket with silver metallic embroidery and embellishment at the yoke, down the front, at the hem, and at the edges of these beautiful sleeves. I adore it, Darling."

Her earrings were black and silver drops with diamonds. On her shoulder was a killer cocktail bag.

She showed it off.

"Bao Bao Issey Miyake black prism clutch-- to hold my gun."

Kayne did a spit-take, missing everyone, including the gathering theater crowd.

"Well, you know, Kayne Darling, the last time we attended the theater...."

"She's not sitting next to me, Nick. All yours, buddy."

Rebecca stepped back and appraised our theater outfits.

"Oh, Darlings, nice try, but it is a good thing you have this fashionable woman in your life. You need just a skosh more fabulous. Too, too Americano. To borrow a word, Dullsville."

She handed me her glass and took a tube of dark red lipstick from her purse. Rebecca turned to me, holding it like it was a weapon.

"Nah, nah, go away with all of that." I lurched backward.

"Come here, my Nicky, you gorgeous boy."

She kissed me hard and slowly on the lips, stepped back, and rubbed the coloring in, telling me to open my mouth a bit so she could get all the corners. She handed me a compact mirror and adjusted her lipstick with the tube. I flipped a look – fey but not too nellie. Glam tough. Oh, Hell yeah.

"Ah, ah, do not touch. Not exactly the right color for your complexion, so the effect is pure decadence."

She held up the stick.

"I have more if you decide to kiss all the gorgeous men tonight."

She added some shadow to my eyes, giving them a bruised, smokey look. Rebecca then opened my shirt three more buttons and rubbed a little red between my pecs.

"A little secret women have been using for years. Such a hot man's chest, Darling. Shall I rouge your nipples in case you want to nip-slip a peek?"

I pushed her away, turning bright red.

Kayne was sputtering with his hand over his mouth, failing to suppress a laugh. The folks crossing the plaza to attend the gala were unsure what to make of this courtyard Helena Rubenstein.

She placed her implements back into her clutch and extracted a fat cylinder of mascara.

She turned on her next victim.

"Resistance is futile," I said.

Kayne, knowing the wisdom of my words, leaned down and accepted her quick enhancement of his already long black lashes. She rubbed some red and black together and lightly dabbed his lips between the arches of his jet-black, close-cropped goatee. She loosened his tie and unbuttoned his shirt almost to his navel. The effect was to make the leather tie fall close to his collarbone above the expanse of his chest and the naked ripples of his upper abs.

"So sexy-Satanic, Darling."

She turned to me, "When the account of this adventure is written, let no one say that Rebecca Quito was the only one doing a European gender fuck."

Kayne looked as exotic and tantalizing as Hell itself.

"Speaking of the Fallen Angel, just where is your date?"

"No, no, no. We are not a couple, Darling. As much as I fantasize that he is Kayne adjacent, no, no, no, Darling. The man has fully embraced the Dark Side of the Force. I pray constantly to Our Holy Mother for his redemption."

I nodded to a couple making their way forward at the far edges of the entering crowd.

"Behold Lord Vader himself."

Kayne and Rebecca turned to watch as Eric, in black formal wear, which included a stunning opera cape, leather pants, and chain-trimmed boots. He entered the theater on the far side of the courtyard with a very fashionable woman. Her head and face were covered with a trailing, deep blue silk veil so that just her eyes peered out – the mysterious woman from Vienna.

She caught our stare as they vanished into the theater.

Chapter Thirty: Cordelia

From the Case Files of Kayne Sorenson, Ph.D.

The audience shrieked with terror.

Nick was the first to race down the aisle to the stage this time. He jumped onto the low wall surrounding the orchestra pit and, from there, vaulted to the performance floor.

"Put her down, Sir Cantwell. Carefully. Everyone step back."

The entire company was in an uproar, as was the audience, many of whom held out mobile phones to capture the murder-like voyeurizing vultures. Rebecca and I fought our way forward.

The actor playing Lear gently laid the body of Cordelia/Elena Janescue on the stage floor. Blood flowed from the gash at her neck, staining her white and blue robes.

Sir Keith Cantwell sputtered, "I couldn't see in the dark. I thought she was already in character, and the blood was a last-minute revision." The shaking lead actor was coming to the full realization that the woman he was scripted to carry on stage as his hanged daughter was, in fact, dead.

Nick's mother and sister raced in from the wings with a doctor. Portia covered her mouth in horror, and my mother made the sign of the cross. Nick let me deal with the corpse and went to them.

"Garroted and in the last few minutes. Have security close the stage doors and allow no one in or out. Get the police here immediately. Portia and Rebecca keep everyone back from Elena. You, sir, show me exactly where you picked her up."

Lear struggled to compose himself and led me behind a tormentor curtain, stage left.

"Get out of the way, please," I yelled as we moved through actors, stagehands, and dressers.

As we passed, I saw Nick holding his mother as she wept silently.

"Why would anyone do this, Nick?"

The lead player led me through a maze of props and set pieces to a corner of the wing near a wall of dressing rooms. The production was somewhat minimal when it came to the scenery. Portia's design team created the castle rooms and storm-ravaged heaths of ancient Britain using lighting and high-tech projection. Some traditional stage pieces that enhanced the production by sliding on and off were stashed in the wings.

I followed a trail of blood behind the very distraught actor. Keeping us both out of the mess of footprints.

"Show me, Sir Cantwell, please."

"Here, I pick Elena up here at the end of Act V."

He gestured to the monumental throne used in the first act of the tragedy and then pushed off into a backstage corner.

"Her dressing room is one of those back there."

I examined the large, elaborately carved chair using my mobile's flashlight. I videoed the prop and the surrounding area. We were joined by the actress who played the part of Goneril, Mia Chan.

"Sir Keith, are you OK?"

The renowned thespian nodded, but I could see that the extent of his shock was just beginning to manifest itself. The blood of the murdered actress had left a large smear on his white gown.

"Yes, my dear."

"Please stay back and mind the blood. No one is to touch this."

As I inspected the throne and its area, Keith Cantwell continued his explanation.

"Cordelia is only in three scenes of the play. Elena had lots of time to kill."

He paused over the awkward word. Mia held on to him, and he continued.

"She would climb up and watch the play from the seat. She said she could see over passing actors and stagehands. Sometimes, she would fall asleep, which is what I thought happened tonight."

"Go on. Describe exactly what happened, please."

"We had a short interaction at the beginning of the last scene of the play, and then I went to my dressing room. My dresser alerts me to my final entrance. Tonight, I was a bit late because he was nowhere to be found to give me the warning.

"I quickly stepped up on the platform, scooped her in my arms, and made our entrance. I thought she was in character, Dr. Sorenson, I swear to God."

I examined the floor of the old theater's stage left wing around and behind Lear's throne and found the trap door. The National had been built in the golden age of public construction of the Austro-Hungarian Empire, 1886. Like the Palais Garnier of *Phantom of the Opera* fame, the landmark still retained the classic Nineteenth-century theater features. Out of sight were the rope riggings, elaborate fly systems, multiple trap doors, and an undercroft with a trap room. The latter allowed actors and sets to appear from nowhere while serving as a crossover for actors to switch entrances.

Hearing the approach of what I knew would be the authorities and production management, I descended quickly into the murky depths of the undercroft and closed the trap.

A string of dim caged lights led the way beneath the stage to the other wing linking opposite sides of the stage. Beneath the performance area were the platforms that were raised and lowered via pulleys to allow actors to appear and vanish in the performance space above. I could hear the movement of the company and law enforcement overhead.

Behind me were the doors leading to the orchestra pit. In front of me was a warren of stored theater properties. My mobile's flashlight illuminated a massive structure that allowed sets to descend into the undercroft from the back of the stage.

I searched for blood and footprints, small drops leading from the space above. The killer's trail led back into the storage area. I proceeded with caution to another stairway going to a lower level. On the first step was a coil of fine wire, and I dropped to one knee to inspect the bloody murder weapon.

The garrotte had taped ends for the killer's grip and was serrated to cause instant and massive destruction. It had been placed at the top of the stairway as an invitation to descend into the darkened depths. I stepped over it and down.

In the space below, I found the discarded costume of a courtier. Blood covered the front of the doublet and the sleeves. I swept the area with my light. It was vast and extended off into complete darkness. Knowing that the killer was nearby and was toying with me, I approached the next "breadcrumb," bloody gloves on the floor before a small door labeled *Dirigent Orchestra*. It was the conductor's entrance to the orchestral pit above.

I heard the movement before the intruder knocked the phone from my hand, bringing on the dark. I took a crouched stance but moved laterally, attempting to find a wall against which I could protect my back. The light spill from the face-down phone was minimal. Instead of cement, I backed into the formidable body of the killer. Instantly, his strong arms put me in a sleeper hold, resulting in the folding of my vocal cords and the compression of my airway.

I broke the hold, spun kicked up into a soft groin area. The killer stepped off and caught my leg. I smashed an elbow into him and wrenched my leg free. I added a double jab but only did minor damage. He was moving fast in the darkness. Stepping back, I lost him. Whatever direction he took, I was unable to discern. My punches and kicks found either empty space or the solid surface of the concrete.

There was a crash of scenery behind me. Turning, I heard a soft but insulting laugh. I directed an assault in that direction only to jab into the open air. I heard another thud from the opposite side, and, with a total reflex response, I struck out with a backkick. Nothing. In the dark of the theater's cellar, the murderous cat was toying with his mouse.

Something light and feathery brushed the right side of my face. Coiled for causing some damage, I struck and caught part of the killer. Then he switched up into a face-to-face clinch, locking his arms behind my neck and pulling my head close to his as he used his forearms to control my head and raised arms.

As close as I was, I could not ID him but knew I had been near this man before. His breath was hot on my face as I broke the hold and spun into a barrage of punches and kicks that, this time did some good. He seemed to fall away.

I came back into my stance, not quite sure where my adversary was. I could hear movement and voices above. A voice came from behind and above.

"Let's end this."

I fought into empty blackness again, making no contact. Then, my head exploded.

Thomas Severino

Chapter Thirty-One: The Riot

Notes from Rebecca Quinto

I saw him.

All attention was focused on the stage, the dead body, and the left wing where Sir Keith Cantwell and Kayne had headed. The arrival of the police, theater security, the first responders, and the press increased the confusion on the stage.

I remember that I was looking out into the brightly lit house where the crowd was still leaving. Some real jerks were coming forward to get a snapshot of the tragedy on stage with their phones. Police officers stopped some of them from ascending the stairs to the stage to obtain a better look. I walked to the apron to ask the thrill-seekers to back off, and that's when I saw him.

He came up out of the orchestra pit, a tall, well-built, long-haired blonde in very disheveled, black formal wear. The mop of his hair fell over his face. He hopped up on the rail and from there into the center aisle. As he landed on the carpet, the slick soles of his patent leathers caused him to slip and fall to his knees.

As he stood, he raked back his blonde hair from a very bruised, handsome face. The stage lights from the theater ceiling obscured my vision. Still, I thought I recognized him from a pursuit almost a lifetime ago.

He sped off up the crowded aisle as I attempted to get a police officer on his retreating ass. I raced for the stairs on stage right but stopped. Eric Sorenson, leaving his companion in a first-tier box, dangled from the tier's outside balustrade and dropped to the lower floor. He raced to intercept the fleeing blonde.

I thought, *Holy shit! It's an entire family of fuckin' acrobats.* He looked like a superhero. Black cape flying, he flung himself through the dense crowd of the theater foyer, disappearing in the crush of the departing audience.

***

Kayne was sitting up in the emergency room bed. He was whispering to Nick and the police officers. Near the foot of the bed were Portia and Viola, talking to another officer. Mia Chan, who apparently had accompanied them now, stood off to the side, staring sorrowfully at the floor.

Kayne was saying, "I guess I need to get to the gym and work on my martial arts. Nick, you and me into some blindfold work soon, what say, my love?"

He was attempting to smile, but the painkillers had yet to kick in.

Nick said nothing, a bit too shaken up for coherence right now. He stroked the right hand of the man he rescued from the theater cellar. A nurse practitioner was winding a bandage around Kayne's head.

She said with a smirk, "Dr. Sorenson, I can get you a hand mirror if you want to adjust your makeup."

This brought soft laughter all around, except for a very distressed Nick.

The police officers shrugged and went back to the interrogation.

"Once more, please, Dr. Sorenson."

Kayne tenderly touched the side of his head and repeated the scenario beneath the theater's stage.

"The clues to his whereabouts led me deeper and lower into the theater's underbelly. Make no mistake, the killer was deliberately leaving a trail. I am not sure if he was wearing night visions or not."

"None were found. If so, the killer took them with him."

Kayne continued, "We fought on the lower level, and he knocked me out. I came to in the ambulance. I was very close several times, but I never saw his face."

Kayne looked off. When he continued, there was something trance-like in the way he recited the killer's description-- like he knew the guy.

"He is my height, about 225 pounds, late thirties, and trained in hand-to-hand. There was a distinct military style to his fighting."

"I think your head injuries are making you a bit confused. How could you possibly know these details, Doctor? You said it was pitch black in the theater's undercroft."

"I beg your pardon, Officer, but my observations are the result of elemental reasoning. An opponent of his skill and body mass must be of a certain age. His combat style is *Krav Maga,* an Israeli military self-defense system developed in Hungary. Fighters must recognize attack styles to provide a proper defense."

The Slovakian police officer continued, "It would seem he left you with some evidence in a highly intimate place, Doctor. My turn to conclude, no? I would wager you two have a history, yes?"

The detective placed on the bed a plastic bag containing blood-soaked leather gloves.

"They were stuffed in the waistband of the front of your slacks. Minus the bag."

Kayne looked at the gloves and then raised the sheet to examine the front of his briefs, confirming their placement.

"Your conclusion cannot be tied to facts regarding a previous relationship. I assure you, officer, I did not see the murderer's face."

"I did, Darling."

Everyone turned to me.

"Rebecca, how could you possibly? You were not in the sub-basement."

I related my witnessing of the escape of the murderer from under the stage. I explained, seeing him flee from the orchestra pit and out into the house. I made no mention of the pursuing Eric Sorenson.

"Kayne, I could be mistaken, but the last time I saw that man was about eight years ago in Budapest on the Danube embankment. It was a situation I will never forget."

I looked directly at Kayne. He, in turn, looked open-mouthed at my reference to the chase and rescue of his naked ass. All this took place in our halcyon days of hot continental sex and perilous European adventures.

"Yes, Darling, it was Haagen. I am almost sure. One does not forget that blond villain."

Kayne looked off again, digesting the information. *Yeah, he knew but was not telling the police for some reason.*

Police work seemed to snap Nick out of his worry. As I translated, he turned from attending Kayne and spoke to the investigating detective.

"Ádám Haagen. Most likely of Budapest. Former Hungarian military. Wanted in the murder investigation of the actress Mira Savic in Vienna. Similar *modus operandi*. I can put you in touch with Didi … excuse me, Kapitän Dieter Pichler of the *Polizeikommissariatin, Wien.*"

The detective continued, "Thank you, Officer Sechi. While I have you all here, what can you tell us about the young woman, Elena Janescue?"

Portia spoke up. "She was new to our company. Elena auditioned and secured the part of Cordelia when we came over in May to form the production in Brussels. I believe she was a German National. We always check our actors' papers following the Ars Europa guidelines."

Viola added, "She was an excellent actress and a very cooperative member of the company. Quiet offstage. Took direction well. Very talented. I foresaw a continued career of excellence in the theater for that poor young woman."

I translated the detective's next question, "Ms. Sechi and Professor Sechi, are you aware of any possible reason that someone would murder Ms. Janescue?"

The two women thought intently before Portia responded. As she did, Portia turned to look at Mia Chan.

"No, officer. I am not aware of any reason for harm to come to Elena.

Mia said softly, "I can. Elena was a wanted criminal. She carefully disguised her identity because she was trying to stay incognito for a while. She knew there were folks out to get her, and it looks like they did."

The reaction was one of surprised concern. The detective asked the young actress in English. "And exactly what was her crime?"

"Pussy Riot."

Thomas Severino

Chapter Thirty-Two: The Ingénue
Nick Sechi's Journal

By first light, despite the shock of the horrible murder of the young actress, we attempted to get back to normal. Kayne was released from the hospital, and we gathered in our hotel room to plan our next moves.

Rebecca said, "It seems Sir Keith's dresser had been locked in a closet. He was overpowered after agreeing to a backstage liaison with our Hungarian assassin and too embarrassed to make any noise. You see, the poor kid's pants didn't quite make it to the utility closet. He confirmed the description of the assassin. It was indeed Major Haagen. So that leaves me with one ancillary question, Darlings."

"And what might that be, dear girl?"

"Is everyone having sex on this trip but me? Even loathsome killers and stagehands? Some Mata Hari I turned out to be."

I chuckled.

"Well, my advice is if you can find a straight guy among this lot, I say put on your red pumps and go for it, girl."

Even my Mother snickered at that one.

"Don't look at me. I am not about to discuss my sex life in front of my son and daughter. What will people think? And speaking of, has anyone seen the Executive Producer or Kayne's brother?"

The apparent implication hit the three of us all at once. It resulted in expressions resembling folks who had just tasted spoiled dairy.

"Nah, nah, nah. The insane brother sings in our choir, Mom. Anyway, Portia has a ton of stuff to deal with, considering one of her players was murdered. Her libido is most likely shut down."

"Speak for yourself, Junior. Sechis are hard-wired for...."

"Portia!"

"Sorry, Mom."

Portia Sechi burst into the suite, very much a woman on a mission. She mocked, "Seriously, the grisly murder of our dear Elena has completely devastated the company. I can't believe this. I have been trying to comfort our folks all morning."

My mother put her hand over her mouth and sank into a nearby chair. The full extent of the tragedy had affected us all very deeply, and our feeble attempts at levity did little to alleviate the horror.

Portia pulled up a seat at the table and said, "Yet another round of interrogation by the local police. And the media is driving me bonkers, kids. I got a show to do. So, do not piss me off."

She launched into corporate speak. "OK. Executive Committee Meeting at this moment is called to order. First order of business: The Medical Condition of Dr. Sorenson." She pointed at Kayne. "Go."

"All cleared, Madam Executive Producer. The hospital kept me for tests and found nothing amiss. X-rays, blood work, everything good."

He thumped his chest, indicating soundness, and announced, "Next issue."

I chided, "Kayne, you are so not telling the truth. You should have stayed in the hospital for continued observation. They warned him to be careful. No exertion and plenty of rest. Even hard-headed Australians need to watch their wild-arsed behavior, as they say. This is not good, Boss."

He rolled his ice-blue eyes at my remarks, and I could tell that action caused him a bit of pain.

"Officer Sechi, you are in charge of keeping your man under control. Limited exertion."

I thought, *One tall order. You have no idea, sister.*

Portia's tone turned serious at this point.

"The remains of Elena Janescue have been shipped to her relatives in Paris. The company, including Mother and I, has voted unanimously to continue the production's run. The arrival in Budapest has been delayed by two days. Although, I will point out the vote was pretty much *pro forma*. The company has requested that the remaining performances be dedicated to the memory of Elena Janescue and everything she stood for. Mia Chan and a few others have created a memorial page for the programs and our web page.

"In any case, the contract with Ars Europa is tough to break. And the actors depend on their salary. Elena would not have wanted it any other way."

Viola placed a comforting hand on her daughter's shoulder. The loss of a company member and the terror of her killing at the final performance in Bratislava were a heavy burden.

Portia continued, "So with clearance from the police, I sent the theater properties and the staff on to Budapest. They can do the setup and just about all the tech before we get there. I thought the two-day delay would give the company a bit of a healing rest.

"We arrive in Budapest tomorrow and hit the boards the following night. They want us to add two performances before leaving for Ljubljana. That totally works. Ticket sales for the Hungarian capital are through the roof. Nothing sells tickets like murder most foul, unfortunately."

Kayne asked Viola, "Will you be filling the role with an understudy?"

"No, Kayne, we are running with a very spare company at this point. The minor players are not up to the role. It must be played with a delicate balance of pathos and style. We have found a new talent that will take over the role, someone quite good if somewhat inexperienced."

Rebecca jumped in, "I told you, Viola Darling, I did Shakespeare all through my undergrad days, at times in Spanish. My co-major was theater, and I know the play."

"Holy Shit, you mean to tell me…." I was astonished. Kayne did a similar take, sitting up with his mouth open.

"Well, my dear beauty, I never would have thought…."

Rebecca moved to the center of the room and did a drag queen twirl, one hand in the air above her head.

"And this is only the beginning, Darlings." She mimed taking thunderous ovations, head bowed into a low curtsey with a delicate hand over her heart.

"There will be another production and another production."

She stopped and pointed to Portia. "Hamlet. Yes, like the legendary Sarah Bernhardt. Ahhh, ... the Divine Sarah.

"No, wait, wait, Darling. 'The Scottish Play!' Yes ... 'Out damn spot'...."

She dramatically wrung her hands, Lady Macbeth style.

"Or, or... wait. Cleopatra, tragic queen of the Nile, in love with the Master of Rome, among other Italian males."

She brought smiles to everyone as she luxuriated in chewing up imaginary scenery. Our beauty vamped an Egyptian goddess fated to love passionately yet unwisely.

"I'd pay to watch you get bitten on the ass."

She lightly cuffed me with a magazine.

"That's bitten *by an asp*, you Philistine. And it was on her breast of which mine are spectacular."

Portia mocked her newborn star, "Hold it, girl. Cordelia is only in four scenes. See what you can do to obey the director here and overwhelm the audience with a tragic portrayal. Then we will talk."

Mother picked up the conversation, "And by the way, no revisions of the Bard's lines. No 'darlings,' Darling."

She added, "Actually, she was excellent at the audition. And another woman of color among Lear's daughters will strengthen the diversity message of our production."

Rebecca was brimming over with delight. I toasted her with our morning juice.

"Break a leg, gorgeous."

"Hear, hear. Cheers, O Divine One."

Portia went back to the business of the company.

"Anyone have other issues before we move out and literally get this show on the road?"

Mother interjected, "Elena's connection to Pussy Riot. What are the implications for the company?"

Kayne spoke up, "According to Ms. Chan, and as corroborated by our private internet investigators and the Bratislava police, Ms. Janescue was part of the group's demonstrations in Moscow and in Sochi during the 2014 Winter Olympics. She was taken out of Russia by family members after being put on probation following the group's Moscow trial for hooliganism. Her fellow 'band' members were sent to one of Russia's penal colonies.

"In addition, our operatives in Colorado have discovered that her real identity was one Olga Solenskya. Outside Russia, she continued to work behind the scenes on the group's unauthorized and provocative guerrilla performances in public places, most recently at the finals of the 2018 World Cup. She was part of a team that marketed the interventions and solicited international support for the collective, carefully staying out of her homeland.

"Pussy Riot has done much to bring global attention to issues like the decline of human rights in Russia. She was especially vocal regarding feminism and LGBTQ rights. The group very dangerously promotes opposition to Russian President Vladimir Putin. I find it surprising that she chose a very public venue as the theater to go underground, as they say. Even using an alias."

I added, "So, a big group of bad guys in the mix. Are we looking at more problems here?"

Kayne and Rebecca knew I had in mind the impending rescue operation.

"Good question, Nick. I think at this point, we need to let your mother and sister know what's going on."

Thomas Severino

Chapter Thirty-Three: Resistance

From the Case Files of Kayne Sorenson, Ph.D.

"I thought I'd find you here."

He was sweating, wobbling like he was intoxicated, and he clenched and unclenched his hands like a potential strangler.

"Eric, considering our mobiles are most likely being monitored, I left word at the hotel. Looks like you just made the train."

"Yes, my dear brother. I learned that the troupe was on its way to Hungary, and I needed to complete a few things between last night and today. Where's the bluey boy?"

"Cooling his heels. We had a team meeting back at the hotel and are having a bit of an altercation, it would seem."

I expected a snide comment from the Nightstalker, but it never came. Upon closer inspection, he looked like "who-done-left-it-and-ran," a closed long-sleeved shirt over his signature t-shirt and the smell of Turkish cigarettes.

Rebecca asked, "Eric, the blonde … last night at the theater?"

"An agent with very secure connections, my girl. I almost lost him in Hviezdoslav Square. However, at the last second was able to track him into the warren of streets that is Bratislava's Old Town. I came across two of his buddies at the Ondrejský Cemetery, and the game changed up a bit. I will forego the boring details of our skirmish and say I lost the three of them at the river. A speedboat was waiting—one of those supercharged cigarette boats, black as the Danube at night.

"And speaking of cigarettes…."

He made a move to stand and winced, falling back onto the compartment seats. I stood over him and opened his shirt. A bloody, improvised patch covered the right side of his rib cage. The wound had been bandaged but badly.

He pushed me off and staggered to his feet.

"Can't keep your hands off me, dear brother? Flattering but perhaps a tad inappropriate." His attempt at an insult was feeble.

He fumbled in his jeans for his pills packet and spilled two tablets on the floor. I retrieved them, handed them to him, and gave him my water bottle.

He gulped water and pharmaceuticals and said, "It's only a scratch. I just need some sleep. Portia got me a compartment. We still have two and a half hours to the Budapest Keleti station. I'll crash."

His eyes drooped. Rebecca stepped between us.

"Look, Batman, you're coming with me. I need you all fit and ballsy as this thing comes to a climax. Do you understand?"

He waved her away.

"Oh, yeah? You put up a fight, and I swear to God, I will drop you on your demonic ass."

He shot a half-deadly look her way.

"Mia Chan is a registered nurse and has tons of first aid for the company. We are gonna get that mess cleaned and some painkillers in you."

"No pills, Rebecca." He looked sincere for just a moment, the tough-guy façade slipping.

"OK. Yeah, I understand."

Her tone softened. "Just come along, Eric. I need some face time with you anyway. Considering Nick's opposition to our exit strategy, the topic is 'Plan B for the Escape.' Then you get to sleep."

***

Alone in the compartment, I backtracked in my head all the way to "the reveal" at the Bratislava Hotel. My thoughts went to Nick and his latest rage. He was wild about how the conversation settled out regarding the rescue of the three gay scientists. I mentally rewound and played the conflagration that erupted just before we left for the train when we explained the hostage affair.

Back at the hotel, Portia and Viola had many questions. Their initial interest was the safety of Nick, Rebecca, Eric, and me.

"Mom, I face danger every day in my profession in law enforcement. We have gone through all of that. This is the same thing."

"It is not the same, Nick. This is an organization of evil that you four are going up against. It sounds like their forces are formidable, and there are only four of you. Four.

"In your police work, you have the backing of a force of men and women dedicated to justice and public safety. It is rather presumptuous on your part to think you can create some kind of Avengers group."

Nick was somewhat mollified. Portia was silent.

Rebecca spoke up, "Viola, these gay scientists will die horrible deaths unless a small force gets to them and frees them. Add to that the fact that they are three of the greatest minds in their field of science and medicine. But the bottom line is they are innocent people, persecuted and in grave danger.

"Kayne is just about the most brilliant mind on the planet when it comes to what makes criminals tick. He can anticipate their every move. I will only say that Eric is a formidable ally. He is Darth Vader, but Eric is on our side. He will get this group fine-tuned for the rescue.

"I got us into this because the FBI and ICPO-INTERPOL believe we can do this. And Nick can keep all safe and focused on getting the job done. Your son is a genuine superhero."

Portia remained mute but looked from one to the other. Viola turned and faced the wall, deep in thought.

I said, "We have had to be careful because of the security surrounding this operation. However, I assure you we have contacts in the Viennese police, INTERPOL, and the CIA if this thing goes awry. I have connections in Hungary, also. We believe the exchange will happen in the next two weeks."

Rebecca nodded.

Nick stepped to his mother and put his hands on her shoulders.

"It's OK, Mom. All will be well."

Viola looked into the eyes of her son.

Portia spoke.

"I want in."

***

"Listen to me and listen to me carefully. I will not allow my family to be put in harm's way over this operation. No fuckin' way! This all is separate. Just complete the theater contract and get home."

Nick was florid. Not only was he addressing his sister, but he also looked at Rebecca and me to make sure that we knew his former position in the matter had not changed. He stabbed at the table to emphasize his points. I saw his blushes begin to rise from his neck to his face.

"Portia, everything that Mother said is very true about the dangers. The four of us can handle this. The plan is good. We will distance all of this from the theater company."

He looked at me for affirmation, but I hesitated to respond.

Portia addressed her brother, "Nick, your plan sucks. No exit for anybody. Are you going to put these three people in shipping containers and hope they arrive alive and in a country where they will be safe? Even you, with your crazy-assed tendency to take senseless risks, have to see that...."

"Wait a minute. Hold on. Just a second... I have heard all of this before."

He pointed to Rebecca and me.

"Have you been talking to them about this?"

He was furious.

I started, "Nick...."

"Darling..."

Portia interrupted, "Nick, stop the hot-head shit. It's simple. We insert the freed captives into the company during the run in the Slovenian capital. Some of the company members are Europeans and will remain on the continent. The refugees take their place when we exit the continent. Ars Europa has a very easy in-and-out policy, and I believe there will be minimal scrutiny as we return to North America. You four provide protection until we leave. Kayne can use his connections for reinforcements."

I said, "Rebecca and I will work on proper paperwork for their exit from Europe and entry into Canada."

Rebecca gave the thumbs up.

Nick said, "This is all too pre-packaged, if you ask me, a bit too rehearsed."

He rounded on me.

"Where is that precious brother of yours? He has obviously been campaigning for this solution– the three of you and your little political rally at the restaurant...."

He pointed to Rebecca, "... for *your* very dangerous scheme."

I protested, "Nick, you are being rather paranoid, my love."

Rebecca rounded on him, "Hey Nick, say the word, and you guys are out. All of you. I will finish this with Eric and meet you both in Florida."

Nick's anger continued to escalate.

"Right, Rebecca. Without Kayne and me, you and the Spy from Fuckville are going to just waltz in there, take on those gangsters, and save the day."

Viola came back into the discussion.

"Nicola, calm yourself. You have no reason to be so upset. So like your Father."

He turned to his mother and sister.

"And he would be the first to tell you both not even to consider this. He would want it my way. Why is that so hard for any of you to see?"

He was spinning in the hotel room, trying to convince any of us. Portia rose to his ire.

"He was my father too, Nick."

Viola said, "Stop! Nick, Portia..."

Everyone seemed to be suspended in the emotion of the very heated exchange.

Viola took Portia by the hand and made as if to exit the hotel room.

"We will see you on the train and continue this discussion then. Cooler heads will prevail. At that time, you will have our decision."

Nick was not to be placated by his mother's pleas for a delay. I had experienced his frustration and anger before, and he had dealt with mine, but this seemed to be a new level of estrangement. Realizing that hyper-emotions are not my game, I was at a loss on how to reconnect with him.

His gaze was poisonous and fiery as he looked from Rebecca to me and had the last word.

"Kayne, Rebecca, I am telling you both – do not do this."

Chapter Thirty-Four: Nick's Passion

Nick Sechi's Journal

I was super pissed.

Kayne was unsure how to continue the discussion once my sister and my mother left our suite at the hotel. He grew silent and distant. Rebecca started to her room to pack and said, "It seems that some major decisions need to be adjusted here. I'll get back to the two of you shortly."

The cab ride to the train station in Bratislava was like a trip to a funeral. I had nothing to say to Kayne and Rebecca. I felt betrayed and was sure that the machinations of Eric Sorenson were foundational to the fracturing of the relationship I had with two people in the back seat of the taxi. He was, indeed, the sower of discord.

As Mother and Portia pulled up behind us at the station, I tried to distract myself by ensuring our luggage was stowed correctly. I also checked that my sister and mother were comfortable in their compartment. All conversation was strained and terse.

As the train started, I returned to our compartment. I stuck my head in and, without looking at either Kayne or Rebecca, announced, "Hey, I'm going to get some air." I skipped the observation deck, deciding on the bar car.

Kicking back into a club chair, I watched the Slovak capital disappear. The summer countryside replaced the urban industrial view along the Danube. Through the doors at the front of the club car that led to our cabins, I thought I saw Eric stumbling up the train corridor to our compartment.

Thinking that this could not get any more disastrous, I ordered another beer, turned in my chair to face the rear end of the train, and fought internally with my feelings. I felt I was the lone warrior on this one.

Partway through my second brew, I felt a hand on my shoulder. I looked up into those Siberian Husky ice-blues. I felt the fire in my head begin to subside at his touch. I wanted to crawl into his back pocket and stay there.

A young male waiter approached with a glass of clear, amber liquid bathing sparkling cubes.

In English, he said, "Here you are, Dr. Sorenson, Nestville Northern, a double on the rocks."

Kayne accepted the glass and moved his hand up to the back of my head, caressing me a bit.

"Take a walk with me, my love."

I grabbed my beer and signaled the young waiter for another, pointing to the observation platform. I followed Kayne to the outside landing.

I tossed a remark over my shoulder, "Looks like your brother showed."

Moving to the opposite side of the platform, I folded my arms and sat on one of the chairs. I watched the night countryside and small villages slide by as we journeyed south in the dark. I had my back to Kayne, but I could feel his eyes on me. We were alone at the end of the train.

I heard the soft clinking of the ice in his glass and felt him come up behind me. He wrapped his arms around me, lifting me into a standing position. He put his head against mine so that his mouth was close to my ear. He could feel the tension in my body as he pulled me closer.

"Here we are again, Nick."

There was an edge of annoyance in my voice. "I'm not sure I know what you mean. What are you drinking, anyway? Smells sweet."

Kayne held the golden glass out into the moonlight. It bounced with the gliding motion of the train. The moon was waning and would be new in a few weeks.

"Try a sip, my love."

I raised the glass to my lips and took a taste while turning my body to face his. My butt rested against the guardrail. I quaffed the whiskey as he taught me, pulling air into my mouth as I sucked the liquor over my tongue to the back of my throat to swallow.

I softened my edginess a bit. "Mmm. That is nice. What am I tasting?"

"It is a Slovakian whiskey from distilleries near the Polish border. One drinks it straight up or on the rocks like this…."

He held up the glass.

"Or my favorite way."

His blue eyes twinkled with moonbeams and starlight.

I smiled for the first time in about 24 hours and said,

"Which is?"

"Like this."

Setting his glass and my beer down on a corner tray, he dipped two fingers in the Nestville Northern and liberally anointed my lips with the golden spirits. He generously applied the drink to my mouth, dripping it onto my chin.

He kissed me deeply and passionately, working his tongue and lips on the inside and outside of my mouth, his hands pressing us together. Some of the whiskey dribbled on my chin, and he went for it. His mouth continued moving down my throat and onto my chest as he opened my shirt.

Damn, I want this scorching hot man right here and now.

He was playing me like a Stradivarius. Why was it that I could so quickly forget my troubles in the arms of this remarkable man? I was panting in the warm night from his creative foreplay.

Hold it. Kayne was lulling me into abdicating my position using sex.

But, before the Boss got to the point of no return, he stopped and stepped back, wiping his mouth with a cocktail napkin, and shot his forelock. He assumed an effete liquor connoisseur stance, head slightly cocked and gesturing to the glass with his fluttering *serviette*.

"While the aroma reminds one of marzipan, brown sugar, and walnuts, the taste is cinnamon, black pepper, toasty oak, and almond. The full mouth and prolonged finish..."

I chuckled as he ran an index finger between my pecs and sucked lightly on it.

He added, "The aftertaste has highlights of dry oak and black pepper with exotic tones of ... of...."

He brought his lips to my collarbone.

I asked, "Of?"

He drew closer again with a full-body press, rocking against me with the rhythm of the train.

"Hot muscle boy sweat."

One huge tease.

I enjoyed his ardor and felt my own excitement stirring to the full. But I pushed him back, trying to gather my thoughts. As we separated, I glanced at the tightening crotch of his slacks and said, "You bastard. Think you can get me to change my mind by getting into my briefs? Give me some credit, Boss."

"Just trying to lighten the moment, my love."

He brought my hand to his crotch. I smirked, "Sorenson family trait? It just never goes down, does it, Professor? You Aussies are some piece of work, mate." I took my hand away.

He chuckled.

I was not about to give ground. I continued, "Kayne, what did you mean, 'here we are again?'"

He cooled a bit, took up his glass, and tossed it back.

"Somehow, we always end up here, my Nick. An impasse. Heightened emotions and grave danger all around, a total obstruction to logic. What's to become of us, lad? Doomed as some great romantic couple out of myth. Soon to be swept up in the maelstrom of passionate primal instincts and be destroyed."

I shrugged.

"Get to the point, Kayne."

He got more serious. "You see, the thing is, this is the part of love and relationships in which I have no expertise. I have earned no distinction in this area. I can sex up like the most dedicated sensualist. Still, heartfelt conversations, putting my guts on the table, all defenses down and ready to risk everything-- it's all bollocks to this bloke from the Outback."

I thought, *Most times, he sexes up like a wild man, pagan and savage.* Lying next to him after our lovemaking, I often felt that all his extraordinary, cerebral abilities needed some regular, wild-assed, crazy release, a carnal downshifting that was both cathartic and energy recharging. One went with the other.

He moved next to me and put his hands on the railing, leaning into the warm darkness retreating behind us.

"I should be able to feel your anguish in the situation in which we find ourselves. All I can feel is the terror that requires the most logical response. My mind bounces from concept to concept, detail to detail. Still, all of this anger and confusion is not my purview and gets in the way of my cognitive processes."

He ran the slender fingers of his left hand through his hair.

"Sometimes... I don't know... I just can't think. And that terrifies me."

He shifted to face the car and turned his head to mine.

"You feel things deeper than me. You explode, fulminate, and lash out, taking any risk that needs to be taken. Your sharp intellect and deep heart are paired with well-placed timing, the strength of resolve, and some serious muscle. I can only observe, analyze, compile, and draw conclusions with as much thought as it takes to solve a problem."

"You keep saying that. So, this means what?"

"It means we are in grave danger yet again and a bit estranged in our hearts. It seems we are disconnected. And that sucks, as you are oft to say."

I met his gaze as he continued.

"As usual, we are responsible for the safety of others, a situation that is not unfamiliar to either of us or one we have never shirked."

He took my arm.

"I will try to feel what you feel and appreciate your point of view on this, but Nick, you must calmly listen to reason."

"Easy Kayne, I will not be infantilized. How 'bout you start off understanding that?"

I shook him off and turned to look into the night. I felt my anger rise.

"Since we got to Hermagor, I have felt like the boy toy."

"Be serious, Nick."

"No! Now, you hear me out... please. Rebecca's tricky duel and masquerade... and your brother. Holy shit! Could he be any more condescending and insulting? He makes me feel so fucking objectified. I swear he'd like me trussed up in one of his bondage sessions in a heartbeat. He should so fucking try."

My hands were balled into fists, and I was getting wild again. I took several deep breaths, attempting to chill.

"And you. What was all that about the Viennese police captain? Sure, he was hot for me, or so I thought. And it felt kinda good. Kayne, I am an adult. Forget that shit. You are my main guy, and you know it."

He started to speak, but I rushed ahead.

"And this exit plan thing with Ars Europa and the scientists. Kayne, it's my family and their friends. I cannot endanger them. I need you in with me on this. Why can't you come over to my side on this?"

He took hold of me and looked into my eyes.

"Because we have no choice, Nick. We all are in too deep. Two murders– all Karadžić."

I tried to turn away in frustration. Kayne pulled me back.

"Listen to me. The deaths of the two actresses and the hostage situation with the three gay scientists are all the work of our nemesis General Raheb Karadžić. None of us, none of us is getting out of this one unless we take that deadly dragon out."

"So, we just walk, Kayne. It's simple and logical. Turn it all over to local and international authorities. Portia's company completes their run, and Rebecca pulls the ingenue-turned-star gig. Eric goes back into the hell-swamp, and we go back on vacation. Or home to Florida."

"Pandemonium."

Huh?

"Eric goes back to Pandemonium. In *Paradise Lost*, it is the capital city of Hell. It also happens to be my brother's favorite leather club in Amsterdam."

"Whatever."

Kayne shook his head.

"You know that your scenario can't happen, Nick. As powerful as government and local authorities are, our General's and his NEO Group's reach is far and all-encompassing. The General's tentacles extend across the globe."

He continued, "Look at the Savic investigation in Vienna. Pichler and his goons are phoning this one in. They just want a gay or an immigrant on which to pin that murder, and they have both. Translation: Mira Savic got what she deserved. It's all political."

I thought about what he said. Kayne Sorenson and his super-analytical mind. My brilliant Aussie prince... *frosty up and listen to the Boss Man, Niko.*

He pulled me close and worked his hands over my tense back, shoulders, and neck. He locked me in his ice-blue gaze and continued.

"Since when have you ever run from a fight, my love? You have told me before. We... us, together. We can take this mother fucker out. And we will.

"Also, Rebecca is astute and willing to confront any action with strength and intelligence. We have seen what she can do against the 'Big Bads.' Eric..."

He stopped and rubbed his chin.

"I have given this a lot of thought. Sometimes, it takes crazy to defeat crazy. He is incredibly strong and can be ruthless. As long as he is on his meds, he will be somewhat controllable."

"He needs to stay the fuck away from me, Kayne. I am serious."

"You represent the good side of the Force, my love. The valorous, truthful, and virtuous. Since he was a child, his Lucifer persona has always rebelled against everything you represent."

"His bicep tattoo," Kayne said, "Better to reign in Hell than to serve in Heaven."

"His sexual interest is pretty scary, I will admit, but I believe he is dedicated to the rescue cause for the right reason, like a true professional. And if it comes down to it, you and I have had some experience keeping the trolls at bay."

The door to the train's observation platform opened.

"I am sorry to intrude."

Kayne spun around to see our best gal pal step through the car door to the outside platform. She had a grave expression and no cocktail.

He said, "This is an entirely new twist, dear girl. Nick, how many times has our Darling interrupted our love play like a card-carrying member of the Legion of Decency? And now we have this refreshing politeness."

He looked to see if I was smiling, broken free of my anger and dark moods. I was easing up. *WTF was the Legion of Decency, Kayne?*

"I need help. No, let me say it straight out. I need you guys."

Her big molasses-brown eyes took in each of our faces in the warm night.

"I cannot see this through without you. Eric is a valuable asset, but I think he may be disintegrating right before our eyes. I've never encountered such an intense individual. He gives the appearance of a crouching predator sizing up his prey. And the personality disorder—Holy Mother! Who knew?"

"Actually, my brother has some very impressive accolades regarding his service to multiple foreign governments. Because he specialized in covert operations, many of his accomplishments and the appreciation they have merited have not been made public."

I asked, "How do you know this?"

Kayne looked into the night.

"In the course of some of the cases on which I have been asked to consult, I have run across government representatives who have recognized us as brothers. In several cases, they have quietly commended my brother and his skills."

His eyes came back to mine.

"I have made it a priority to keep track of the black sheep. I suppose, on some level, I am hoping for a grand reconciliation with Ace and my brothers, but I think we will see the Second Coming first."

I asked, "I sure would like to know how 'scary guy' has distinguished himself as an undercover."

After a pause, Kayne continued, "In the last 10 years or so, the kidnapping of diplomats, American tourists, and members of the press have increased in developing nations. On more than one occasion, Eric has assisted in returning such individuals. Two come to mind, the daughter of a Swedish ambassador about three years ago and a distaff member of the Saudi royal family. In both cases, he minimized the violence, contained the media storm, and returned the captives to their respective families.

"I would posit that right now, he is just about the best there is-- a combination of brutal strength, fearlessness, and intelligence. My brother goes head-to-head with powerful oligarchs at their own game. His relentless pursuit of the killer in Bratislava is testimony that he will get the job done, no matter the cost. The trade-off, of course, is that without his meds, he is dangerous to himself and to those who care about him."

Rebecca asked, "Kayne, your bother talks in his sleep."

We looked in shock at our friend. She rolled her eyes.

"Boys, I am not that crazy. He drifted off when we were patching him up. Like deep sleep, Darlings. He kept calling for Chris. I wonder who that is?"

The deep voice of the man in question broke the silence as he joined us. "It is a matter of no consequence, Rebecca. Best to forget it. Do not bring it up again."

He blew a stream of blue smoke into the night and settled a hip against the far railing. His back to us before turning and throwing her a look that assured us of his seriousness.

"Seems I arrived here just in time. My ears were ringing. Discuss me much?"

Kayne said, "How is your side?"

"Also of no importance, dear brother."

This time, he eyed me with a slightly challenging look. His free hand clenched three times and then settled on the railing. He spoke away into the night, but his remarks were directed at me.

"What say you get us that sexy waiter boy, Nick? You three look like you need another round of drinks, and I need a diversion."

Jesus, this guy knew how to press my buttons. Nevertheless, I stuck my head in, and our waiter soon had two fresh ones and a Marie Laveau on the side table.

Eric turned away from the view to accept bottled water from the young man. His accepting hand lingered against the youth's fingers as he threw the kid a panther-like assessment, his silver eye cold and calculating. The flustered boy exited quickly.

We were joined by Portia and Viola.

Eric said, "A meeting of the principals. Excellent."

Viola folded her hands at her waist and said, "Mr. Sorenson, how are your wounds?"

Eric muttered, "News travels fast, it seems, Professor."

He waved her off and exhaled a white-blue cloud of smoke.

My mother frowned and took a step toward the tall spy.

"When this is over, we need to have a sit-down, you and I...."

In a somewhat high-spirited mood, Portia smirked, "Go get him, Mom."

"... the subject of our conversation will be manners, civility, and decency. And how to attain these virtues."

Eric turned his back to her.

She touched his shoulder and softly turned him. She stared at him briefly.

I felt the others stiffen as I thought: *One does not touch this man, not causally or affectionately anyway.*

"You have a good heart, I can tell. You disguise it well, but it is there. My children and students will testify to my understanding of the human condition. I am seldom mistaken."

She stared directly at him as Portia put a hand on my shoulder and whispered, "Relax, brother. This is going to work out fine."

Eric held her gaze and said dryly, "Another being of light sent to redeem the fallen. Please do not waste your time, Professor Sechi."

My mother continued facing him. She stepped back, clasped her hands at her waist, and said, "Mr. Sorenson, my family, my company, and our two dear friends here are so very important to me. After extensive consultation, Portia and I have agreed to provide the exit strategy for your plan to free the three hostages."

"Fuck, no, Mom!"

I caught "The Look," the one that can stop a bus at five blocks. Her glance was stern and formidable.

"Nicola, watch your language. Remember to whom you are speaking. Please remain silent and listen to me."

Kayne came over and stood between Eric and me. He looked into my eyes and said, "Nick."

I started to shake off both Portia and him but stopped. I had seen my mother like this before, and she was indeed a controlled force of nature able to handle any crisis.

"Son, three incarcerated people whose only offense is that they are gay are in grave peril. Who am I? Who are any of us to refuse assistance? How can any of us walk away?"

She took a step closer, touched my cheek, and said, "Did not the good sisters at St. Nicholas of Tolentine Grammar School teach you the meaning of the Bible verse, 'Greater love than this has no man than to lay down his life for another,' remember? Besides, these captives have research that could change medicine as we know it and relieve countless numbers of suffering and dying. I repeat. Who are any of us to say 'no'?"

Portia added, "And, to take Rebecca's point, even if these there were just ordinary folks, their lives matter."

My mother stabbed an index finger at the sky.

"Yes. Exactly."

I could see Rebecca's eyes brimming over with tears. Eric stared at my mother as she turned back to him. He was entirely out of his element.

"Love calls us to be heroes and heroines for the sake of others, and that is a constant commitment. You know that, Mr. Sorenson. You have taken many self-sacrificing risks in your work."

I imagined a Satanic tail twitching behind him as Eric's eyes became slits. He hissed, "Quite true, Professor, for pay, always for pay."

Her turn to wave off the remark.

She continued, "My assessment stands, Sir.

"My son, daughter, Rebecca, and your fine brother are no strangers to risk for another's sake. When all is said and done, there is no alternative here. It is a test of our humanity."

She gazed into the retreating night and continued, "When my husband and I were raising our children, we often spoke privately about our aspirations for our children. I remember we taught them never to look away from the poor and the suffering. We urged them to consider, 'There but for the grace of God go I.' And we were not kidding."

Portia broke in, "Eric, Rebecca, I will let the company know as circumstances dictate, but I imagine the confidentiality of this affair is of paramount importance. For our part, we will follow the procedures that the four of you think best."

I shifted uncomfortably, fearing the worst. My mother turned her attention to me.

"Nick, your father wanted heroic, loving children, and he got them. This I know very well, my dear. You would have made him proud."

I felt a tear hit my eyelids and spill over. Kayne pulled me tighter. The night countryside was gradually transforming into the early-morning urban landscape of the suburbs of Budapest.

My mother lifted a hand to Eric's face.

He stepped back, raising his hand to the place she touched as if his vampire's countenance had been burned by the rising sun.

She persisted wordlessly and again touched his cheek gently.

No one spoke. I felt Kayne go tense against me.

"Eric, you just have to keep everyone safe."

Lucifer turned away, cloaked in the remaining shadows of the lifting darkness.

Thomas Severino

Chapter Thirty- Five: CRISPR

"You have had three weeks to finish the project. What is the status?"

The conference room held the medical team seated at opposite sides of the large black laminated, rectangular table, Ruslan Dudayev, Eteri Patarava, and Ioane Abkhazi on one side. Seven medical and biochemical professionals sat opposite. Three nondescript staff sat on chairs along the wall that contained the door.

At the head of the table sat the Lieutenant. On the far wall was the media screen. Behind her was a mirrored wall.

Dr. Patarava spoke up, "It must be understood that the trials for this protocol with human subjects do not have the depth nor the longitudinal studies to justify it as a safe medical procedure. However, the indications are very positive. At the cellular level, we have copious evidence that the deformed red blood cells are being replaced in the animals' circulatory systems by normal shaped cells capable of carrying oxygen."

Dr. Dudayev moved the video display forward, showing microscopic views of blood samples from treated animals. Crescent-shaped blood cells appeared in fewer numbers as the gene therapy progressed.

"As you can see, the nanosurgery on the genes works, but there still remain many risks. Because of the newness of this experimental therapy, we do not have complete data on the side effects caused by removing defective chromosomal DNA and replacing it with the coding that will cause the bone marrow to produce spherical RBCs with concave centers. Shown here."

He indicated the screen display, reviewing several slides of magnified blood cells.

"We have followed your instructions and placed the documents associated with our work on the secured site for your team of scientists and physicians."

The Lieutenant's mobile vibrated. She picked up the call.

"Yes, Sir."

She listened.

"I understand. Sir. It will be done."

She ended the call and placed the phone on the table. She turned to address her medical team.

"You have worked with these three in the labs. If you have questions, I will leave you to discuss this. We have clearance to move into the implementation phase on humans. Patient #1's medical records have been made available to both components of this project's team. I urge you to prepare for this phase with the utmost care and haste."

Ioane Abkhazi spoke, "I have a question, Officer. The research for this medical treatment has been shared with your scientists and physicians. It represents our life work. It is worthy of universal acknowledgment that would bring to our careers and continued research to...."

"Now, now, now, Doctor, your Nobel Prize aspirations are showing."

The ice-cold voice continued, "Please allow me to be clear, Doctor Abkhazi. Two things. This is indeed a life's work for which your lives will be spared, and you will be allowed to go free should Patient #1 improve. There are no laurels in prison, Sir, and death comes in many ways to the incarcerated.

Finally, if you have considered lethally sabotaging this project, allow me to inform you...."

She pointed to each of the scientists.

"... that you are Patients 2, 3, and 4."

Chapter Thirty-Six: *Systema*

Nick Sechi's Journal

"The waiter from the train was delicious, Nick. Too bad you are so faithful and pure. You would have enjoyed his lust-filled destruction. And he confessed while in the throes that he likes groups."

Holy fuck, this asshole does not quit.

Sitting much too close for my liking, he sounded like Gollum in *The Lord of the Rings*. I half expected the signature sibilant "s" of Tolkien's mysterious denizen of Middle Earth.

My preciousssss ...

I half turned and said, "Ease back a bit, Hell Boy, you are dripping sweat into my ear. Or is it brimstone? You gonna burst into flames or what?"

Eric and I stretched out on the bleachers against the martial arts training area wall at Izom Gym on Holo Utca, close to our Budapest hotel. We watched Kayne work out on the body bag. Both brothers were shirtless and sweating from intense workouts. Eric had extended his free weight training a full 90 minutes as Kayne and I moved on to cardio.

Kayne and I spared a bit between instructions doing some blindfold work. While I took a break to check in with my family and Rebecca, I tried desperately to move beyond my fear of involving them in this dangerous case. Over pillow talk this morning, I could feel myself coming over to the view that this operation would be challenging but successful.

As Kayne ramped it up on the body bag, his sweat-wet, black hair shaken loose from his tie-up, I imagined him as a graphic novel hero, vigorous and intense.

I said aloud to his always frisky brother, "He's good. Beats my ass just about every time, but not for long. The two of you are getting to be old codgers."

I stood up and looked at him.

"Dude, make way for young muscle."

I flexed a biceps/triceps posedown move in a brilliantly immature move. *The dude himself is rocking an impressive set of guns, Niko. Who are you trying to kid?*

Eric stared briefly, checked out my ass, smirked, and did a scan of the immediate vicinity. He was constantly assessing his surroundings. He turned his attention back to me and pointed to the source of the impact sounds on the training floor.

"Watch and learn."

Kayne did a brilliant series of spins, placing kicks at the top of the heavy bag. The balance and power were pure artistry, his body moving like a superb athlete, focused and sharp. He came back with a fierce barrage of jabs, hooks, knees, and elbows. The impact of his blows filled the gym space. Two trainers stopped working with their clients and pointed to the master at the center of the floor. A small admiring crowd began to gather.

He attached a double-end striking bag and dazzled the spectators with his timing, accuracy, rhythm, speed, and power, all in choreographed moves of breathtaking beauty. The mat beneath his bare feet was becoming slick with his sweat. A trainer offered him a water bottle, and Kayne slipped his mouthpiece to take a swig. He turned and raised the container in a toast with a slight pause at seeing his brother next to me.

Kayne did a small head douse before handing back the water. The trainer took up a set of punch mitts and put him through some advanced moves, calling for a series of maneuvers designed to further perfect his striking and lower-body moves. Glistening, he danced.

"Mr. Garber, pardon me, sir. Your room is free whenever you are ready."

"Did you get the equipment I requested, boy?"

"Yes, sir. You will find them there for you."

The young staffer and Eric exchanged a few sentences in Hungarian. The instant sexual tension needed no translation.

***

When we got to the private room, I pulled my tank top over my head and removed my workout shoes and socks.

Eric gulped water and washed down a couple of pills.

His upper torso was chiseled, ripped, and impressive, with a road map of scars that testified to his combat skills. He clenched and unclenched his hands.

"Let's go. Some 'cals' for warm-up." A series of squat thrusts, jumping jacks, push-ups, and chin-ups got our hearts racing and our muscles warm.

Boot camp with the Mayor of Crazy Town.

As Eric and I did a bit of a challenge on the training straps in one corner of the room, Kayne walked in and stood back against the wall, observing and wiping himself down.

Eric taunted, "Well fuck, Boyo, you sure flush up like an Irisher. Thought the 'Eye-Talians' were a dark race."

"Fuck you. We gonna train or what, old man?"

Eric sobered a bit and said, "Look, Nick, as a police officer, I know you are exceptional at H2H. I just want to sharpen you up a bit, learn your style, and have you learn mine as we may be fighting the 'Big Bads' side-by-side."

He looked over at Kayne.

"You too, brother, get in the mix, mate. Or are you worn out from your dance session with trainer boy?"

Kayne narrowed his eyes, bowed his head, and approached his brother with fists clenched, and Eric launched into a flurry of attack moves before I could assess any danger in the situation. They fought with loud and powerful gusto, finally collapsing to the mats and laughing, a knot of two very wet, identical bodies.

"Just like back in the 'Woop Woop,' when we were ankle biters, eh Bro?" Kayne rubbed his brother's military buzz and disengaged their entwined bodies. "Couldn't take me then and can't take me now. But you've gotten better.

"You are right there, Kayne, the Brain. The body remembers– muscle memory."

Kayne looked at me and smiled.

"Not much to do growing up in the Outback but sport and martial arts. I was easy on you, brother, due to your recent injury. How is your side?"

Eric waved away concern without speaking. I noticed that he had changed to bandage to a smaller one.

Kayne asked, "So, what do you have for us, James Bond?"

Incredibly, Eric smiled.

"OK, Lads, so this is *Systema Spetsnaz*. It is a method of H2H, hand-to-hand combat used by Russian Special Forces. Lower levels focus on methods of self-defense. I know you blokes are trained fighters, so we're going to the highest level used by the military. Level Five teaches strategic defense against multiple assailants, weapons neutralization, and lethal aggression."

Apparently, either his meds or my mother's interchange on the Budapest train last night had chipped away the ice of his demonic personality, or Eric was at his most human when teaching combat. The menace and acerbic mocking seemed to drift away to be replaced by a focused pedagogy in fighting styles. Even his features softened as he spoke to us.

He squatted, knees to the floor with Kayne and me sitting to his left and right, respectively.

"We will be dealing with a well-equipped militia armed for terror and destruction. I am informed that we will be contacted for the next phase

218

of the plan as we get to the Slovenian capital, Ljubljana. I want us on a regular training regimen over the next week. I have reserved this exercise venue for the duration of our stay."

I rolled back, pushed off in a kip-up, and landed on my feet. I liked to impress, I will admit.

"So, let's go, muscles, bring it. I've been so looking forward to dropping you, old dude." I hit my stance with a quick check of my superhero look in the mirror.

Eric brought his gaze up to meet mine and slowly stood up, his body unwinding and his visage turning cold. A sinister smile curled his lips.

He sighed and turned his back to me. Kayne shifted on the floor next to us like someone bracing for a car crash.

I tensed. So gonna enjoy serving up some well-deserved whomp-ass on this....

"Yiii ahhh!"

No fuckin' way!

I was lying helplessly flat on my back on the mat, looking up at my assailant. He was standing with a foot on my neck and leveraging my right arm up and away from my torso so that I rotated almost face down on the floor. His body was a blur, and his red face clenched in a power yell as I hit the mat.

I could feel Kayne smirking at my ballsy brashness without looking at him.

Instantly, Eric released the tension on my wrist and let go of my arm. He stepped off and came to a relaxed stance.

"Huge mistake, Captain America. Save the ego for your graphic novel masturbation fantasies. Your opponent will always take advantage of your emotions, your wild-arsed risk-taking, and your lack of concentration. No anger, no swag, understand?"

He continued, "In *Systema*, the body has to be free of tensions, filled with endurance, flexibility, effortless movement, and explosive potential. Let me repeat: the 'spirit' or psychological state has to be calm, free of anger, irritation, fear, self-pity, delusion, ego, and pride, my bluey bucko."

Kayne, now standing, agreed with his brother. He said, "Eric, so much has been going on with us. Guide us through the breathing and relaxation techniques."

"Right, then we can move on to the Level Five body positions and movements."

He extended a strong arm and pulled me to my feet next to him.

Eric looked into my eyes but spoke to his brother.

"Theater at eight?"

Kayne nodded. "They are doing the dress and tech tonight. Tomorrow begins the week of performances.

"Rippa. We have lots of time then, my lads, to turn you into a true fighting force."

He clapped my back.

"Let's go, Bluey. Gonna put that hot body to work."

Chapter Thirty-Seven: Crisis

"Can you tell me what I just saw? What the hell was that?"

"You ask too many questions. Be very careful. You have your assignment. That is all you need at this moment."

The woman stood smoking in the twilight, staring down at the rugged terrain of the Dinaric Alps that rose above and behind the fortress and fell away to the south and east.

"Are you confident he is still in control? His health seems to be a big concern. He takes fewer audiences, preferring to use technology to meet with his operatives. He seems unable to concentrate."

"Step very carefully, Sir. You are close to speaking disloyalty."

The Lieutenant and the dark-haired man turned to see a blonde figure emerge from an alcove of the ancient building and draw near to them on the flagstones.

The woman stepped on a cigarette butt and continued, saying to both men, "The General wants his prize. He is a collector, among other things. He has a passion for art and history and an equal lust for eliminating the forces that oppose his plan for Europe and beyond. You are charged with a small piece of that to rid him of key members of his resistance and spread the necessary propaganda to coerce public thought."

The dark-haired visitor asked, "Does his passion for collection include the professor, the American police officer, and the museum director?"

The arriving soldier spoke up, "Why do you taunt us? You know it does. We have agreed that that is to be left to me. Garber has turned and will soon take his place in the movement, reporting to me as one of our assassins. He will soon provide us with all we need."

The Lieutenant shifted uncomfortably. She said, "I have no desire to play your games, gentlemen. I am needed elsewhere. You have your orders."

The men bowed slightly as she turned and walked back to one of the arched entrances of this upper story of the fortress.

"Irena is as unsure as we are, Ádám. As head of the Assassins Corps, are you ready to step in and lead the enterprises of the *Paukova Mreža?*"

"The Dragon's web of terror is in no danger here. It has survived the meddling of the Sorenson-Sechi-Quinto team. The Neo Group is re-forming after considerable losses. Still, arms supply, technological warfare, detention facilities, and regime funding are not at their full potential. Right now, Karadžić is still very much in charge. The face of Europe and the world is changing."

"And there is money to be made, correct?"

"Yes."

The former soldier moved closer and offered the dark-haired man a cigarette. He pulled in close to Major Haagen to take the light. Their hands were touching.

Ádám walked to the broken balcony and watched night settle over the mountains and, with it, a slight chill. A slim crescent of a dying moon shone brightly in a dark velvet sky. With the two fingers that held the cigarette, he gestured to the breathtaking landscape.

"A wall of soaring limestone, wild and unpopulated, sitting atop a vast labyrinth of water-carved fissures, escarpments, channels, and caverns. You can see Jadro Spring to the north. Did you know it was the source of water for Diocletian's Palace at Split?"

His partner walked up behind him but showed no interest in the visual tour. He stepped forward so that they were side-by-side.

The soldier continued, "Ancient Illyria, two millennia of warfare and these fortresses providing refuge from the Romans to the Ottomans to the Nazis. This stronghold was once occupied by Hitler's puppet in the

Balkans and the eastern Adriatic coast. It is favorable terrain for covert warfare, the Web's center, and the Dragon's Lair."

"Yes, yes. All very nice. But your romantic reveries are boring. So, fortunately, I must return. I am happy you are a man of few concerns as this project comes to a head. No fear of our friend, Mr. Garber?"

"You jest surely. Eventually, Garber/Sorenson's mania will be his exquisite downfall. Then again, you always underestimated me."

"Unless something should happen."

Haagen waved away the last comment and pulled the man into a tight embrace, his strong arms raking the other man into a tight clinch.

"Who shall we kill next?"

***

"We must hurry. He is in deep crisis again. Spleen, major organs, massive pain."

The Lieutenant donned the surgical gown and sat on the gurney. The medical staff attached the transfusion apparatus to the shunt in the crook of her left arm. She settled back.

"Let's go, Dr. Veke."

She was pushed into the surgical theater and attached to the General, who occupied the operating table.

"I have placed him under sedation. Following the transfusion, I will administer the first of the bone marrow protocols. He will receive seven throughout this week. If the research we have gained is accurate, he should show improvement very quickly. We will be vigilant."

"Have the other patients received the protocol?"

"Yes."

He could not meet her eyes.

"Assure me, Dr. Veke."

"I have the videotapes for your review, Ma'am. Please relax and stay quiet now."

Thomas Severino

Irena Jerzak closed her eyes.

Chapter Thirty-Eight: Pearl of the Danube

From the Case Files of Kayne Sorenson, Ph.D.

I insisted Viola and Portia stay with us at Budapest's Corinthia Hotel. Over protests ("Kayne, Nick, we can stay with the company at the Marriott.") I explained that it was my gift to such warm folks who had welcomed me. Nick and I spent the first few hours in our suite talking about the decision to involve the "Lear" company in the rescue affair. In the remaining days, I hoped that his confidence in the team's efforts would ease his mind a bit more.

Realizing that Nick needed to be near his family, I indicated that I longed to learn from such a renowned Shakespeare scholar. Truthfully, Viola and I enjoyed many post-performance conversations in the hotel's rooftop Sky Lounge. The first was after the opening night party featuring Ars Europa's newest star, Ms. Rebecca Quinto.

Her performance was spectacular. The company seemed to rally from the recent tragedy, and the program announced the dedication to the slain Elena Janescue. The house was packed, and the media crowded the approach to the theater. The BBC interviewed Viola, Portia, and cast members, as did Euronews.

At curtain call, Rebecca raised the hand of Sir Keith Cantwell and, with the other Lear daughters, took their first bow. As the curtain rose a second time, a spear-carrying extra rudely walked in front of the newest Cordelia, upstaged her, and did a foppish bow. He stepped on her train, knocking her back and almost off her feet to the laughter and increased applause of the audience.

As the curtain descended, Rebecca turned on the joker and knocked off his helmet. She was about to scramble back into place for the third call. However, she screamed and jumped into the arms of the actor. At the third rise of the main curtain, the audience applauded the ingénue's hug kiss-up in the arms of the award-winning journalist, Mark Gadarn.

"You are a wonder, Boss. You fuckin' knock me out."

Nick handed me a second Hibiki on the rocks and clicked it to his beer glass. He looked so scrumptious in his tux vest, shirt sleeves, and a loosened bow tie. I so longed to do "Nick Shots" with a rare Hungarian Brandy. I thought I saw a bottle of *Pálinka Szilva*. Yes, definitely, the plum brandy dripped on his white muscles-- a tasty morsel and prelude of things to come.

I came out of my reverie and said, "More security for the safety of the company, and he was about to get thrown out of Turkey. Their tolerance of Americans in that republic, during the age of Trump, is quite erratic. CBN will rest easier now that he has left. He is a journalist with what many find to be disturbing questions. Cheers, my love."

Kayne had great respect for the Welsh-American reporter. He was a very cool guy and excellent in a fight. With a brown and gold mane and turquoise blue eyes, he was a dead ringer for Bradley Cooper. *Rebecca loved her some hot men – to be sure.*

I met Kayne's toast and said, "And she was fantastic-- a... a... a rippa. That's what you Aussies say."

"Bloody oath, Kiddo. Rebecca was that. And you were bonzer at the gym yesterday and today. Looks like the truce is holding."

I gestured to my brother a distance away in the dark, smoking with one of the company members who seemed to be mesmerized by the Prince of the Night.

"Yeah, he seems changed a bit, Kayne. He is at his best when he is instructing combat training. I am learning a lot– making gains."

"Not bad for two old codgers, eh, lad?"

During the day, the three of us worked on strikes, punches, kicks, defensive and counter-attack techniques, releases from grabs and chokes, attacks with knives and sticks, as well as advanced knowledge of blade and stick fighting.

I kissed him as he flopped on the couch next to me. He brought his lips to my ear and whispered a bit of lust.

"Officer Sechi, I am appalled. I know of at least three states in the US where what you describe is illegal."

"I'll be gentle, Boss. No one will ever know, and anyway, this is Europe. All sorts of decadent behavior go on here. I wonder if the good people of Budapest remember a naked runaway not too many years back."

"That again? You are a devil, lad. With your bad Italian ways and bedroom eyes. What's all this interest in my arse anyway?"

"Just one of the best on the planet is all. Can you move over one, Darling? Thanks, awfully. Ohhh, male arousal! How heavenly. Well, anyway...."

Rebecca inserted herself between a very embarrassed Nick and me. Mark plopped down opposite, delighted to be reunited with his lady love and his friends.

"S'up, boys?"

Nick's fist-bumped our delightful friend. "Doin', bud?"

"Darling, Kayne. Thank you again for arranging for Mark to join us. What a surprise. You are so very thoughtful. And having him to blend in with the company was excellent."

Mark spoke up, "Portia let the cast and crew know that I was more than just a struggling actor stuck in the Balkans. She told them I was there to help keep a watch on things. She intended to calm their fears for the rest of the run here in Budapest and Ljubljana. Turning on the badass for ya, boys!"

He popped a gunz flex.

"Ummm... We are about to head to our room for... well, let's just say I will not be at the gym tomorrow morning for our training with Eric, Darling. Or late if we show at all."

She positively simpered.

"I thought not, my girl. Abstinence suits neither of you. Do not shout the walls down, and don't be late for the theater."

"Looks like your trainer may be late also. Is that my King of France he is making out with so furiously over yonder?"

In the shadows, Eric had pinned the young actor to the wall, holding his wrists imprisoned and kissing him up like he was eating the lower half of the lad's face.

"Darlings, cuckolded and murdered all in one night. And the body isn't even cold. Oh, the Bard, the Bard! How I suffer for my art!"

Even Mark was amused by the Divine One's Bernhardt-esque rave.

Nick said, "Oh, brother. Get her."

I stood up and doffed my jacket as the warm night air. My Japanese whiskey was having an intoxicating effect. Likewise were Ms. Quinto's histrionics. I settled back down.

Mark could not resist joining in a chewing-up-the-scenery style as he said, "Come, my Cordelia. We have much to do anon."

Nick did an eye roll and said, "Oh, do you two really have to go? Awww. Well, g'night, you raging heterosexuals."

He practically pushed Rebecca up and off the couch and scrambled back into my embrace.

Rebecca stood regally and extended her hand to her handsome Welsh man. She turned to the very excited lad in my arms and pointed.

"You, Officer, need to chill all that fresh and nasty vibe. Your mother and your sister are headed this way."

She twirled her fingers and smiled fiercely.

"Later, Darlings."

***

A DJ was spinning some excellent music, and the party guests were taking advantage of the ambiance of the rooftop perch over the dazzling Hungarian capital. Nick turned as his mother and sister approached, our renewed make-out destined to be interrupted yet another time.

"You remember how we stopped the show at your sister Sylvia's wedding reception, Nichola? C'mon and dance with this old lady. You boys can neck later."

Nick groaned, "Mommm."

Viola lightly pulled her smiling son from the couch, and they began to "bust a move," as the Americans say on the dance floor. The crowd was admiring the gyrating Yanks, with more than one cast member mentally undressing my sexy ginger.

"And you are all mine, handsome." I stood and took the arm of the delightful Portia and parted the small crowd to show them a few things.

The Sechis were excellent dancers, and I managed a few moves that brought smiles, stares, and comments. Portia pulled me close as both females and males sought to break in. We eventually embraced in a slow number.

"A few things, Kayne. First, thanks for the beautiful hotel rooms. Wasn't Rebecca smashing?"

I nodded. I sensed my mind was getting overstimulated again. On the other side of the dance floor, Nick and Viola were talking to a man who had been watching us dance. He was apparently a Hungarian, and I assumed he was associated with the local management of the National Theater.

Portia noticed that I was observing them.

"Also, thanks for this opening party. The cast is beginning to relax after the murder of Elena in Bratislava. And Mark is wonderful. He and Rebecca took rooms at the Marriott to be closer to the company."

I shook off my mind's confusion and said, "Mark Gadarn is not only a brilliant journalist and exceptional man, but he is military trained and has assisted us in more than one dangerous case."

"I am sure you know I am using you, Kayne. I have to confess. I am trying to gain the attention of György Siklós, our Ars Europa representative. He is adorable and straight. Thank you, Lord. No offense."

"None taken, my dear. Cheers."

"I was hoping that he might show me the sights of the Pearl of the Danube."

We were interrupted by Mr. Siklós, who did a short bow and said, "May I cut in, Professor?"

I returned the bow, and they glided away.

As I turned to look for Nick, Eric and his somewhat nervous actor companion, Marc Blane, aka the King of France, approached.

"Kayne, bright and early tomorrow, yes, Mate?"

"We'll be there."

"Marc, I will meet you at the elevator. Go there, now, boy."

The young man walked off, nodding to me in a silent goodbye.

"Be kind to this one, brother. He has to perform nightly for a few weeks. No broken bones, bruises, or scars, eh?"

"I am appalled, my brother. You know my *liaisons dangereuses* are always consensual-- the sexin' ones anyway. However, it's not my style to hold back, but perhaps you are right. A switch to vanilla might be interesting. Although, I will say, the boy expressed an intense interest in exploring the ways of darkness. Like many of his age and sexuality, he is hungry."

In my mind, I could hear Nick. *Right. As if....*

"So that we may experience the limits of physical exhaustion tomorrow during training. I have asked three mates, former members of CEPOL, to come and play. You and Bluey Boy will have your hands full. You think that hot Welshie will join us?"

"Not likely if my chemistry predictions are accurate. And hands-off, brother. He is taken."

"Speaking of the Bluey, where is he?"

Nick said, "Right behind you, bud. Thought we were gonna behave ourselves. S'matter, you run out of pills?"

Eric turned and faced him. He smirked and dropped his cigarette. "Save some of that swag for tomorrow, Pretty Boy. You'll need it."

He headed for the elevator.

Nick was about to launch into commentary, but I pulled him close and placed an index finger against his lips.

"Moms Sechi?"

"Bed."

"I am tired, also, my love. Let's go."

"Not too tired, I hope, Boss."

I smiled. *Leave off and let the boy anticipate...*

As we left the rooftop, I snagged a bottle of *Pálinka Szilva* plum brandy.

Sweet and delicious.

Thomas Severino

Chapter Thirty-Nine: CEPOL

Nick Sechi's Journal

I was in fitness heaven.

Kayne and I showed up late, but we were psyched. Breathing and stretching exercises with Eric got us warmed up. About 30 minutes into it, Rebecca and Mark surprised us, arriving in their gym outfits. Their night of love still created an afterglow aspect as they joined in the stretching, exchanging cute little hetero signs and words. Kayne and I exchanged knowing looks. *Such a display, LOL.*

All four of us deferred to Eric as he explained, "The purpose of this series of training sessions is to become further acquainted with the *Systema* protocols for disarming an opponent or multiple opponents. So, let's try some moves with each other to get the feel of how we fight."

It turned out that Mark was skilled in hand-to-hand, something he worked on as an embedded reporter in the Middle East, from Syria to Afghanistan.

"C'mere mate."

Mark approached the secret agent. Together, they threw a series of offensive and defensive moves, ending with Eric taking the younger man to the mat beneath him. He pulled off Mark's t-shirt and pressed on his right shoulder and back. Mark winced as he allowed Eric to examine his latest wound.

"The bullet went straight through, just soft tissue. I can do this."

"How old?"

"Few months."

Eric stood and pulled Mark to his feet, sending Kayne a glance that said, *"This is the best you got, a wounded reporter?"* Rebecca watched intently.

Mark said, "No drama. Given a few days, I will knock you on your Aussie ass."

"Fuck me, another arrogant Yank blighter." He stood with hands on his hips. Kayne and I watched the mercenary build his team.

"Rebecca, come."

She jumped up beside them.

"Remember those moves we practiced? Show me."

Rebecca had been trained by the FBI's civilian programs, stayed incredibly fit, and was impressive against the 6'2", 210# Aussie. He could not intimidate her.

"Not bad. So, look, Mark. If you modify the move like this, your weak side will not be in jeopardy. Try it on her. Yeahhh. That's got it, mate, but turn in more with your weak side."

He switched his attention to Kayne and me.

"You girls gonna sit there and watch like a pair of debutants? Get those bodies in heat. Hello? Fight somebody."

Kayne gave a mock salute and leaped on top of me. We tumbled Greco-Roman style, rolling and grappling. I heard Eric continue.

"No, Mark, she is setting you up for a fall. Like this... try it... that's better. Again... Rebecca, do not hold back with him... you know he is weak on that side. Make him compensate... higher, Mark... Yeah, yeah. Do it, Lad."

Moving to upright positions, I started to spar a bit with Kayne, aware that we were suddenly joined by three very fit men.

Eric left off with Mark and his glamazon warrior opponent. He yelled, "Bring me their heads, mates."

I spun away from Kayne and was taken into a headlock by a powerful man who was at least 4" taller and bested me with some 25 additional pounds of muscle. He danced away from my legs as I tried unsuccessfully to break the hold. I gasped for air and strained as he tightened his grip.

He said in heavily accented English, "You will not escape, puny earthling. Let's go, Pup. It's ass annihilation time. I am coming for you, bitch."

Kayne was attacked by a similarly fit jock who was joined by his buddy in trying to bring the whirling, jabbing, and kicking professor to the mat. With incredible speed, Kayne moved between them, fending off attack after attack, left and right.

I broke free and tossed the muscled doofus over my head but soon found myself pretzeled up in another hold. This was the ultimate in martial arts fighting, an incredible rush. So great!

Eric was standing hands-on-hips and yelling, "What the fuck's taking you lads so long? I want them obliterated. Now!"

He turned to his trainees and pulled Rebecca into a hold. She fought back, but he was getting the best of her with his superior upper body strength. Eric looked up at Mark and said, "What are you bloody waiting for, ya mug? Fuckin' rescue her."

Mark landed a kick on Eric's upper body as Rebecca ducked, but the spy kept his grip. He had her in a deadly neck hold, locked tight with one hand, ready to snap her cervical vertebra.

"Don't make me hurt her unless you want to wear that princess costume in her place tonight."

I broke again with my attacker and flipped away, coming back with a kick that sent the studly diving to the mat. I jumped on his back, gripping my legs under and around his while using my arms and hands to choke him. He tapped for release, and I rolled next to him, matching his panting and sweating with mine. We smiled at each other, acknowledging our respective skills.

The big bear sat up and offered me a beefy arm to pull me into a sitting position next to him.

He said, "You're good, kid. You throw it all in with some real skill. You and I need to do a cage match for the fans."

He roughly tousled my short hair.

"Then I'll take on your buddy over there." He nodded to the three-person fight a few feet away.

"Name's István, by the way."

"Nick. You guys must be friends of His Satanic Majesty."

The big jock laughed. "He's a trip to the asylum, right? Deadly as shit."

He pointed to the other two jocks. "That's Ferenec and Karl trying to beat your bud's ass. Yes, he is good. Wait a minute...."

He pointed from Kayne to Eric.

"Twins?"

"Yeah, sorta."

"They appear to be the Yin and Yang. One good and one bad. Cain, is it?"

"Yep. Only with a "K" and a "Y.""

He mentally spelled it. I liked this big guy.

We watched as Karl and Ferenec brought Kayne to the mat in a three-way sprawling hold. Kayne was spread out like a starfish between the arms and legs of the other two. They pulled on him in opposite directions. He laughed between panting.

"I yield, ya Blighters! Crikey! Leggo!"

We all took a water break for introductions. We watched Eric and Rebecca train Mark, who intended to get lethal.

"Mark, get back over there. Further. Do the run-and-dive maneuver I showed you. Use your opponent's body to nail your impact."

Eric added with a yell, "Let's see it!"

Mark sprinted at the combination of Eric and the imprisoned Rebecca. At the last moment, he flew off the floor, twisted his body, and landed, separating them and rolling with Eric to the ground. Rebecca stepped away, unharmed. Superb!

Kayne said to our companions, "My brother mentioned that you gentlemen agreed to train with us for a few days. We appreciate your assistance."

Ferenec answered, "Your brother's a man to be respected in a fight. We have a bond with him as nutso as he is. Saved each of us at one point in our careers."

Kayne said, "CEPOL, the European Union Agency for Law Enforcement. Very impressive credentials."

István grabbed me and faked a neck hold. He said, "Yes, we are former trainers for the Agency."

He looked into his captive's face but spoke to Kayne. "We joined up in 2012 after the Agency moved here to Budapest. Hold still, kid, or I'll wallop you again."

I pushed at the muscled goof, but more out of play than anything serious. With my closed fist under his nose, I did my best street fighter from da Bronx and said, "You're cruising for a bruisin', shit-for-brains. Don't make me throw ya a beatin'." István did an 'Oh-I-am-so-scared' face and then pulled my threatening arm behind my back in a hammerlock.

Kayne's eyes danced.

"Eric said you guys were good but needed some fine-tuning. Got some good moves, Professor, but we can make 'em better." Karl smiled and rubbed his shoulder where Kayne had landed a kick.

Ferenec, a dead ringer for the hunky Jason Statham, addressed Kayne, "Your right is a bit loose, sir. Try tightening it up. Let me teach you the "Superman Punch." You're a leftie, so let's do this with that troublesome right."

He demonstrated, "So, you are going to use this move to close the distance on your opponent and take him out. Bring the rear leg forward to fake a kick, then snap the same leg back and throw a straight punch. Watch it again."

The soldier executed the move, and Kayne picked it up quickly.

"See? You're getting both greater power in the punch and providing a way to jump into range against an opponent who is reluctant to engage. You will bring him to the mat every time. Try it on me again. Excellent. Same move with your left... Hey, for an egghead, you're not bad. C'mon, Man of Steel, bring me that bad shit."

Ferenec and Kayne were a work of art as they battled, working combinations off the new move.

"Show it to me again. Now, yeah... yeah... that all you got? Fuckin' hit me, Aussie. Ouch! Shit! Nice."

Karl approached Kayne and felt up his head. "Got some issues here, too, dude. Recently clobbered, I would say. Do a neck roll for me. Again. Too much pressure? Good. Headaches? Naw? Good. Keep it out of the mix for a while as best you can."

He turned to Ferenec. "Don't kick him in the head, Bud."

Meanwhile, I slipped István's hold and tried the same hammerlock on the big ape. He smiled and broke it slowly, staring into my eyes as he poured on the power. He delighted in my astonished look. Then he put me back into yet another neck hold as I sputtered with frustration.

Holding me at bay, he said to Kayne, "All of this yours?"

"Yep. All mine, in a manner of speaking."

István laughed and tossed me into the middle of this jock circle. I stood panting and eyeing the four fighters. Karl remarked, "Look how red... so funny."

I hit my best fighter's stance and rushed each one, in turn, catching the empty air just in front of them. The CEPOL guys faked fear and stepped back. Last was Kayne, who sidestepped, flipped around, and pulled me into a hug up. *I so let him.*

"He is, in fact, his own man, this one, and quite a man at that, gents. I just have the pleasure of loving him."

Ferenec said, "Then we must not hurt him too much, eh, lads?"

Karl nodded to the other Sorenson brother.

"Ahhh, so it runs in the family, eh?"

Kayne smiled. "Yep."

"You girls gonna do slap and tickle all morning, or are you gonna train?"

Eric took a dominating drill sergeant's stance and looked us over, arms folded.

Karl mocked what he expected to hear from the tough and uncompromising coach, "Thank you for coming today, Ferenec, Karl, and István. It is certainly kind of you to help us...."

"Yeah, yeah, yeah. I need fighters, not polite Marys. We clear here?"

I said, "So butch, Mr. Sorenson, Sir."

Eric did a two-finger, his-eyes-to-my-eyes move.

"You're caving for the ultimate throw down with me, Bluey. I am what you have always feared. Do not push me."

This brought dramatic "Ohhhs" from the rest of us. I used my right hand to brush imaginary dust off my shoulder and met his eyes in an expression that said, "Bring it, sucka."

"This is Mark and Rebecca. They also fight like girls."

Kayne and I cringed as Rebecca got in Eric's face.

"All righty then. I swear, fucko Darling. One more disparaging remark about my sex, and I will make good on my threat to drop you in a matchless demonstration of woman power, you Stone Age mess. So, are we clear?"

We all laughed, but Eric. His silver eye stared from his poker face. He ignored the moment.

He came back with, "OK. Here's the drill-- man... ah... person in the middle. The rest in a surround. There are sticks, fake guns, and pads. The object is to neutralize and stay alive.

"Our opponents will surely have firearms, so we need to perfect moves that will disarm while staying unhurt. Karl brought us some

239

Kevlar. It's restrictive, but work with it. Put your mouthpieces in. Let's start with you, Wonder Woman."

One by one, we did the circular gauntlet. The opponents, the CEPOL guys, and Eric, took out Team Sorenson quickly at the start. Kayne was a superstar, I will admit. I was fascinated by his defense moves when Eric would call in two and three opponents simultaneously. Kayne lasted the longest. There came a couple of times when he and his brother were in a flurry of one-on-one. The first bout went to Eric, the second to Kayne.

I held my own against strength and numbers, as did Rebecca. She used her petite size and lower center of gravity to her advantage. Big male attackers needed to modify their moves to take on the beautiful Fury, who ducked, dodged, and struck with expert skill. She had actually ended up on Ferenec's shoulders during one round, his head in a scissor lock between her thighs. She rolled them both to the mat to the cheers of the rest of us.

"Naw, naw. I so let her...."

"Oh, bullshit, Darling." She slapped his broad chest and gave him a hug-up.

I ignored Eric's taunting remarks when he and I were matched, concentrating on the martial arts. He bested me each time, bringing me to the mat but not without a show of super exertion. It was Superman vs. Batman.

Rebecca repeated her performance as Michelle Yeoh in "Crouching Tiger, Hidden Dragon." She and I were evenly matched. Once we figured out her moves, she ended up losing at least half of the time. However, at one point, she brought each of the men to the mats except Eric.

Mark improved rapidly, stopping one or two times to favor his injured side. We kept this up with rapid changes for each defender for a long time, with breaks for water and breath-catching.

"Let's do twos in the center."

We alternated our pairings, back-to-back, as the opponents moved in for the attack. István did his Papa Bear routine when we pared up.

"Let's show 'em how we do this, eh, Nick?"

We dominated, and after we high-fived it, he pulled me into a hug up and rubbed my head. I saw Kayne's eyes roll again.

"One-on-ones. Pair up and switch off when I call time. Use the entire body, folks. I want to see some unbreakable clinches. Mark, you and I need some time together. Come over here to me."

I wanted to send Rebecca a bitchy look over Eric's last comment about her man, but she was grappling on the mat with Karl. She was gonna be one tired actress tonight.

The three of us and the former CEPOLS trained like Delta Force until all six of us were sweating, panting, and lying around on the mat. Behind us, Eric and Mark were shouting as they practiced moves and battled.

"Get up. Mark in the middle. I wanna see it. You take every one of them out or answer to me, and you do not want to answer to me."

He was indeed much improved, and the NCO from Hell shouted encouragement of his gains.

"Laps. Get off your arses."

Mark panted and pulled at the waves of his sweat-soaked hair. He said, "After a week of this. I am so going back to Syria."

Rebecca playfully swatted his butt. "The hell you are, Darling. Run."

As we rounded the practice area, I noticed the trainer from the Izom Gym, who had secured us the training space, standing back to the wall as Eric leaned in one hand placed above the young Hungarian's head. His other arm was at his side, hand clenching. They finished a brief conversation, and the trainer nodded and left.

On the next lap around, I noticed he slapped pills to his mouth and slurped his water bottle, making good on his promise to Kayne to keep on his meds.

We all sat back, hydrating after the last drill and making small talk. Rebecca rested with her head on Mark's good shoulder. He wrapped an arm around her. Eric walked over and put a hand on István's head, who did not seem to mind.

"Not bad for day one. Same time tomorrow. Thanks very much, lads. I am in your debt." He made this last remark with a slight bow.

He pointed at Mark.

"You'll be ready, Welshie. I've trained worse."

I said, "I am as hungry as a Hungarian Brown Bear, dudes. Sarge, how 'bout some lunch?"

"Protein. Watch the carbs-- good before, not so good after. Build muscle and rest up. Kick in a nap before the evening. Rebuild. I have an appointment, but I will see you at the theater tonight. These blokes will get some goulash in you."

He headed to the changing rooms.

Karl said, "Folks, this gym is attached to one of Budapest's geothermal springs, accessed through each of the changing rooms. I could use a soak, and then we take you to a wonderful *étterem* within walking distance, known for local cuisine. It is near the Matthias Church. Everyone in?"

We stood up in agreement and made our way to the changing rooms.

"I hear the Sarge. I so need a nap, Darlings, before the theater. By the way, Saturday night's performance is a fundraiser for the *Commission Consultative des Droits de L'homme of Luxembourg,* a European human rights group connected to Ars Europa. Get out your best frocks. Do you boys like Shakespeare? You are looking at the star of the show, and I say this with all humility, Darlings."

The CEPOL guys were entranced.

Kayne said, "Hold on, Madam Sarah, may I remind you, you are in four scenes, and you die."

As he finished the sentence, he stopped at the *faux pas.* He, Rebecca, and I felt a shadow fall over our graves but shrugged it off.

The CEPOL dudes were excited about joining us at the theater, and Rebecca said she would leave tickets at the box office for them.

242

"Bring dates if you like."

Mark anticipated a concern and said, "Jacket and tie, men. Black tie is optional."

István smiled. "In our work with CEPOL, we all had the 007 tuxes, and speaking for myself, mine still fits."

His buds gave him mock jabs.

We stripped in the changing room, grabbed towels, and headed to the baths. The facilities were segregated by sex, so we agreed to meet Rebecca in the club's lobby.

As we left the changing room for the spa, I noticed Eric's trainer boy, also in a towel, heading for one of the steam rooms.

Thomas Severino

Chapter Forty: Topaz

From the Case Files of Kayne Sorenson, Ph.D.

I felt like my body was made of melted butter after the thermals. The former CEPOL agents were affable, and it was evident that István had taken a liking to Nick, who hated the boyish role but kept falling back into it to the delight of the rest of us, I will admit. Ferenec and Karl were entranced by Rebecca. She relished the attention, and Mark adored that she was so aggressive and charming.

I asked Mark about his injury, and he shrugged it off. We exchanged remarks in Welsh, and he said he was coming along and did not want any of us concerned, especially Rebecca.

We had strolled from the fitness club along Budapest's historic Archduke József Embankment. Our guides pointed out the Hungarian Parliament Building with its landmark Gothic Revival style, the most massive parliament building in the world.

Nick said, "I've seen this on PBS, those European River Cruise advertisements. Budapest is so freakin' beautiful."

"Listen to how I pronounce the name of my city, Nick," István said.

He pointed across the river.

"It is actually three cities joined centuries ago, each with a powerful history. That is Buda." He pointed across the river to the west.

"Say it like me. The 'u' sounds like the vowels in the English word food."

"Buda."

"Good. To the northwest is the modern district made from the ancient settlement of Óbuda. Try it, lad."

Nick hit the accent perfectly.

"And, here on the east bank is the ancient city of Pest. In Hungarian, the 's' is like the 'sh' in the English word wash."

"Pest. Budapest."

He nailed the "sh" sound.

"Yep, now, with some Hungarian food and wine, you will be swaging like a true Magyar."

The Hungarians pointed out the sights as we headed to the restaurant, Buda Castle, Fisherman's Bastion, Gresham Palace, and the spectacular Széchenyi Lánchid Chain Bridge. It sparkled like twin strings of diamonds in the warm summer evenings as viewed from our hotel and its rooftop lounge.

As we drew near the Matthias Church, Rebecca sidled up next to me and said in a stage whisper, "It seems I remember you bare-assed and on the run somewhere around here a few years back, Kayne Darling. It's so important that one has friends, Darling, who have your back or, in this case, your hot Aussie butt."

I stopped and said rather too loudly, "Must I be constantly reminded of my naked run? OK. OK. I was frisky. He was hot. We were rutting. I decided to break it off and, in my expediency, forgot one little thing. There. It's all out in the open."

Karl guffawed and said, "And so, it appears, was your *fenék,* bud."

Rebecca patted my arse. I advised, "Decorum, my dear. You are, after all, the toast of the Budapest theater set. And your Mark is right here."

"Oh, bother, Darling, he knows I am incorrigible when it comes to a well-muscled man's butt."

Then Mark gave me a pat, and the line seemed to form, each taking a turn to grab my arse until I threw up my hands and said, "Bloody hell, ya mugs! Objectify, much?"

Tourists stopped to find out what the hilarity was all about, cameras at the ready.

Crikey!

***

Topaz Bisztró was just off the Embankment and boasted a cozy venue with excellent local cuisine. Karl, it seemed, was well known to the staff, so we were given a table in the back near the show kitchen. Overhead mirrors showed diners the preparation of exotic Hungarian dishes by chefs clad in white with scarlet toques.

The walls were hung with bright red braids of Hungarian paprika peppers. István said, "Brought to us by the Turks many centuries ago, it is the symbol of our national cuisine. The red is for babies. Orange paprika will make you cry."

Karl and the waiter spoke in Hungarian as he ordered for all of us and called for wine. His CEPOL buds commented favorably on his choices.

Ferenec said as golden bottles of wine appeared at our table, "Our spices come from the south, but it is the white wines from the north that are the specialty of the Hungarian cuisine. Ahhh, here we are. This is *Cserszegi Fűszeres*. A delicious and formidable example of our wine. The grapes are high in sugar."

He poured. I did not tell Rebecca that only men poured the wine in Hungary.

I nosed the golden varietal and spun the glass to observe the "legs." Nick watched me and did the same.

Mark sipped and said, "Spicy, sweet, and tart. Excellent choice. *Egészségére,* folks."

Each of us made eye contact, raised our glasses, and toasted the quaff.

Nick decided to perform our character, The Affected Wine Connoisseur-- an inside joke. He sniffed his glass, held the wine to the light to observe the color, inspected the label, and sipped.

"Is that the stone fruits I am tasting? Peach and so on? A well-structured, dry little vintage if somewhat self-conscious. Nice signature spice. My palate is reminded of Gewürztraminer. Well done, boys. Can I get this in da Bronx? Box-o-wine?"

We all laughed at his caricature.

Karl said, "Do not compare this Hungarian nectar to that German piss water, or I will fight you, New York boy."

Rebecca said, "Kayne Darling, you need to lighten up on our virile, young Officer here. You are causing him to slip his macho more and more."

Nick laughed and did a chest thump, playfully growling at Karl.

We dined on *hortobágyi palacsinta*, savory Hungarian pancakes filled with spiced stewed chicken, curry with eggplant and tamarind, and a chicken and ginger stir-fry.

We discussed Mark's time in Turkey.

"So much going on there. Erdoğan is tightening control as the national strongman and is annihilating the resistance. Syria and the Kurds remain huge problems for them. Their economy is in trouble, and the state is clamping down on tighter immigration policies. In many corners, Americans are seen as troublesome."

"I am so glad you are here, Darling. I've been having nightmares about you in a Turkish prison *a la* 'Midnight Express.' Ouch!"

"Yes, sweetheart. All this is good, very good."

He took her hand.

Nick asked, "Rebecca, tell us about the gala on Saturday night. Sounds like a media moment. Are you excited?"

"Yes, completely. Oh, I forgot to tell you. The cocktail reception before the play is a masquerade. Due to recent circumstances with the company in Bratislava, the Budapest police asked that no masks be worn. There will be a presentation afterward, and security must be at its best."

"Excellent strategy, my girl. We all need to be on high alert."

I could see from their expressions that Ferenec, Karl, and István had been briefed by my brother on the company's troubles.

"Mark and I will be in our 'King Lear' costumes, and I thought you both...."

I abruptly stopped her. I looked at Nick to make sure he was listening.

"OK, Rebecca. Because I want to make sure that we avoid any of your high jinks with this. Listen to me carefully, please."

Rebecca, hands clasped under her chin, elbows on the table, batted her long lashes and said, "Oh, yes, Professor Sorenson, I am all ears, Darling."

"Here we go."

Kayne counted off on his fingers.

"No drag or female clothing of any kind; no party boy, gay boy outfits; no leather; no jock kit and no American cowboy get up. I do not want the two of us to look like the last two surviving members of the Village People."

Nick said, "And no fuckin' ABBA."

Even the CEPOL lads missed that one. Mark caught it and laughed, raising his glass. *Priscilla Queen of the Desert-- not popular in the EU?*

I turned to Nick and said, "And no superhero crap, my love. I have no intention of parading around the National Theater of Hungary, commando, in tights and a cape. Clear?"

"Yes, Boss." He pulled a mock frown, turned to Rebecca, and said with a wink, "I got this, doll."

Ferenec said, "Tell us about the gala. You mentioned the Commission *Consultative des Droits de L'homme of Luxembourg.* They do great work."

"Nick's sister, Portia, is thrilled with this connection. The honorary chair is a major funder of the Commission and spokesperson on occasion. She is Her Royal Highness, the Dowager Princess Margarita of Turnovo, Bulgaria, a very mysterious figure but passionate about human rights. She leverages her philanthropy big time, Darlings, advocating for those who are voiceless in this part of Europe."

I said, "She is the daughter-in-law of the present Tsar of the Bulgarians. Her husband, Prince Kirill, died in 2005, I believe. His family line is the House of Saxe-Coburg and Gotha-Koháry. I understand she is an American."

Karl asked, "There will be extra security for Princess, yes?"

"Interesting, Karl Darling. One would think. I have found out that our dear friend, Eric Sorenson, is a personal friend and confidant of Her Royal Highness and her grandson. He will no doubt accompany her again."

"Again?"

Nick snapped his fingers and continued, "Kayne, that must have been the woman in the pashmina in Vienna and in Bratislava. Curious."

A waiter approached and began speaking to Karl in Hungarian. He shrugged and then pointed at me while handing over an envelope. I opened the message.

A white, folded card bore the stylized image of an eagle or a falcon. A hush fell over the table. István was the first to speak just a single word.

"Turul."

I opened the card and showed our friends.

In the center of the page was a scarlet dot.

Chapter Forty-One: *Maskarázik*

Notes from Rebecca Quinto

I reached through a small group and touched Nick's shoulder. He turned away from a cluster of gala-goers and followed me through the National Theater's arc-shaped glass central façade. I hiked up my Cordelia train and moved us to a less crowded spot.

The outer plaza formed the prow of a wonderous ship stretching over a water feature giving the arts complex the feel that it was floating on one of the Danube's many tributaries. Servers, performers, guests, and the media paraded by in masquerade chic.

"So, what do you think, girl?"

Nick stretched and turned in his Dr. Watson costume. Male Victorian drag did nothing to disguise his hot jock and devilishly handsome form. Security checked his medical bag (only protein bars) and walking cane (no hidden sword).

He began with arms outstretched, saying, "It was a compromise. I wanted Kirk and Spock, but the Boss said no Com-Con. I need to work on his more playful side."

"Nick, listen, Darling. I am shocked to shit. What else is going to happen in this caper? Oh, my God!"

"Rebecca, easy does it. You have stage fright, girl, and are freaking. Where's Mark, and what's going on?"

"Last I saw him, he was with Eric, the Princess, and her grandson. Portia was briefing the company on the stage positions for the presentation. Kayne?"

"Hanging with theater security and the police for any sign of Major Haagen or his henchmen. Oh yeah, and the CEPOL dudes. They clean up excellently. Major studlies looking good in those tuxes... You get their flowers?"

In my excitement, I ignored his question.

"Nick, have you seen the Princess? Have you taken a good look at her?"

"Yeah, love the Hamlet's Mother outfit. Gertrude, right? So Katherine Hepburn in *The Lion in Winter,* complete with that head and neck covering. Rocking some spectacular cheekbones. Classic bone structure. And that little guy, cute as a bug."

"Nick, listen to me, Darling. Anything about those cheekbones that look familiar?"

Nick pondered and took a swig of his beer, and then the light went on.

In my mind, I heard Kayne say to Nick: *Your problem is you see, but you do not observe.*

"Holy Shit! You don't mean to say … Nah, nah, nah. No way in hell she's… then she would have to be… but Rebecca, Kayne would have noticed, right?"

"Hold up, Darling…"

We were interrupted by Portia and Viola dressed as Juliet and the Nurse. Nick's sister was gowned in light fawn and pink with slit over-sleeves and trailing brocaded trains. She adjusted the eponymous cap, which collected ample curls of a blonde wig at the top of her head. Her makeup suggested the innocence of puberty.

His mother was swathed in yards of chestnut brown and gold. Her headpiece was brilliant white, cascading to her shoulders and halfway down her back. It suggested the livery of an overdressed female servant in 15th-century Verona. She appeared both formidable and comic.

Viola said as she twirled, "Amazing what theater costume shops can do in a pinch. What do you think?"

Neither Nick nor I said anything, just staring like two fools. Our minds were on tonight's shocker.

Portia/Juliet said, "Hey, what's the matter with you two? We are stupendous, and this is all we get? You both look like you have seen a ghost."

Again, we were interrupted, this time by a member of the theater company staff.

"Ms. Sechi, Professor Sechi, and Ms. Quinto, you are wanted for pictures with the Dowager Princess on stage. The performance will begin in 20 minutes. Her Royal Highness will address the assembly after the last curtain call."

Three of us hiked up our voluminous skirts and followed the staffer into the theater. Trailing the group, I grabbed Dr. Watson and whispered, "Say nothing, Darling."

***

The performance was one of the best. The company was stunning, responding to the presence of so many European VIPs. At the final curtain, Portia asked the audience to be seated and brought up the house lights. I could see security throughout the house. Ferenec, Karl, and István had left their seats in one of the Royal Boxes and were spread out in the side aisles. I saw Nick and Kayne in the wings.

Portia introduced the Executive Director of Ars Europa, who, in turn, introduced Princess Margarita, benefactress of the arts and activist for human rights on the world stage. The audience rose in ovation as the house lights went up.

The Bulgarian Dowager was escorted on stage with her grandson, a tow-headed boy of about 14 or 15. The young man looked dashing in burgundy and grey with accents of black in an exquisite rendering of a Danish courtier from Shakespeare's Danish kingdom of Elsinore. His deep blue eyes were dazzling as he accompanied his grandmother, a woman with a regal bearing.

The Dowager's other escort was a resplendent Eric Sorenson entirely in Hamlet kit – gold and black brocade doublet open to his sternum over an unbuttoned white silk shirt. The jacket sported striped, black satin, full sleeves, and white ruffles at the wrists. A short, tasseled cape attached to one shoulder, black breeches, and thigh-high leather boots completed a dashing figure.

Eric led the Princess to center stage and kissed her elegant hand, then gently taking the boy's arm, he stepped back. Princess Margarita moved forward in her beautiful, scarlet medieval gown. A flowing white cowl pleated from her shoulders, around her face and neck, and gathered into a golden crown. The diadem secured her russet hair into a top bun and framed a handsome face with those telltale, exquisite cheekbones. Her clear voice rang throughout the auditorium.

She began by greeting the theater guests in 15 languages, each receiving applause. She continued her address in Hungarian. She was indeed *Neĭnoto Kralsko Visochestvo*, Her Royal Highness. Her message to the world was a live broadcast across the internet universe.

"Fellow Europeans and members of the human family, it is an honor to address you this evening on behalf of those throughout the world who have no voice to petition justice. I want to thank Ars Europa for using its voice to encourage change and peaceful discourse through inspiring productions like the one we have just seen."

The audience applauded, and the "Lear" company bowed.

"My dear friend and countrywoman, Irina Bokova, former Director-General of UNESCO and passionate advocate for gender equality, improved education, a firm opponent of racism and anti-Semitism; this defender of the power of the arts has given us these thoughts."

The Princess extended her arms upward, taking in the performance space as she quoted.

"Theater has the power to move, inspire, transform, and educate in ways that no other art form can. Theater reflects both the extraordinary diversity of cultures and our shared human condition, in all its vulnerability and strength."

She continued, "In this historic house of the Muses: poetry, theater, dance, and music, let us speak out and join together to push back the gathering forces of darkness and ignorance that divide us and promote hate, corruption, imprisonment, and torture across our land. We are called to remember our history with honesty and put aside the war that rages in our hearts."

The audience was astounded by the power and passion behind her pleas to resurrect human compassion, civility, and the defense of the disenfranchised. Her voice rang out with the skill of a trained thespian as she walked across the stage.

"The concentration camps are rising again all over Eastern Europe – we call them detention centers-- prisons for refugees and minorities.

"Europe! Awaken! We have seen this horror before."

She extended a hand to indicate her grandson.

"We must, for the sake of our children and grandchildren, begin to cast out the hatred and evil that divide us. We must embrace charity and compassion, the heritage that once knit us together as Europeans and citizens of the world.

"This evening, we have seen an immortal tale of family, greed, and what happens when political ambition replaces a genuine love for each other. That love abides within each of us – our better natures. We must make sure that love is forever victorious, or our lives will descend into a fearful and bloody tragedy."

She paused to allow her words to echo in the theater and sink into the minds of the audience.

"Tonight, I am pleased to join with my father-in-law, Tsar Stephan II of Bulgaria, and the members of our family to take this occasion to announce the €3.2 million gift. This donation will establish the Prince Kirill Koháry Royal Endowment for the Preservation of Human Rights to be administered by the *Commission Consultative des Droits de L'homme of Luxembourg.*

"My husband, the Prince, let no stranger pass without opening his hand in fellowship. Let this gift, in his name, be an inspiration to all of us on behalf of the voiceless throughout the world. And I plead with all of you to open your hearts as he did. Do not cast out the stranger as other. Embrace them as family. Let us challenge the politics that created hatred and suspicion.

"I urge you to...."

She never finished.

Thomas Severino

Chapter Forty-Two: Circles

Nick Sechi's Journal

In the end, it was pure stagecraft that prevailed. My mother's blocking of the closing ceremony resulted in a clear view of the speaker by the folks on stage. This detail ended up being a lifesaving arrangement.

Within the group arranged in a semi-circle around the speaker, Eric had stepped back behind the young Prince Alexander Kristof and had a complete view of the illuminated house. Kayne was in the left wing, and Mark was on stage right nearer to the Princess with members of the company.

When the bright dots appeared like blood-red bees, one swarming on the gleaming white of the Princess' neck covering and the other on the boy's chest, members of our team sprang into action.

Mark rushed the Princess, flying across the stage. He knocked her into Kayne's arms as the latter dashed forward, covering the distance between him and the speaker with lightning speed. Eric enfolded the boy in his body, dropping them both to the stage floor. The company and the audience erupted in pandemonium. Portia and Rebecca did what they could to get the company to hit the floor.

I looked up into the balcony and ran to a stage door on the west side of the building. To my right and toward the front, a runner pushed through the crowd and made for the surrounding park. I was off in pursuit, jumping obstacles to gain on the assassin. He ran between the dimly lit trees and into a garden of green and black shadows. As I drew closer, he entered a hedge maze, the walls of which grew at least ten feet high.

I could hear the mercenary's running footsteps on the gravel and behind me the calls of security forces also in pursuit. It did not take long for me to lose my direction in the many switchbacks of the complicated structure of the gigantic labyrinth.

It was then that I remembered something Kayne taught me.

Nick, the labyrinth is an ancient, meditative symbol that creates wholeness. It combines the imagery of the circle and the spiral into a meandering but purposeful path.

Put your right hand on the wall and move forward, never removing it. You will eventually find your way to the center and back out into the world.

The shouts of law enforcement officers came at my back. Searchlights from helicopters began to crisscross the confining yew hedges. After frantically twisting and turning back and forth in the living puzzle, I saw the theater killer in the center of the winding structure, pulling agitatedly at a drainage grill on the ground. I called out.

There it was, the red circle on the man's forehead. He raised a hand in surprise and fear. A pop came from above and behind.

The assassin in front of me dropped to the gravel path, dead.

***

The soldier explained in Hungarian, and Mark translated. The military detachment had set up on the front plaza of the Theater. The crowd had dissipated, and the police held the media at bay. The entire theater and the surrounding park were considered a crime scene.

"He was on the top of the Ziggurat and had a clear shot. It is a wonder he did not take you out also."

Mark pointed to the other structure in Bajor Gizi Park, a five-leveled spiral of a building that served as an art gallery. The spotlit Ziggurat overlooked the maze. The construction featured a rising circular ramp leading up to an observation deck. A stairway led up to the top of the structure on the far side.

"It seems there were two shooters. The other got away after killing the first in the maze. The dead man is a wanted criminal in Croatia, a sharpshooter, and an assassin."

Who assassinated the assassin?

I asked, "And the Princess and the boy?"

"Her Royal Highness and His Highness have been taken to Saint James Hospital in Buda. Eric is with her. I do not know of her condition to be honest. The boy was not harmed, thanks to Eric. Your mother, sister, and the rest of the company are safe. Rebecca is trying to calm them."

"Kayne?"

"I don't know, Bud. After the Dowager was shot, she fell into his arms. Then, Kayne lowered her to the floor. She was bleeding badly, but the EMT folks arrived quickly. That's the last I saw him. He seems to have disappeared."

Thomas Severino

Chapter Forty-Three: The Danube

Nick Sechi's Journal

I asked around for a guy dressed like Sherlock Holmes, an anomaly in Victorian clothes. Karl and Ferenec mentioned that they saw him headed to the riverbank. I jogged to the west end of the park and found a pedestrian bridge that crossed over the tram tracks to the Danube embankment. Due to the lateness of the hour, there were few strollers on the promenade. The dazzling lights of the Hungarian capital were reflected in the waters of the famous river. Like siblings rivaling for attention, Buda, Pest, and Óbuda glittered in the night on the banks of the shared waterway.

I saw him above me on the walkway of the Rákóczi Bridge. I scrambled over and took the stairs to the span that links Buda and Pest in the southern regions of the capital. He was leaning over the railing and gazing into the black and midnight blue of the Danube. The river was alive with the cascading lights of the city. Kayne saw me approach and turned back to the hypnotic waterway flowing to the south beneath our feet.

"István mentioned Óbuda. That's it up there on the horizon. We should go see it. There are Roman ruins of the first settlement. We should go... get lost... and ...."

I embraced him from behind, holding him tightly, my face buried in his neck. Our breathing synced, and words were not needed.

After a time, he asked, "Did you know?"

"No. Not until I saw her face this evening. The resemblance is pretty fantastic, Kayne. Had you not met the Princess before?"

"No. When she collapsed and looked up, I could not deny what my observations should have clarified earlier. I believe I almost did not want to know. I was in denial, someplace in my unconscious obscuring my cognition... OH, BLOODY HELL!"

He grabbed his head with one hand.

"Eric was holding out."

He struggled to regain control, looked down, and sighed. He said, "My brother wrestles with many demons in his life. He courts death and terror with an insane relish. He was cast out of paradise at the ripe old age of 17. Who knows what his motives have been over 18 years? Sometimes, reconciliations are impossible. There are times when forgiveness has no chance and no meaning."

"No one ever heard from her?"

"We were only allowed to know that she left when we were two years old. Da saw her abandonment as a treasonous betrayal and considered her dead. One of the many rules that Eric contested. He pestered Ace, wanting to know why we had no mother. He decided that our father drove her away."

He gasped for breath, still struggling to control his emotions. After a bit, he continued.

"You met Ace, Nick. You know he is a bloody force of nature. He is capable of the utmost folly. As are each of us, I guess."

"What do you want to do, Boss?"

"I don't know, my love. I am again in the very unchartered terrain of the heart, and I am baffled. My cognitive talents are utterly useless.

"I have so many questions. I feel like a child wanting his mother, who never wanted me or any of us in the first place. God, this hurts. I want to run away from anyone and everyone-- get permanently lost."

He turned in my arms, his blue eyes awash with tears.

"But then, I would not have you, and I would be in the utmost peril."

A tall man dressed in black, 17th-century royal garb approached from the Pest side and stopped about ten feet away. The darkness obscured his facial expression only to be revealed as he lit a cigarette against the railing. He crossed his long legs at the ankles and leaned back, blowing a stream of smoke into the summer night.

Kayne muttered, "To ask you how you knew where we were would be a ridiculous question."

"True."

"Your business is to know where interested parties are at all times."

"Also true."

We stood in silence. A barge moved beneath our feet, following the river deeper to the south. Eric approached his brother and touched his glistening cheek. He inspected his fingers as if he were encountering a new and profoundly meaningful substance. He longed for this moment but was surprised by its raw intensity, nevertheless.

One word broke the stillness.

"Why?"

"Brother dear, I have no idea. Hate, jealousy, revenge, they are all inside of me, and all the pills in the world cannot rid me of the animosity I feel towards you, my family... and myself. It is a beast that has raged inside me for as long as I can remember. Some are born with love in their hearts. I am not one of those."

He spoke with deep anguish, "Perhaps Our Father, who art in Inala, was right. There is something unfixable inside of me."

Silence.

Suddenly, Eric let out a tormented cry, which soared out over the waters.

"The great Thomas Sorenson! Ace! Master of Paradise. Lord of Inala Ranch, the giver of love and mighty withholder of affection. Lawmaker and dispenser of justice. Yes, Kayne, ours is a wrathful and terrible God."

He stabbed in the darkness toward his brother.

"You and the brothers he loved. Even the one not of his blood, Mitchell the Archangel. Me and poor Jane Sorenson, he did not.

"Mother, aka Her Royal Highness, the Dowager Princess Margarita Koháry... We left. Driven from Eden. *Non serviam*, brother. Fled the Red Center, the Outback Hell. All contact prohibited."

The specter in black flashed a silver eye in a tormented face. Eric hissed with finality, "There is no regaining Paradise for the utterly damned. We continue to create our own personal Hell."

He tossed his cigarette into the Danube. Kayne looked away from his brother to the opposite end of the bridge. The rage and insanity seemed to dissipate like the moving lights in the swirling waters.

Kayne said quietly, "She created her own redemption. She raised your son with love and devotion. She did so, it would seem, before the very crowned heads of Europe."

Another silence.

Eric said, "Yes, Prince Alexander Kristof is not of the Bulgarian blood royal. In his veins flows the blood of convicts as it does in yours and mine. He, too, is fatally flawed. Our Aussie lineage, eh? His mother was Danish. That is a story best not told."

"Another boy with no mother and an absent Father. Talk about the sins of the fathers ... Excellent."

"Yeah, Jane raised him with love. Prince Koháry was kind to the lad for Jane's sake. Giving them both non-inheritable titles. The Kohárys were childless but loved each other, and he doted on Kris. Sent him to the best schools with the princesses and princes of the blood. For that, I am thankful."

I asked after the Princess.

"The bullet caused some damage to her right upper arm passing through. As she fell from Mark's expert tackle and into Kayne's arms, her body position was such that the assassin's target was sent off-kilter, missing her heart. The fact that she moved around the stage a lot during her speech was also to her advantage. The other bullet meant for the Prince hit the scenery behind us."

He lowered his voice to a near whisper and said to Kayne, "She is in hospital. She asked to see you."

More silence.

Then, Kayne held up a bloody right hand, staunched with a wet handkerchief.

"Yes, let's go to St. James'. I believe I have captured some ballistic evidence for the Budapest police."

Chapter Forty-Four: Margarita

Nick Sechi's Journal

"Come closer, please."

The Princess took my hand and looked into my eyes with a familiar ice-blue gaze. She spoke with effort and some weakness. Her arm was bandaged to the shoulder. She sat up in the hospital bed. Two attendants stood nearby, and outside the room, three guards protected the occupants. The Prince sat quietly near his grandmother, eyes shining.

"I have heard much of you, Officer. I follow your blog. You, my son, and Ms. Quinto are fearless in standing up for justice. You are indeed... what is it now, my little love?" She looked at her grandson.

"Superheroes, Gran. Like in the movies. Bam... bam."

The boy threw a few punches and kicks my way, which I caught and playfully defended.

"You'd be amazing, Your Royal Highness. Just need some training, MMA style."

"I am not a Royal. Sir. Just a Highness. Please call me Kris. May I call you Nick?"

"Hey, cool, bud."

We exchanged a buddy fist pound.

"May I ask, are you gay, Nick?"

"Through and through, bud."

"That's cool. I saw the way you look at Professor Sorenson. By the way, 'King Lear' blows, dudes."

"Kristof, would you go with Eric back to the hotel, please? I need to speak to Officer Sechi and Dr. Sorenson. You need to sleep. You will be safe. Our guards are there also."

"Yes, Gran. Good night."

He kissed her.

"I will see you tomorrow, my boy. We are going to discuss Shakespeare for a long time. I will call you, Eric."

"Good night, Your Royal Highness."

The man in black bowed and left with the boy.

***

"Officer Sechi, please help me into that chair. This bed is very uncomfortable. Emma, will you and the others leave us, please?"

The Princess was wrapped in a soft, cream-colored robe with her auburn hair unpinned and fashioned into a single, thick, long braid extending down her back. Her bandaged arm was held in a sling. Her makeup was understated – a Grace Kelly look from the '60s.

She raised her eyes to Kayne, who stood and shifted against the back of the hospital suite. She pointed to him and instructed me.

"Officer, please wheel me closer to Professor Sorenson."

"Your Royal Highness, I suspect what you have to say is very private, and so I will leave you and the Professor..."

"No, please. From what you describe in your notes and journals, you love Kayne very much and are favored by the Sorenson family. I suspect you share a remarkable love. It comes through in your writing, young man."

Kayne was looking up.

"... and so, there is no reason for you not to hear what I have to say. Please remain."

Princess Margarita turned her attention to her son. She turned her head slightly from side to side, looking at Kayne. He broke the uncomfortable silence, saying softly, "I am here at your request, Ma'am, but I do not see the point, and so, I will leave you to rest and...."

"Please allow me, Professor, to thank you and your friends, especially Mr. Gadarn, for saving my life and the life of my grandson."

She extended her left hand, palm down to him.

He made no attempt to reach for the Royal hand as he dropped his gaze.

She lowered her hand and, sounding more like a Jane Sorenson than Her Royal Highness Margarita, the Dowager Princess of the Bulgarians, said, "Yes, that was a pretty presumptuous move, I will admit."

She sighed deeply and continued.

"May I ask, have you ever felt completely overwhelmed and trapped? No way out? After you and your brothers were born, I struggled with feelings of intense imprisonment and unrelenting hopelessness.

"Thirty-three years ago, I ran out on my husband and sons. I will not disparage Thomas, your father, in explaining why I left Central Australia. His relationship with his family ceased to be my business long ago, and I can hardly judge anyone who has been a single parent. The years change one's perspective but not all of one's feelings.

"Please allow me only to say that at Inala, I was unable to live the life he had demanded of me. So much was beyond my abilities, no matter how hard I tried to fit into the role of dutiful wife and mother. I was destroying my own spirit and any semblance of who I was. I abandoned my sons because I sought an end to a sense of confinement to overcome my soul-filled pain of despair. When one cannot be what one is inside, death replaces life – one dies from the inside out.

"I knew that my children would have the finest upbringing. Thomas Sorenson would use the wealth of his vast resources to ensure that the boys had the best of everything, including a strict military-style education.

"I have wrestled with that decision for many years. The most severe criticism of what many would consider a supreme act of selfishness has been my own. The self-loathing was exceptionally destructive. "

"Really, Ma'am, I don't…."

Margarita continued, "I disappeared for many years and worked in the theater in Europe for a time. I met my late husband, the Prince, a kind and loving man. He worked behind the scenes to secure the divorce, which came with one stipulation – total custody of the children went to Thomas, and I was to make no attempt to contact them.

"My husband convinced the Tsar, my father-in-law, and his family to allow the marriage. As Kirill's wife, I was treated as an equal, and I loved him dearly. With the Prince, I could become someone authentic. Our work to promote human rights enabled me to feel good about who I was. Finally."

She attempted to gain eye contact but failed. "Fifteen years ago, Eric and the infant, Alexander Kristof, came into my life. His connections made finding me easy. My husband and I took the child and raised him. The boy's father lived a perilous life, and many would have killed either or both. I was able to cloak my grandson in the State Security of the Bulgarian Royal Family.

"Recently, Eric has resurfaced and has been more involved in the life of his son. But Eric's mental condition has deteriorated over the years. About the same time, my second husband died. My grandson and my human rights advocacy work became the only thing that mattered."

The Princess entreated her son with her eyes, stopping only to brush aside a few remaining strands of hair from her forehead.

"You should know for many of your childhood years, I was unable to find out any information about any of you. I was blocked at every turn. Eric showed me a wonderful blog earlier this year, *The Kayne Sorenson Mysteries*. Then, when I found out you were in Vienna, I felt I could risk seeing you, even as I feared rejection."

The distraught woman's message took on a fearful tone.

"Now, it seems I must go into hiding. Our opponents are a powerful force aligned against democracy, peace, and solidarity. I know this movement and its leaders. Apparently, they can breach the security I must have for Kristof. Dr. Sorenson, I fear that Eric and the rest of us are doomed. This is far from over."

270

Kayne remained silent. Now, his blue eyes examined her, trying to assess her veracity. I moved next to him, aware of the emotional turmoil that boiled beneath his stoic exterior.

No one spoke for what seemed like a long time.

"How is your hand, Professor? I understand the bullet passed through me into you."

Kayne said nothing at first. He continued to search her face for answers. She sat back, seeming to realize her entreaties were futile.

Finally, Kayne held up his bandaged hand.

"I am fortunate that there is only minor damage, Ma'am."

"Officer?"

The Princess gestured that she wished to stand. I assisted her, but as she rose, she sank to her knees before her son.

"I realize that you must feel this is a self-serving and theatrical gesture, but tonight, I feel if something should happen, I could not leave this world without...."

He looked down at the woman at his feet and struggled as he said, "All those years... wondering... not knowing or understanding why...."

He shook his head as his eyes glistened. He struggled to regain his composure as a mask of indifference seemed to descend.

"Yes, Ma'am. It would appear you are much too late."

Jane covered her face with her free hand and spoke over him softly, "I beg your forgiveness, my son."

"Come, Nick, we're out."

He started for the door leaving Jane kneeling and looking up through silent tears.

As he pulled the door open, the security retinue looked into the room but did not intervene. I watched Kayne's back as he stopped in the doorway for a long minute.

Then he turned. As she knelt, Margarita reached toward Kayne's retreating figure.

He dashed to the devastated woman. As I stepped into the hall, I attempted to close the door behind me. I saw Kayne go down on one knee and pull the grieving woman into his arms.

"Mother."

Chapter Forty-Five: Ice and Madness

From the Case Files of Kayne Sorenson, Ph.D.

I spoke into our suite's phone.

"Please send him up."

Nick and I were joined by family and friends, all of whom had been awake all night. The first lights of dawn were stealing through the large windows. No one had touched anything on the breakfast cart but the coffee. Eric stood on the open balcony smoking, wrapped in contemplative silence. I fought to process the thoughts and emotions of my meeting with the Princess.

Replacing the receiver, I announced, "It would seem we have a visitor. Portia, Professor Sechi, perhaps…."

I gestured to the connecting door to their suite.

Portia raised a hand.

"No, Kayne."

There was a single knock at the door.

"I got this, Boss."

Nick opened the door.

Ádám Haagen stood in the doorway, taking in the seven occupants. His disciplined and handsome figure, tall, muscled, and sparklingly blonde, was a sharp contrast to the disheveled appearance of the rest of us. He took each of us in turn into his gaze. His smile and his bow mocked.

He boldly strode into the suite very close to Nick. Eric came in from the balcony, reached behind to close the doors, and took up a position between the Hungarian and Nick's family. Mark pulled Rebecca close to him.

Nick brought his arms up with clenched fists and said, "Cool. Rock and roll time. A bit outnumbered, Dracula? What say? Let's check you out. Arms up, asshole."

Ádám laughed and allowed Nick to frisk him. Nothing.

"This is the boy toy, eh, my Kayne? A diversion but a tantalizing one, I will admit."

Portia raised her mobile.

"Ms. Sechi, if you call the police, I assure you so many more will die."

I interjected, "What is it you want, Ádám?"

"Let's have all of the women out."

Viola moved around Eric and said, "In the words of my son, fuck you, sir. Say what you have to say and get out."

She pointed to our group and continued with passion, "This is family, and we have encountered more of your evil than necessary tonight."

The assassin bowed.

"Ahhh, the hot-headed Italians. Like mother, like son. Nick, is it?"

Nick turned red but did not answer as Ádám sank into a chair.

"Ms. Quinto, so good to see you again. It has been years. And this must be the heroic and renowned media pest, Mark Gadarn. You know, I honestly thought we were going to get rid of you in Afghanistan last year. Pity, the Afghans are such terrible shots even when well paid. And Colorado? A sad farce. You should have died, you know. Perhaps the third time's a charm."

Major Haagen's voice was silky smooth. He lit a cigarette and used a coffee cup as an ashtray. I noticed an almost imperceptible tremor.

"Mr. Sorenson, or is it Mr. Garber? The aliases in these spy games are so confusing." He looked at Rebecca. "Wouldn't you agree, Your Excellency?"

Rebecca offered no reaction. The Major pointed to Eric, saying, "Your eyes seem to be spinning in your skull, dear boy. Perhaps it is time for another psychotropic. Tell me, is the boy prince a person with schizophrenia also?"

Eric said nothing. His silver pupil seemed to jolt with light.

Looking at the group, the intruder continued.

"Please allow me to introduce myself."

He stood and clicked his heels with a mock bow.

"I am Major Ádám Csaba Artem Márton Haagen-Báthory, a former member of the Royal Hungarian Guard and a direct descendant of the Hapsburgs. Now leading a private mercenary group in the region."

He paused and pointed.

"The once and future, and I might add extremely, very accomplished lover of that bitch with the bandaged hand."

Nick rushed him, florid and cursing. I stepped forward, but Eric grabbed him in full flight.

"No, Nick. Easy lad."

"Oh my, such bravado, such manliness. You will be a lot of fun, boy, before this is over, a shared party favor, perhaps."

My mother turned away.

Nick said, "You are a total shit, you fucking vampire."

Ádám shook his head and said, "So, may we agree that Mr. Stoker's monstrous villain was Transylvanian and not Hungarian, though most likely of Magyar blood? Let's get our name-calling straight. I assure you I will not immolate in the rising sun."

While still being restrained by my brother, Nick countered, "One lives in hope, fuck wad. Oh, wait. Not doing too well for your boss, asswipe? Poor performance assessment is coming, I would guess. The only fatality tonight was one of your own agents."

"Yes, that is unfortunate. There will be another day for the Princess and her cause. Of this, I can assure you. But let us turn to other things."

"Ms. Sechi, your theater company is in total disarray. The performances in Ljubljana will be canceled within the hour, and the actors and staff will be disbanded. Our association has pretty much ended the struggling Ars Europa consortium and its liberal propaganda. Take your sister and your mother, the Professor, and return to America immediately. Do not come back to Europe."

"You very much underestimate the power of the arts, sir."

I stepped forward and interrupted Portia.

"You are here to warn the forces arrayed against you, Major. I perceive that as extremely interesting. Your intimidation and threats, you will find, will fall on deaf ears. Please, enough with your games."

I waved a hand in dismissal.

"It is also quite apparent that you are having doubts about your role in the General's organization of terror. Your appearance is telling, Sir. You seemed to have shaved in haste this morning. I detect a nasty cut just below the left ear. There is a trace of freshly spilled whiskey on your lapel. So early to be imbibing in spirits, Major. Finally, your usually immaculate boots' shine is dull and scuffed. I conclude you have been seriously distracted of late."

I continued, "Our alley encounter in Vienna? In the bowels of the National Theater? Either the work of an amateur or of someone whose allegiance is conflicted. How many times will it take for you to kill me, sir?"

I knew this man and his fragile ego. I pressed further. "Your warnings are becoming more plentiful, and you are, in fact, working against your own organization. How incredible. Your hints of tonight's attempted murder were those of a naughty schoolboy. They brought what was meant to be a carefully planned assassination to the level of broad comedy. The red target dot and the Turul Bird of Death note, Major? How quaint and so elementary as to the meaning."

I walked the room as I spoke, addressing my remarks to the group.

"In 1920, the right radical students of Budapest established the *Turul Bajtársi Szövetség,* the Brotherhood Association of Turul. The favorite pastime of these thugs was beating up their fellow students of Jewish origin. The Turul Association had an essential part to play in enacting the laws discriminating against the Jews of Hungary. We are seeing more of this conspiracy in Europe these days. And the Dowager Princess Koháry, in addition to being an outspoken adversary of the General's hate operations, is, in fact, Jewish. Ashkenazi, to be exact."

I turned back to the constant soldier.

"No, you are an agent who is turning, Major, and will soon be on the run. The Viennese authorities are in pursuit of you for the murder of Maria Savic despite the attempt to frame Uwe Müller. Tonight, you killed one of your own top snipers, shooting from the Ziggurat into the maze. You were not aiming for Nick. You are a decorated marksman. You are in a self-destructive death spiral, and these acts are ridiculous attempts at salvation."

Ádám's façade began to slip. He said with some anger, "I did not kill Savic. You have been played, my Kayne."

Eric burst out with, "Bloody hell, man. When is the meeting?"

Haagen attempted a laugh. "I yield. Enough. Two of you are two too many, and this ginger one... ouch, so delicious, distracts my attention with thoughts of exquisite torture."

"Bring it, Boris."

Rebecca urged, "Spill it. You are wasting time with your theatrics. I have the documents. We want the scientists. What's next?"

"You will be contacted in two days for the exchange. The General is anxious for his treasure, and the captives have served their purpose. He will see only you four. Bring the manuscript and be prepared for the unexpected."

The major stood and made to leave.

"Of the rest, I can tell you nothing. Farewell."

Chapter Forty-Six: The Rog
Notes from Rebecca Quinto

"No, György, it has to be the Rog. The Tivoli Festival doesn't send the same message. It is not edgy enough... Yes, I get it, no 'Lear.' We do not have the cast anymore. My mother and I have mounted a new production. Yes, this will work. Trust me."

Portia was speaking animatedly into her cell phone on the train to the Slovenian capital of Ljubljana. We had spent last night planning for the recovery of the captive scientists and our collective escape from Europe. Finally, we were pulling together as a team, agreeing on strategic moves and alternatives. Our CEPOL friends were committed. The catalyst seems to have been the appearance of the Hungarian assassin.

"Wait, listen to me. The Rog Factory and its collectives represent an alternative space. Right ... resist, organize, create change. The Rog space signals all of that. It's fuckin' historic."

Portia paced the cabin as she spoke to the Ars Europa executive. Last night, she explained that the cancellation of the "Lear" performances in Slovenia was a setback. Still, the festival had had enough of the terror and was feeling some political pressure to end all its many European summer productions. This meant a considerable loss of funding.

The abandoned Rog Bicycle Factory near the center of Ljubljana was a controversial, cutting-edge community venue. The legal status of the use of factory spaces had been contentious from the very beginning. It escalated in 2016 when construction workers entered the areas to begin the demolition process on the mayor's order. A week later, the local court decided to halt the demolition due to public outcry.

Since then, the Rog has become an alternative space in a heavily institutionalized city. It provided housing, multiple gallery spaces, art studios, two skateparks, various concert and club venues, a bicycle repair shop, and the Rog Social Center, a haven for disadvantaged groups such as migrants and refugees. The building and its environs have become a symbol of a vibrant program of social and cultural activities.

"Yes, small cast … I just need a platform, lights, and sound… five speaking performers max … the rest will be non-speaking crowd roles… No, György, I want them dressed as refugees, people without housing. The "Lear" costumes and sets are on their way to Brussels and are totally unsuitable for the piece, anyway."

She paused.

"But it *is* Shakespeare. Yes,… a lost work… Because my mother is one of the world's foremost authorities of William Shakespeare, that's why I am sure."

Viola said, "Tell him I will send him the research proving this section of the play was written by the Bard, and yes, I should know."

"You heard the scholar. Right… for the website. Mother will take care of the rehearsals. The cast is already learning their lines as we speak. It is simple to stage."

She listened again to her boss.

"Me? The marketing, György. There will be such a spectacular turnout that the cause for Ars Europa and everything we stand for will go viral… yeah, now you're talking. We're hitting back, baby."

A pause, and then, "Where there is social media excitement, there is crowdfunding, my friend. I have the contacts to get this all covered, including broadcast media. The buzz has already begun. Let's do this."

Portia broadly smiled as she said, "You bet your ass. Resist!"

Chapter Forty-Seven: The Dragon Rises

"Has the capture taken place?"

"Yes, my General, they are waiting for you in the lower hall."

"Have them brought to the Outlook."

The White Dragon stirred. "Her Royal Highness?"

"Also taken care of, sir."

"I want it clear that I get it all. Do you follow, Lieutenant? The Major is to be detained, as well as the hostages and the captives. Haagen will be the first of my purge after this project is complete. The Dragon's dungeons are hungry. But, primarily, the manuscript will be secured. Is that not a lovely display case next to the Klimt?"

"Yes, sir."

"Has 'Mr. Garber' turned to us?"

"Our recruitment of the agent Eric Sorenson has been successful. He has brought the others to the Fortress, earning their trust. His price is the American Police Officer."

"And mine is the insidious Kayne Sorenson. The others are of no consequence. I will enjoy flaying the Professor alive for his meddlesome resistance to our cause. I need amusement. Did you know that one of my ancestors preserved the skull of one of his opponents, a Turk? It was fashioned into a drinking cup. How deliciously savage. "

Although momentarily excited, the Director seemed to fade and needed time to gather his breath and his thoughts. He sipped his Narcissus Wuyi Oolong tea and said, "I believe this bone marrow protocol has hurt my taste buds. My tea seems unnaturally bland."

"General, I have a recent update on the matters in Vienna. You know that the Major has become a suspect in the death of the actress-activist Savic, and the previously suspected young actor has been released.

What you don't know is that our agent in Vienna has disappeared right after he met with us at the Fortress."

"Is Haagen responsible?"

"We have no knowledge of that."

"The agent must be found."

"With all due respect, General, we need to hasten this matter along. Our cells in the Caucasus are stalled in their cyber warfare operations. Many of our other activities are seeing major setbacks because of occurrences in Colorado. We need to retool and refine our efforts globally. We stand on the threshold of...."

His response was forceful, cold, and deadly.

"Do you presume to tell me how to run this organization, Irena? The caverns of the fortress prison below us will hold more bodies tonight. You do not want to be numbered among the fallen, my dear."

The Dragon of the Balkans continued, "Take me to the Outlook."

"Yes, my General."

Chapter Forty-Eight: The Outlook
Nick Sechi's Journal

Kayne and I were ambushed in our hotel room at gunpoint not long after arriving in Ljubljana. Our captors made sure that we were securely trussed up in their SUV in a matter of minutes. Portia and my mother were setting up the performance at the Rog, thankfully far from the violence.

Eric was put in a second vehicle also under armed guards. Major Ádám Haagen oversaw the abduction, keeping it out of the public eye. He traveled in the second vehicle with the former spy.

He was incensed that the fourth member of our group, Rebecca, had escaped his tentacles. As we were pushed into the conveyance, one of his comrades held up a parcel. It was the manuscript. They had ransacked our rooms and found the Major's cap. Haagen seemed to say only to himself: *She will be eliminated later, a mere inconsequential woman.*

The two black vehicles sped out from an alley at the rear of the hotel and into the moonless night.

***

General Raheb Karadžić's Fortress stood black in the warm twilight that settled over the Dinaric Alps to the south. The trip up the mountain brought us to a lower courtyard. It was there that we were escorted up a set of broad steps to a series of elevators. I noticed that there were several floors below us on the lift's panel and six above. The guards hit the button for the parapet at the top of the structure, and we ascended.

We alighted high in the castle on a paved expanse that opened to the valley on one side behind a stone barrier. Electric torches illuminated the place where, in the past, boiling oil and volleys of arrows were poured down on enemy soldiers.

Three sides of the outlook were the castle walls with medieval crosses, swords, battle axes, and heraldic flags covering the stone. A gothic cloister of archways created recesses filled with night shadows. An ominous figure in a wheelchair spoke as he came out of the darkness.

"Am I to be deprived of the voluptuous Ms. Quinto, Major Haagen? Have you failed me again?"

"My agents are bringing her, I assure you, my general. I knew you would want the manuscript as soon as possible."

The oligarch was not placated. "Why do you continue to disappoint me? Why can I not get what I want? Do you realize if you had managed to recruit Dr. Sorenson all those years ago, his meddling in my affairs would not have prevented my activities in the world? That magnificent mind would now belong to me. You annoy me."

He waved away the Major with a gesture and had the Lieutenant take the manuscript. She carefully unfolded it with gloved hands and said, "It appears to be authentic, but I cannot tell in this light."

"We will examine it closer below. If Ms. Quinto has been false, coercion will be in order. Do I make myself clear? I will have to wait, but I have my real treasure right before me."

The White Dragon rolled slowly forward. His head seemed to vacillate slightly from side to side, with red eyes glistening like a snake hypnotizing its prey.

He hissed. "Good evening, Dr. Sorenson. Please excuse my manners. Welcome to *Zmajevo Ježa*, the Dragon's Lair. We are very high up, as you can see. Those lights over there are Ljubljana. And in the opposite direction, you can just make out Trieste on the sea. I cannot tell you how excited I am to see you again. And your... friend."

He turned to the two men and one woman at the far side of the court. "I don't believe you have met Ruslan Dudayev, Eteri Patarava, and Ioane Abkhazi, distinguished members of the global scientific community, but alas, deviants like the two of you. I suppose they are what this is all about at some level."

Feeling my rage boiling over, I lost it.

"You have the artifact, fuck head. Live up to your word and release the scientists, or are we all gonna stand around jackin' off?"

Eric stepped forward and turned me to face him. He administered four very powerful bitch slaps to my face, knocking me to my knees and picking me up each time.

Kayne yelled for him to stop, struggling against his bindings. Ádám subdued him with a chokehold, making him watch the assault.

Eric pulled me into a mouth-raping kiss and said in a husky voice. "You have had this coming for a long time, muscle boy. What I am going to do to you will hurt, and I will not stop. I will make sure your family gets a copy of the tape of our interactions. I wonder if I will keep you drugged for multiple sessions until you bore me."

I staggered against him as he pushed my head back and spit into my face.

"My General, I have been true to my word. Now, I will take the boy below for my amusement and then return to Ljubljana for Ms. Quinto, the sister, and the mother."

"Excellent. Mr. Garber. You have my permission to do so."

Raheb Karadžić turned again to the vast open space of mountains, sky, and clouds. "Tonight is the second new moon this month. It is a time of ceremony, and our blood rituals will be all that more powerful and effective. For thousands of years, the Black Moon has meant death. I feel its power in my body and in my soul. Tonight, we continue our efforts to make the world anew blessed by fresh blood and the Black Moon."

I tried to kick away and use my upper body to take Eric down but was met with some powerful blows against which I was helpless.

Kayne succeeded in wresting himself from Ádám's hold, only to have two guards knock him to the ground.

It seemed to grow darker as the White Dragon reached for refreshment from an attendant. Karadžić sipped his tea and spoke again. His voice dripped with sarcasm as he said, "All this violence. You are upstaging my grand finale. Please, you are upsetting my scientists.

Yes, by all means, conclude your torturous play in private, Mr. Garber." He waved Eric away.

I struggled in his arms as Eric pulled me toward the elevator. I called out for Kayne at the top of my voice.

The Major said as we passed, "Mr. Garber, no last words for your dear brother?" The Dragon chuckled in the background, a dry, lifeless laugh.

Eric again spat. This time into the face of his brother.

"Rot."

The last thing I heard was the General saying to the captives, "Have you ever seen the skin of a man removed while he is still living? Major Haagen is an expert with knives. His flesh carving is simply exquisite, and he goes ever so slowly."

He waved a hand and pulled a bored expression.

"You may proceed."

Chapter Forty-Nine: Black Moon

Notes from Rebecca Quinto

"Quick, get in here. There is not much time."

"Holy shit, Nick, what's happened to your face?"

"Just some acting. This dude's a pro." I hiked a thumb at Eric.

Eric said, "Is this all the gear, lads?"

Karl said, "That's it. István has the truck at the base of the mountain."

The doors closed, and we rose to the topmost floor.

Kayne was in his briefs and hanging from an archway. His clothes had been sliced away and lay at his feet. As the elevator opened on the parapet courtyard, Ádám Haagen spun around. Kayne used this moment to kick up and grip the soldier by the neck, choking with his legs. I sprinted to them and did a flying kick to the Hungarian's knife hand, knocking him to the ground. He hit his head against a stone column and seemed dazed. Retrieving the blade, I released Kayne from his captivity and turned on the guards.

Mark, Karl, and Ferenec ran to the hostages and brilliantly took out their guards. They opened the duffel bags and began to strap each other into harnesses. Eric and Nick ran at security surrounding the General. The Lieutenant grabbed the wheelchair and made for an alcove. I remember hearing a door in the recess close.

The shooting started and ended quickly. The *Systema* paid off as one-by-one weapons, and soldiers clattered to the floor. We did our best to neutralize Fortress Security, holding them at gunpoint and forcing them to rapidly tie up their comrades with rope from our gear.

Karl, Ferenec, and Mark strapped themselves in tandem to Drs. Dudayev, Patarava, and Abkhazi gave Eric the thumbs up, mounted the low parapet wall, and dove into the abyss, manipulating the parachutes' triggers and bringing the winged transports safely down the mountainside.

I found the alcove empty and could not find a latch for a secret door. Behind me, Nick called my name and tossed me an assault rifle as he and Eric stood back to back, attempting to hold off another wave of security guards. I returned and did what I could to break the stalemate.

Kayne was now on the attack.

"Get up, ya mug. Get over there on the floor with your buddies."

The Hungarian Major started to respond, but he reached for a pair of crossed swords that hung from the wall above the kneeling guards with lightning speed. He tossed a saber to Kayne, who, in his briefs, took on the armed soldier. They battled behind us and up onto the dizzying heights of the balustrade.

Eric, Nick, and I backed up to the opening with the guards approaching like a creeping tide. Access to the remaining parachutes was tenuous at best. Eric sprayed the courtyard and overhangs with rapid fire, which bought me a few seconds to toss chutes to Nick and one within Eric's reach.

Haagen, using a pillar for shielding, dashed beyond Kayne's reach. He rushed next to me while fighting the pursuing, whirling Kayne. I felt the saber blade at my throat. Out of breath, he rasped, "She dies, Kayne. You or her. Decide."

Instantly, Kayne tossed his blade over the head of the struggling Major to Nick, who caught the hilt and drove the sword into Ádám Haagen's back. I broke free and reached for the last chute.

The Lieutenant had appeared from the alcove side with more guards. Eric shouted over the gunfire, "We're leaving, Mates. Hit the silk."

Gasping and spitting blood, the Golden Hussar staggered in the middle of the courtyard, gunfire exploding around him. Blood oozed from his back and his chest; the sword still impaled in his body. In desperation, he reached for Kayne's lower legs as he fell. Nick came from behind and flew at his darling, leaping into space while grabbing him to his body.

Eric, the Dammed Angel, pulled me against him, and as I fastened the tandem straps, he turned to fire a deadly volley again into the crowd. It was raining bullets as we hoisted together up and onto the ledge.

We leaped.

Thomas Severino

Chapter Fifty: Trieste
Nick Sechi's Journal

The chute was torn by the bullets from overhead. Kayne struggled for purchase as we descended 900 feet into the valley below. I could not hold him and steer the chute. Our safety depended on his upper body strength to hold on and my ability to see in the dark and get us down. The wound in his hand made things even more difficult.

The spotlights from the base of the mountain fortress served as both assistance for our descent and illumination for the shooters above. I fought with the rigging to control the speedy fall of our chute, spiraling in the night winds and through the tree-covered tors, searching for a landing. In the end, I got us hung up in a pine tree.

"Jump, brother, I have you."

Rebecca later described what followed from her place on the ground:

> Kayne looked like an angel descending from above, that practically perfect body in only his Aussie Bum briefs. He landed in the outstretched arms of his mirror image, clad totally in black. Eric held on to his brother in a very uncharacteristic loving embrace, pressing his face into the neck of his brother as he caught him.
>
> Nick released his harness and fell into the arms of a reaching István. The big Hungarian said, "There you go, boy."

So, yeah. So, I was severely bruised from the tree landing but was concerned about Kayne and ran to his side. Eric seemed not to want to let him go. And I could see that Kayne was bewildered as well as fatigued. His arms moved up to hold on to his brother.

"He's OK, Nick. Nice flying, Bluey. So, what the bleeding hell happened to your vertigo shit, wuss boy?"

I said with a considerable amount of bewilderment, "Fucked if I know. You musta slapped it outta me."

I rubbed my swollen face. "Remind me to take you apart later, old man."

The dude almost smiled.

Ferenec handed Kayne a pair of overalls and boots from the extra gear in the truck. He also outfitted the freed scientists with casual tourist-type clothing, stowing their lab coats and hospital whites. We quickly made our way to the troop carrier. Mark assisted us into the conveyance as Karl yelled, "Incoming." A rocket shell slammed into the tree we had just vacated. It exploded in flames.

As the General's forces sped down from the fortress in pursuit, Rebecca reached for Mark. It seemed the full effect of the rescue she organized began to overwhelm her. Mark gathered her in his strong embrace and said, "You did it, gorgeous, straight out of the annals of courage and bravery. So 'Scarlet Witch.' Let's get the folks out of here."

The last in the truck, Eric shouted and waved to our driver. "They're coming. Go! Go! Go!"

István raced the troop conveyance through the mountain pass to the south toward Trieste.

***

The scientists sat huddled in the front of the transport.

Kayne said, "How are you doing, my friends. I imagine you never glided before, but these gentlemen are the best."

"We are in your debt, Dr. Sorenson and friends. We owe you our lives," said Dr. Abkhazi, still very breathless.

"I only wish we had brought an end to General Raheb Karadžić."

"Not to worry, Sir. That has been taken care of."

"I am not sure I know what you mean, Doctor."

This time, it was Dr. Dudayev who spoke.

"Professor Sorenson, we were forced to use the CRISPR technology to splice the genetic code into the General's bone marrow to create normal red blood cells. He suffered from acute sickle cell anemia. To ensure that the treatment contained nothing fatal, a hidden toxin, for example, we were required to undergo the same marrow procedure. There is no incipient danger. Healthy bone marrow is not affected by this DNA manipulation."

He explained further. "Dr. Patarava did, however, manage to dust the General's prize tea leaves with thallium. It only required a small amount, and the application took only a second when no one was looking."

Eteri Patarava demonstrated a unique characteristic of the opal on her left hand. The top of the "poison ring" flipped open to reveal a small cavity. She turned her hand palm up and shook it.

Kayne said, "Thallium. The most pernicious element on the periodic table."

"Precisely, while he will appear to make progress with his blood condition, he will most assuredly and painfully die soon."

"Darling, how can you text at a time like this?"

"All the news while it happens, gorgeous. I am, after all, not a superhero but a humble journalist. Jimmy Olsen to your Supergirl."

Mark called out, "Listen to this, folks."

HuffPost World Politics

With the European Union divided by extremist and right-wing political movements capitalizing on a wave of anti-immigrant feeling, the delicate social contracts that underpin multiculturalism were the subject of an avant-garde arts performance that has brought Slovenia to center stage tonight.

Ars Europa, a continent-wide festival of the arts, created a viral groundswell over its performance of a lost Shakespeare text, a selection from The Booke of Sir

Thomas More, the only surviving literary manuscript in the Bard's hand.

Staged at the infamous Rog Factory venue, an alternative space for liberal expression in the Slovenian capital of Ljubljana, 15 actors took to the small outdoor stage. They performed the most moving plea for the plight of immigrants ever put to paper and expressed in dramatic form.

In the current political climate of Europe, this provocative piece of theater focuses on xenophobia and the expulsion of social "aliens." In the play, the heroic Thomas More pleads with the crowd to accept and welcome the asylum seekers in their midst.

> *'Imagine that you see the wretched strangers,'*
> *More cries,*
>
> *Their babies at their backs, with their poor luggage,*
>
> *Plodding to th' ports and coasts for transportation,*
>
> *And that you sit as kings in your desires,*
>
> *Authority quite silenced by your brawl...*

Tonight, the actor playing More spoke to the crowd, turning the current argument back on the intolerant mob. If they were refugees, where would they go? Which country would want them?

> *'Why, you must needs be strangers,'* finding no *'abode on earth'* with *'detested knives against your throats, Spurned like dogs.*

Ashamed and contrite, the angry mob in the play backs down. It is a show-stopping piece that quickly went viral and has begun to create increased cyber funding for the liberal voice of Ars Europa.

In the 21st Century, we have no way of knowing if More's sentiments were the playwright's too, but he makes a case for tolerance with blazing force.

The events at the Rog tonight have shaken the world's conscience over the current refugee crises, the apparently endless flood of asylum seekers from the Middle East, and destinations as far-flung as Afghanistan and Eritrea-- on how to respond with compassion and tolerance.

Mark tapped a link and held up his phone, saying, "Check out the video."

In the clip, actors dressed as refugees included Mia Chan, my mother and sister (both in hajibs), Marc Blane, and, in a t-shirt sporting the rainbow flag, Uwe Müller, all the way from Vienna.

"Holy shit, this is fantastic!" I said.

"I am adding this story of the rescue to CBN's online. The net has gone insane on this."

Eric said, "Let's make sure our escape is successful, mate."

"Bus coming up, folks, this is where we get off."

We were on a back road near the port of Trieste. Alongside were abandoned container trucks. We scrambled off the transport to find the cast and crew from the Rog performance a few hours ago. They welcomed us with open arms.

Eric yelled, "They're up our arses, mates. Make it quick!"

Kayne hopped into the truck's driver's seat as the CEPOL guys unloaded and reloaded the gear onto the bus. He turned the transport to face the way we came and tied the gas pedal to the steering wheel. Kayne hopped in and steered the carrier, careening up the road to smash into a fuel tanker. He rolled out a split second before the impact.

The explosion set up a pillar of fire and smoke, blocking the way with burning debris. We held our breath as Kayne appeared as a silhouette backlit by the inferno, wiping road dirt from his overalls and running to the bus. So freakin' *Mad Max*!

"Let's go, Boss. Got a ship to catch."

István sped into the port parking lot about two miles further on, and we began to disembark. Nearby, a pier-tied yacht rode the black waters of the Adriatic.

The Inala Princess.

Chapter Fifty-One: Absalom, My Son

From the Case File of Kayne Sorenson, Ph.D.

Finally, I suppose the sheer force of personality got us through port security and on *The Princess*.

Uwe and the CEPOL lads bid us farewell but held back to watch us move through the gate agents to the docks. I found out later that Reverend Tomás Sanger was transferred from Vienna to Oslo by his religious order.

Ace explained to the three security agents that he was taking some friends down the Dalmatian coast for a pleasure cruise. He pressed a thick envelope into each of their hands. Portia was behaving like a seductive Sophia Loren, distracting the Italian guards.

"*Ma voglio così tanto vedere i panorami, stallone Italiano.* But I so much want to see the sights, you handsome Italian stud."

Eric held back, ensuring everyone headed for *The Princess* and to safety.

Cleared for disembarkation, the small parade hurried down the pier. A lone gunman stepped from the shadows after most of us had passed.

"No."

The intruder's identity was revealed as he stepped from the shadows into a circle of light beneath one of the dock's lamp posts. Dieter Pichler trained his firearm on Eric, the last of our escaping group.

Kayne and I turned. Using a pile of shipping cargo as cover, Mark scrambled into the open hold of the tanker moored directly behind *The Princess*. Ace, at the head of the fleeing group, was in the process of giving instructions to Viola and Rebecca to get the folks on board. As he watched the drama unfold from the gangway of the yacht. He backed up and growled, "What the fuck is this? Who the bloody hell are you?"

The German accent had vanished and, in its place, the higher intonations of the Australian patter.

"I am my father's son, Mr. Sorenson. Surely you remember him. And he..." He choked with emotion and motioned to Eric with the gun, "And he, unfortunately, is yours."

The engines of *The Inala Princess* roared to life. I said, "Dieter, think about what you are doing."

"For what purpose? He destroyed my father with his lust and defiance. My mother drank herself to death-- such was the community's outcry against us.

"Did you know my father left a note? Not expressing regret and sorrow for taking up with a 15-year-old boy but with sadness that he could not be with his precious Eric."

Eric raised his hands and stood still.

Ace said, "Lad, what's done is done. Killing never..."

"Solved anything, Captain Sorenson? Oh, hell yes, I will send this bloody demon back to hell. And take the rest of you with us."

He waved the gun to make his points. "I killed the actress, Savic, to get nearer to Sherlock here, where I knew I could plan the destruction of his brother. I also wanted to please Karadžić. I planted the Rorlan vial on Haagen at The First Floor. The Hungarian can be so pliant."

My mind was distracted by an image of the dying Hussar.

"So, that and the recent hospital accident with the Princess Margarita of Bulgaria. You know, they never searched me for a weapon. Comes with being a police officer from Vienna, I imagine."

He parodied the conversation with her guard at St. James Hospital. "I just want to ask Her Royal Highness a few questions about her assault tonight... Why yes, we believe there is a connection to the death of the actress Mara Savic in my city of Vienna."

His voice hit an insane pitch. "So incredibly easy. I am such an excellent dirty cop."

He sneered as he continued. "An eye for an eye... your kin for mine, yes, Captain? Oh, sorry, did you not know? So very sad... such a family tragedy."

I covered my eyes and bent forward as tears came. I could feel the rage building in my father and brother. Eric cursed and moved to disarm the man, but Dieter switched the aim to me.

"Come on, you piece of filth. He dies, you die, we all fuckin' die. Makes no difference. I have been dead inside ever since I can remember."

Eric stopped.

"And so here we are."

Dieter stepped closer to my brother, and his tone of insolence gave way to ultimate rage. He waved the pistol at the Lord of Hell.

"Let's dance, you fuck!"

Instantly, the old deck shuddered with an explosive sound. A massive cargo net suspended above our heads crashed to the flooring a few feet from where we stood. The tanker behind us started its huge engines with a startling roar of massive churning steel blades against roiling water. There was an explosive backfire.

Mark!

I did the most unpredictable thing I could think possible. I flew at Ace, knocking him to the deck and trying to throw Dieter into a state of more confusion. Ace, as predicted, roared in profanity-laden anger. Nick vaulted over us as Eric high kicked the gun, sending it skidding across the deck. Dieter pulled Nick into a stranglehold and screamed, "I'll fuckin' snap his neck. I swear, I will. Stay away!"

I pulled off my bewildered father and cried, "No, wait... wait...."

Nick looked at me with his beautiful hazel eyes and smiled. I knew then that he was about to die in the arms of a vengeful maniac. He closed his eyes meditatively and seemed to grow limp. His hands gripped the choking hold limply as if for support as his body sagged. I remember the killer's grip was somewhat awkward, given his hold on the gun.

As Pichler rocked his seemingly lifeless prisoner, Nick changed his stance so that his feet aligned with the murderer, who still held the gun. With sudden force, Nick stomped with his heel on the right instep of his attacker and broke the hold, exploding out of the grip of the rogue Viennese police officer.

Nick screamed, "Systema!" And Eric closed in. Mark swung from a rope tied high on the tanker. He landed on the pier, adding a third fighter to the mix. Our heroic warrior went for the lost gun, kicking it into the water.

Dieter tumbled forward into Eric's uppercut and fell off the deck behind the moving tanker. Eric grabbed the rope and jumped in to try to save the man as he was drawn under the churning propeller. Blood spurted up and onto the stern of the vessel.

Ace flattened himself on the edge of the pier and offered his hand to his dangerously floundering son. I grabbed the big man to anchor his lower body. With extreme effort, the former Marine grasped and pulled Eric up from the water as the engines cut off. The Prodigal clasped his father, locked and dripping against our Da. The exhausted couple stood for half a moment, staring into each other's eyes.

At first, neither could speak. Eric stepped back, blinking and coughing. Next, he raised his arms above his head and looked at a very confused Ace. Eric said softly, "Go. Go now. Go, Father."

As we ran up the gangplank guiding the resisting Ace, Eric turned, hands still raised. The big spy, soaked and disheveled, faced the approaching port authorities.

"*Mi arrendo.* I surrender."

Epilogue: A House Built on Sand

Nick Sechi's Journal

"Where is the Prince now?"

"Mom, he prefers 'Kris.' Remember, his title is non-hereditary and was given as a courtesy to his grandmother, the late Dowager Princess Margarita. He is there in the water with Portia."

"Too bad. The young man just looks like a prince. Such a gorgeous boy."

After Malta and the departure of the three scientists to Canada, Portia, Mother, Kris, Kayne, and I decided to hide out for some R and R in the Naples region of Campania. My mother's people were from Santa Maria on the Tyrrhenian Sea of southern Italy. We sat together for lunch at the *Ristorante Lido*. Mark and Rebecca had headed for Nice on the French Riviera for their getaway.

"So sad about your mother, Kayne. I lit a candle at *Santuario Santa Maria a Mare* up the street. May she rest in peace, dear."

Kayne said solemnly, "Thank you, Viola. She will be remembered for her continuing support of human rights, especially regarding the Koháry Endowment."

I flipped through my phone and said, "Did you see the crowdfunding totals since we left Slovenia three weeks ago? Ars Europa-- $10 million, The Prince Kirill Koháry Endowment for the Preservation of Human Rights-- $5 million, and the Center for Liberal Strategies in Sofia-- $8 million. Money talks; nobody walks."

Kayne looked out at the running teenager in his boardies, diving into the turquoise waters, chasing Portia, and catching the eye of many beachgoers.

"This is the first day he has shown few signs of depression. His grandmother's murder by Pichler at the hospital will have life-long effects on my nephew, I fear. The funeral at St. Nedelya Church in Sofia was well attended. Her Royal Highness was interred beside her husband, the Prince."

He poked at his food.

My mother asked, "No sign of Eric?"

I volunteered, "At the church, I could sense his presence. With Ace there, he would have stayed out of sight anyway. Kris said he saw him and that he had been asked to leave for smoking in the church."

My mother smiled slightly. "Sounds like our Fallen Angel."

She switched gears as Portia and Kris toweled off and made their way to the covered deck and our table.

Placing a hand on Kayne, my mother continued, "What you have done, dear man, this summer is a very selfless and heroic thing. You have saved lives and made a public statement for justice, love, and compassion."

"We have done this together, Viola."

He reached for my hand. "You lead a brave and fearless family, Professor Sechi, and I am a very lucky person to have found this wonderful and powerful young man. It seems you brought them up properly."

"Umm, humm. The family is important. Here in the sunshine, the sea, and the fresh air of Campania, you both can heal from your injuries and the aching of your hearts. Here, eat something."

Good ole Mom...

"And that brings me to an important matter. You must give that boy a warm and loving home. Kristof has suffered a great many losses. He has lived on the edge of unreality for far too long. We must keep our doomed, pampered princes solely among the characters of Shakespeare and other ancient lore. There are new masterpieces to be written. He has the potential to be a shining prince."

Professor Sechi quoted, "He was the mark and glass, copy and book, that fashion'd others."

Kayne said, "Henry IV, Part 2."

She smiled and looked off at the frolicking prince, running toward us in the sunlight and on the white sand. Viola smiled.

"I am speaking of the ultimate self-sacrifice, Kayne. Make a family for this boy. It looks like you will not be alone in this project."

My mother looked at me as I squeezed and kissed Kayne's hand.

"You guys should hit the water. It is awesome." Kris shook his already sun-bleached hair and sent a spray over the four of us.

"Uncle Kayne... oh, sorry, just Kayne and Nick, right?"

I mocked, "Hey, we're casual, Your Hind Ass."

Kris reached and threw a breadstick at me.

He said, "Don't bust my royal rocks, you. I have my armies."

Killer smiles, and gorgeous eyes ran in the blood. I chased him into a corner and tickled him into a mock fight. I threw him over my shoulder and raced into the water.

We returned breathless and wet, having wrestled in the surf. Kris started again, "So, Kayne, any word from my... um... from Eric."

Kayne placed an envelope on the table in front of his nephew.

***

My dear son,

I am a soldier, not a writer, and definitely not a father.

Once, before I left Australia, your Uncle Kayne gave me a book. It was Henderson the Rain King *by Saul Bellow. I remember a line from that book:*

"The forgiveness of sins is perpetual, and righteousness first is not required."

So much has happened these last fifteen years of our lives. You must have had so many questions for your grandmother. Just when exactly did you realize that I was your father? They say that one of the worst unknowns is not knowing who you are– where you come from.

So, that is my first huge sorry. I left you to figure all this out, lad, without me.

When I was 17, I did something that cost a man his life and destroyed the most valuable thing there is in life, one's family. The toll of the punishment for my sins included my father and brothers, from whom I have been estranged for more than 15 years.

And so, that is also a very big sorry.

I am not sure how long I will be on the run, and I profoundly regret that I will not see you grow into the most fantastical Sorenson man ever. I am grateful to your grandmother and the Prince. They raised you with love and taught you to be a man, a good man.

My brother, Kayne, is just about the finest person one could ever know and love (until you pass him up). And Nick is likewise an incredible dude. (Grow strong and give him a good clobbering on the mats when he gets to be an old codger in his mid-thirties. Tell him it's from me. LOL.)

Yes, Kayne and Nick are true-blue blokes, lad, and are committed to each other with some pretty unbreakable bonds. They will continue to keep you safe, loved, and growing strong until we meet again, which I promise you on my life, we will.

Many times, I have not made the right decisions in life, my son, and I fear that I may have to spend the rest of my days fighting to come back into the light. Nick and Kayne are true heroes, and they will keep you close until we can be together again.

I will never stop loving you, my son.

Eric

Kris Sorenson looked up at the cobalt sea, the azure sky, and finally into the ice-blue eyes of his uncle and wept.

Kayne embraced him.

Stage Blood

The End

Thomas Severino

Appendix: A Reflection on the Family

At the end of *Moonstruck*, the 1987 comedy, the Castorinis, the Cammareris, and the Cappomaggis, after a hilarious romp through love, fidelity, and the meaning of life and death, come to an understanding as old as the soil of their ancestors. As the music of "Musetta's Waltz" from *La Bohème* swells, the camera pans from the kitchen to the dining room pictures of the family immigrants from the Old Country. We hear the voices of three generations as they raise a glass.

"Ah, la familia, eh? To the family!"

Stage Blood is a dark mystery that plays against a "stage set" of family life in all its wonder and tragic dysfunction. The dynamics of Shakespeare's classic, "The Tragedy of King Lear," sound like a motif of what can go wrong when family love is replaced by greed, lust, betrayal, murder, and a parent's tragic suspicion of filial ingratitude rejecting a child's pure expression of profound devotion.

The relationships of the Sechis and the Sorensons sometimes wander very close to destruction and despair, struggling for authenticity, forgiveness, and redemption. The tragic anti-hero, Eric Sorenson, is lifted right from *Paradise Lost* by the poet John Milton. A poet Johnson says has "the power of displaying the vast, illuminating the splendid, enforcing the awful, darkening the gloomy, and aggravating the dreadful." Samuel Johnson. <u>Lives of the English Poets</u>. New York: Octagon, 1967.37)

"The Tragedy of King Lear," Milton's epic "Paradise Lost," and Brecht's "Mother Courage and Her Children" all address the catastrophe of war. Lear and Edmund, Eric and Ace, Satan and God, Mother Courage (the female King Lear), and a world gone insane are all caught up in an impious civil war. They are angels in revolt. The advocates for human rights in Dr. Sorenson's mysteries square off against evildoers, the "Big Bads," who threaten to rip the global human family asunder and destroy the love, acceptance, and decency of a charitable and faithful community.

Into this conflagration comes "Nick Sechi's Avengers," a group of broken yet courageous and intelligent individuals with the guts and smarts to challenge one another, speak out, and face incredible dangers on behalf of the defenseless. What better way to engage the conscience of humankind ("The play's the thing …") than a story of family, love, death, and evil set against a monumental backdrop?

Stage Blood suggests that it is the love and devotion of a family that holds us all together, bridges differences, and conquers hate, division, and alienation. Family, the one we are given and the one we create, are those we hold as most beloved, who are called to proclaim solidarity with one another with a fervent prayer for harmony and peace.

Acknowledgments

Viola: What do you say, Tommy?

Tommy (age 3): Thank you.

... to my sister, Janet Neary, who taught me to read at age four. I was bored in kindergarten, and subsequently, I remain very grateful. Throughout my life, I could not get enough of literature. Also, thanks to my teachers, who introduced me to the wonders of Shakespeare, the classics, and other inspiring works.

Shakespeare: The Invention of the Human by Harold Bloom (Riverhead Books, 1998) inspired this story with incredible insights into the writings of the Bard.

My mother, Viola, herself an avid reader, brought me to Latham, New York, in 1961 for "theater in the round." That live production of "West Side Story" made such an impression on my young mind. I became a lifelong theater junkie.

My husband, Tony, opened up an exciting and beautiful world in our many travels while putting up with my fear of flying. Thanks, dear, for your enthusiasm and your patience, as well as your ability to advise my writing with insight and love.

To my dear friends, Bob and Jack, I am humbly grateful for more than fifty years of friendship. My life would have been pretty dull without Bob's humor, keen insight into the human soul, and spirit of self-giving. Rest in peace, dear friend.

From our years as undergraduates, my little buddy, Jack, has provided much love and a profound spiritual insight into our shared lives and professions. You are an inspiration for love and kindness.

Both of these men are devoted to their families, friends, and the people they serve with generous hearts. I am so lucky to have been a part of their lives. They have taught me so much.

Many thanks to Rob LaLonde for his expertise in formatting the cover of <u>Stage Blood</u>. Your time and talent are much appreciated, Rob.

Finally, my father-in-law, Anton, inspired much of this work, especially the geographic setting and the cultures it depicts. Not a Thanksgiving goes by that he does not gather his family at Milwaukee's most exceptional German restaurant. There, we raise a glass of *Deutsches Bier* or *Wein* in loving memory of family and friends.

His stories of growing up as an immigrant in America are as thrilling as they are heartfelt. He is a warm and loving man with the superior determination of a Hapsburg-- qualities shared by his son, Tony, and his daughter, Liza, and lovingly endured by Pat, my late mother-in-law. She has been Big Tony's love since their high school years. Love endures.

Finally, this story is a humble homage to two families, the Wallers of Slovenia and the Severinos of Santa Maria. The church mentioned by Viola Sechi in the epilogue is where my grandparents were married.

"Ah, la familia, eh?"

Afterword

Thank you for reading <u>Stage Blood</u>. I hope you enjoyed it.

I invite you to take a first look at <u>Ancient Blood: A Kayne Sorenson Mystery</u>. Kayne and Nick find love, murder, and intrigue in "The Lucky Country," Australia.

Cheers, mate!

Thomas Severino

Ancient Blood

A Kayne Sorenson Mystery

Thomas Paul Severino

Thomas Severino

Prologue

"What I need you both to know is that this is a very dangerous pregnancy. Multiple births are always risky. With triplets, and given the anatomy, there is an increased possibility of complications."

The woman looked away from both her husband and her obstetrician and absently ran a hand over her abdomen. The husband called to the toddler investigating the doctor's office, pulling a small box of medical supplies to the floor.

"Mitchell Andrew, get over here to your Da, lad, and stop being a nuisance."

The handsome boy gamboled across the office floor, giggling and with arms raised. He jumped and was pulled into the arms of his father. He squirmed a bit and reached for his mother. She tempted him with a teddy bear, and the boy took it into his arms.

The young Marine said, "Speak plainly, Doctor. What are we looking at here?"

The doctor explained. "Your wife's pelvic area is small, to begin with. This tends to bring on intrauterine growth restriction. The babies will be small, with low fetal weight. IUGR can cause congenital disabilities or, in some cases, chromosomal abnormalities

The boys will likely be born prematurely. We are looking at 37 weeks as opposed to 40. The longer your babies are in the womb, the better the chance they will be healthy. Babies born prematurely are at higher risk of brain and other neurological complications, as well as breathing and digestive problems. The earlier in the pregnancy a baby is born, the more health problems are likely to develop."

The man grunted, "Not good, mate. We needs 'em strong in the Outback."

"What will happen to me, Doctor?"

"Our biggest fear for you, ma'am, is a condition known as Preeclampsia or Pregnancy Induced Hypertension. While you are in fairly good health now, the risks are considerable because you are young, a first-time mom, and carrying identical triplets. Without treatment, this high blood pressure associated with your pregnancy can be life-threatening. You are both Catholic, so alternatives are not a possibility."

"Bloody Hell, no!"

"Ace ..."

The father became agitated and spoke over his wife. The toddler squirmed and lightly stroked his father's face. His mother took him, trying to alleviate what she knew would be an explosion.

"Crikey, Doc, this is 1983. You guys outta be able to handle this. I mean, shit. We are talking about my family here– four lives in the balance. We can pay for the best care and specialists. I may not look it, but I run one of the largest cattle stations in the country, for shit's sake. Just give her the best plan, mate."

"Mr. Sorenson, the first thing is, Jane must be moved here to Melbourne as soon as possible. She cannot receive the prenatal care she needs in the bush. Your business requires you to be away from the station for weeks on end. This is not possible if all four are to come out of this healthy and happy."

He looked at his patient. Her internal struggles with the situation were just below the surface and not helped by the volatility of her husband, whose aggressive, military personality tended to want things his way with a monumental stubbornness.

Ace said aloud. "I have some property near Port Melbourne, a nice house, and near the tram."

"Do you have family here?"

"Naw, just us. Jane is a Yank."

The energetic youngster tossed his teddy across the floor and slipped off his mother's lap to stumble after it. The woman looked defeated in her attempts to keep him under control.

"I have an excellent nurse, I can recommend, Mr. Sorenson. She is an expert in prenatal care. The only thing is, she is black. Is that, ahhh..."

"I don't give a shit about that, Doc. Is she good, is all?"

"As I said, she is one of the best in her field. You will be very satisfied, Mr. Sorenson. Here is her telephone. Her name is Kirra Yugambeh. You can also count on her to look after this little guy."

Ace stood and reached for the baby.

"We'll set it up and move this thing along. Let's go."

"Mrs. Sorenson, please see the receptionist for your next appointment."

The women nodded. The doctor would remember that Jane Sorenson left the office as if in a trance. He also recalled that he forgot to reassure her that all would be well.